A Little Bit Married

DEBRA BORDEN

A Little Bit

 Three Rivers Press

Married

A NOVEL

NEW YORK

Copyright © 2007 by Debra Borden

All rights reserved.
Published in the United States by Three Rivers Press, an imprint of the
Crown Publishing Group, a division of Random House, Inc., New York.
www.crownpublishing.com

THREE RIVERS PRESS and the Tugboat design are registered trademarks
of Random House, Inc.

Library of Congress Cataloging-in-Publication Data
Borden, Debra
A little bit married : a novel / Debra Borden.—1st ed.
1. Married women—Fiction. 2. Middle-aged women—Fiction. 3. Midlife
crisis—Fiction. 4. Domestic fiction. I. Title.
PS3602.O68L58 2007
813'.6—dc22   2006034200

ISBN: 978-1-4000-8224-7

Printed in the United States of America

Design by Lynne Amft
10 9 8 7 6 5 4 3 2 1

First Edition

FOR NEAL, ERIKA, AND DAVID . . .

a little bit perfect.

ACKNOWLEDGMENTS

AFTER MY FIRST novel was published, I took a seminar on publicity. The moderator declared that if she ever wrote a book, she'd use pages and pages for the acknowledgments, her theory being that such accolades create instant ambassadors and free publicity for the book. As I contemplated such a strategy, it became clear that employing it, moral implications aside, would create its own kind of hell, in much the same way that creating a guest list can take the joy out of the party. The big difference is that a guest list usually imposes limits and in this case the opposite would occur. I would be charged to discard them and thank everyone I'd ever met, concentrating on those who might be of literary, celebrity, or media benefit. What followed was a descent into gratitude madness. Late at night, half asleep, I would suddenly remember that my husband's tailor had a son who'd done films and that the dermatologist's assistant's sister interned at *The New Yorker*. By the time I found myself thanking Cousin Robin's neighbor Ruthie and the crossing guard in front of Smith Elementary School, I had no choice but to abandon the idea. I have since resolved to thank only those who have intimately impacted either me or the words that follow. Besides, I am certainly above shameless pandering and would never stoop to such base and mercenary tactics.

Having settled that, I would like to start by thanking someone I consider to be a dear friend, although we've never met . . . Oprah Winfrey.

As always, thanks to my friend *Ann Malbin,* from whom I receive excellent advice about nuance, structure, and style as well as the repeated admonishment on how to make all of my manuscripts better: "Good, but it still needs more sex."

Thanks to *Dayna Colameo,* who single-handedly improved my Amazon ranking with her buying habits (Who knew I'd turn out to be the perfect birthday/friendship/holiday gift?) and is the living definition of selfless friendship and support.

To *Jayne Petak,* as always, because we all deserve one great girlfriend who cannot be insulted or offended, one great girl-friend who is for life, one great girlfriend who, no matter what you do, still shows up.

To *Lisa Weiss,* for all things arty, for the accelerated crash course in heat cones, glaze, and bisque, but most of all, for letting me into the sacred inner sanctum known as Mad Dog's Studio.

To *Leslie Engel,* for her spirit, her generosity, and her upbeat personality, not to mention her mean chicken salad.

To *Barbara Stein,* for her endless knowledge and profes-sionalism. Thanks to you, I would no longer rather bungee jump or eat worms than speak in public. However, I would still rather have a colonoscopy, because they give you good drugs.

To *Janet Jacobs* because her favor has a very long shelf life.

And to *Michael Jacobs,* who taught me "it's all in the pack-aging" and then happily and generously provided it.

To my *Golf Girls,* for keeping me grounded and laughing. As anyone who plays golf knows, being either grounded *or* laughing on the course is no small feat, but thanks to you I am:

Arlette "let's double the stakes" *Nudelman*

Gretchen "can we play a little later" *Sloan*

Ina "my handicap's going the wrong way" *Marcus*

Lisa "God help you if I'm straight *and* long" *Weiss*

Lauren "I don't think we're laughing enough" *Satnick*

Shelli "almost on the par four in one" *Bettman*

To *Steve Bennett,* my techno knight in shining armor who has excellent taste in literature and prime-time TV, but who still owes me a Grande Latte, and to everyone at Authorbytes.com for the best website and hand-holding instruction any author could ever hope to have, many thanks.

As always, I feel lucky to be part of two wonderful teams: At ICM, *Lisa Bankoff* always has my back and instinctively knows how to calm me down or spur me to action. As far as I know, she's not even a therapist. Her assistant, *Tina Dubois,* is unmatched in multiple areas, from literary to logistics. Both are always available for support or triage. (Note to self: next time, less triage, more lunches.)

At Shaye Areheart Books and Three Rivers Press, thanks to my consistently excellent editor, *Shaye Areheart,* for her personal (and soft) touch, to *Jenny Frost, Steve Ross,* and *Carrie Thornton,* for their support, and to *Kira Stevens* and *Campbell Wharton,* who, although the busiest people I know, make things happen where and when it counts. Also, to the incredible art department and *Whitney Cookman* and *Laura Duffy*— thanks for your creativity and persistence, and to *Amy Boorstein* and the production editorial department, specifically *Cindy*

Berman and copy editor *Jim Gullickson*—you make me look better than I am and I'm grateful for your excellent and careful attention to detail.

Finally, thanks to all my *friends and family* for their continued support, and just so nobody is offended, thanks to everyone I thanked in the first book!

Peace and love,

D.B. April 2006

"'I am' is reportedly the shortest sentence in the English language. Could it be that 'I do' is the longest sentence?"

—GEORGE CARLIN

"[Harold] didn't want to get lost in the woods, so he made a very small forest . . . with just one tree in it."

—CROCKETT JOHNSON
Harold and the Purple Crayon

"Being a woman is hard work."

—MAYA ANGELOU

A Little Bit
Married

ONE

It happened quickly and suddenly, as most life-altering events do: with not even five minutes to process that everything you know to be your life is about to change. I sensed it, knew it, maybe, when I bent to touch him; something in the way his head just fell to the side, something in the way he didn't flinch. And then I was backing up and backing up, unable to stop moving away until it was as if the wall came forward and smacked me right in my shoulder blades, forcing the air out in a little "Oh." I bounced off and was propelled back in the direction from which I'd just come, like a duck in a shooting gallery. Back to Alan. That, in itself, was a metaphor, though I didn't know it at the time.

Later, amid the shock and the blunt force of the pain and disbelief, as I found myself clinging to that same bedroom wall while the paramedics attempted to *revive* my husband, I had the very strong sense that things would turn out okay. Some*one* or some*thing* would intervene and everything would be all right. If this was a dream, I would soon wake up. If not, then Alan would simply snap out of it. I could picture that; it might start with a cough, then a sputter, and, finally, Alan opening his eyes, sitting up, shaking his head, and forming his signature grin, that not-quite-a-smile, more-of-a-smirk, I'm sorry grin, the one he adopts when he realizes he's screwed up—the one I used to find charming and not irritating.

It could happen. It *should* happen. I even closed my eyes and willed it to happen. Yet when I opened them, there was no satisfying surprise, only the paramedics continuing to yell his name and pound his chest. A cacophony of events. The driveway that just yesterday I had lined with the most delicate purple and yellow pansies was beginning to overflow with police cars whose black rubber tires were alarmingly close to the dainty blooms. Heavy-footed boots thumped up and down our spiral staircase, the force of which resonated brutally but also hopefully, as if each ponderous sound might discharge help. For one, noisy, overwhelming moment I did wonder if we'd never actually installed the Aubusson runner on the stairs; but we had, of course we had. And the thought of that elegant weave was somehow reassuring. Silk threads and fine wool—these are the trappings that keep trauma and disappointment at bay. A family with trimmed hedges and fresh paint and four different types of insurance cannot possibly be at risk, right?

As if in answer, my thoughts began to get a little crazy. Trimmed hedges and pansies are like Passover symbols of today, the lamb's blood of suburbia, signaling that evil should pass over our homes. Therefore, perhaps, this unlikely catastrophe had simply arrived at the wrong address by mistake and wasn't meant for us at all. Down the block at the corner is the Lewis place. They have children's toys all over the yard and green rubber fencing for the dog and Tom Lewis has three Harleys and a rottweiler and their place is one big mess. "That's the house you want," I whispered to myself or to God or to the evil spirits. Then deep breaths. Deep breaths as I leaned against the wall, which is silk grass cloth, by the way. Not that I wish for any harm to come to the Lewises. But it would certainly make more sense.

AND THAT'S WHERE I got stuck. My hand was rubbing up and down on the grass-cloth wall with some urgency, the way a toddler strokes his blanket when he's anxious, and I couldn't get my mind around the thing that was happening. I did know that once this was over I'd be ripping the grass cloth out; that it would always remind me of this moment, this choking moment when I didn't know if Alan would recover, and of the waiting to know, in itself almost more intolerable.

I thought about my fellow residents in upscale Glen Vale, in the middle of their ordinary days, just as I should have been. Glen Vale is consistently voted one of the Top Ten Most Desirable Towns in the Northeast. People here are insulated from the miseries too commonly reported in the *Bergen Record* and the *Star Ledger;* so insulated that all but the most brutal robberies, scams, and murders have lost their shock effect. They are perused almost casually between bites of a low-carb bagel and sips of hazelnut decaf, the way you might read about a movie plot. I, myself, pass over the headlines from places like Paterson and Irvington with barely a glance at the small print. Why read about these places? They have no impact on my life. And yet last week I read about a teenager in Montvale who will miss his senior baseball season because of a car accident and I cried all morning. I suppose something's skewed, off-kilter. But ask any psychologist about pain and they'll tell you it has to seem possible. In the mob and gangster movies, nothing freaks out the audience more than someone getting stabbed in the hand. That's right, you can have two hours worth of executions and gunfire, but when Luca Brasi gets nailed to the bar by a knife to the back of the hand people start to pass out.

SO I WASN'T thinking about accidents, I was thinking of paint colors. I could rattle off the names still: red delicious, marshmallow, butter cream. At the time I'd thought the fact that they were all named for foods was ironic, like there was a sadistic skinny girl at the paint factory intent on creating one more conflict for the women of the world already lost in the maze of twenty-three hundred color choices to now also abandon their diets.

Two years ago, the paint samples had been my constant companion, spread out in every room in the house, some even painted in patchy swatches on various walls and trim. I'd laughed to myself that I was so immersed in decorating to the exclusion of all else that surely Alan was going to ask if I was having an affair, and I had my answer all ready: Oh yes, I'd say, with my new lover, Benjamin Moore. He never did ask. But it would have been funny if had.

Still, no matter what chips away between us, the house has always been a source of comfort, a thing to rely on. I have an eye, that's a fact, especially for color, but for scale and shape as well. There isn't a person on the planet who walks into this house without exclaiming over the furnishings or taking just a little longer to focus on the conversation, unable to peel their eyes away from the various pieces or overall scheme. It's been more than a source of pride; it's been sustenance in those moments of self-doubt, when the nagging little voice clings fast.

It is possible to exist with two voices inside you for years and ignore one. No matter that the one ignored may have been the one to listen to, the one that might drag you up into the light; it's the dragging, the action verb of that voice, that terrifies me. And though it shames me on some level, too, the settling I've done, I haven't been in a coma. I know I've been making a choice each time I think to myself that it feels wrong and then do nothing. There are moments when I think I can't take any more. When I turn, burning inside, leave the room, and run through the options. But the real truth is that I can take more, and do, on a regular basis. I wash my face or find a chore, turn on the TV or try to read and wait for the time to go by and the heat to fade so we can slip back into the disconnect, which feels preferable to the discord, at least for the time. Because I am just not up to the verb.

Call it the devil you know. And sometimes the devil isn't all that fiery but is hellish just the same. Sometimes the devil looks quite human, sits at a dinner table, drives a car, and washes the patio down with a hose after a windstorm. Sometimes the devil burns you with just a look, or the lack of a response. This I know with all my heart. It's not as if Alan beats me; that would be easy to leave. I hope. It's something else that gets wounded, something inside, both subtle and cumulative. I couldn't see it for years, but now it's as if my self-esteem has shape and color; black and blue, of course, and lumpy, like a toxic mass just below my heart. As it begins to rot, hard pieces of it chip off and are lost forever. I can visualize this. Still, I try to forgive myself for not fighting harder. I think it's highly unlikely that even the most confident of souls, which I am not, can survive certain kinds of unhappiness. One side effect is that now I don't trust anything I think. I never know if I'm right or wrong, and I question every thought, feeling, and decision. In an effort to be open-minded and understanding, I believe I've lost sight of seeing things my own way. Am I possibly ungrateful, or unappreciative, or any of the other "un" words he splashes over me? The only thing I know for certain is that I am *un*able to tell.

The only tool I have is to ignore and focus on the positive. That's worked for so long, and right or wrong, it's all I have. So I'm not giving it up just yet. We do have trimmed hedges and purple pansies, and even this event can possibly be rewritten. After all, we live in *Glen Vale*. I believe I mentioned that.

SO EVEN IN the face of all that noise, all that terribly intrusive rubber and plastic and white polyester and metal, I reflexively perceived (or decided; I'm not sure which) that what was occurring was a small setback, a blip. Things happen. A shrub dies and must be replaced, a gutter clogs and overflows, a slipcover fades. Alan's predicament was nothing more or less than any number of household malfunctions. If I remained calm, I would figure out how to fix it, who to call, where to go. And that's exactly what I did.

Well, maybe not entirely. The panicky feeling came back, accompanied by a twinge of nausea, and for an instant I dipped one slim finger into an unseen pool of hysteria.

And it reminded me of the only other time in my life that I panicked. The only other time that fear had an actual mass and taste and weight. *There was a bed then, too, only it was in my apartment, and it was fifteen years ago, and even though Alan wasn't there it had to do with him, with his suggestion that we "see other people," and "take our time." In my anger and hurt, I'd gone out with someone I knew to be a little dangerous, a third-year law student from Columbia with a killer smile and a reputation for placing video cameras in his bedroom to film unsuspecting conquests, later sharing these tapes with friends. There was even a nasty story about Gary leaving some poor girl stranded overnight at the beach, with no clothes and no purse and a blanket as her only resource for both staying warm and getting home. I thought I was smart. I brought him to my apartment. I thought I could handle him. Right up until the Quaaludes kicked in and we began to experiment with the scarves and my four-poster bed.*

When I heard the door to my apartment close, I didn't believe Gary had actually left me there, tied up and exposed. I called to him several times over the next hour, at first angry and brave, later falsely so, eventually pathetic and pleading, but even though he never responded, it was like my brain wouldn't grasp that someone could do this, leave me to die or even worse, be discovered after days by my mother and the superintendent, who, I reasoned, would eventually force open the door. I thought it might be better to die than to be discovered like that. They'd probably have my father with them. Definitely better to die.

Lying there, beginning to choke on the fear and humiliation, I realized that if I survived this, I'd survive anything. There is only so long that you can house fear before it turns into something else, something just as uncomfortable—evil, perhaps, but not quite as paralyzing. I eventually calmed down and thought about my options. I tested all my silk shackles; they were tied so tight I began to imagine the circulation being cut off as my ankles and wrists started to swell. But breaking free was not likely. Screaming. I could wait to hear the elevator open and time my screams to attract someone walking by. My door would be locked, it would have done so automatically when it closed, so they would still have to break in, but strangers and the super would be preferable to my parents and the super. There were no other options except screaming and waiting. So you'd think I would have started screaming right away, then, but you'd be surprised how hard it is to muster up a good, life-saving scream. It's just like in your dreams, reluctant, raspy; it gets stuck, jammed between denial and dignity. Besides, I was like a hiker who first gets wedged in a crevasse: I was worried, but still certain that an escape plan would reveal itself.

BY THE SECOND HOUR, *which, thanks to Gary the sadistic sociopath, I could chart by the lit digital numbers on the Sony clock radio he turned toward me before he left, I started to practice my scream. "Aaahhh," I called out, at about the decibel level that accompanies a stubbed toe. "Hellp," I tried again, maybe as loud as calling to your friend across the street. It was pretty pathetic. A few tears leaked out. Alan, I thought, this is entirely your fault. If you hadn't forced me to get back at you, I never would have gone out with Gary in the first place. I would never have thought of bondage as something a sophisticated single girl should try. I was close to panicking once again. At that point, my neck hurt and my wrists and ankles hurt and I was getting cold. My nipples were so hard from the cold that they burned. I told myself to get a grip and go back to trying to train myself to scream. And suddenly, instead, I began to laugh. I got quite hysterical, actually, giggling and crack-ing up, the kind of laughter where people look at you and wonder if everything's all right, the kind where you bend over and hold your stomach, except, of course, when you can't because you happen to be tied, spread-eagled, on top of your brown and tan, psyche-delic, $200 Wamsutta quilt: a quilt you practically had to beg your mother to buy and which she finally did, but only after you assured her that you would treat it with the utmost care; a promise from* which I was certainly now disqualified. And to think, she was worried I might eat cookies on it . . .

ALTHOUGH I DIDN'T mean to, I found myself thinking of all my mother's admonitions. There weren't many. Don't tweeze above your eyebrows. No man buys a cow when he can get the milk for free. I think that might have been it. I laughed some more. And then, even more shocking, I head a voice.

"Wow."

Just that. One word. "Wow." I became instantly, intensely silent. My hearing was suddenly as acute as a cheetah alert for prey. Gary had been there the whole time. The bastard had been just out of sight, standing by my door, for almost two hours, watching me deal with this horror. What kind of psychotic maniac was capable of that kind of control? Now the fear came back. But also some relief. Even though I knew I was dealing with a total sicko, I also had someone who could get me out of this mess. Now I really wanted to scream, and threaten him, but something kicked in that told me this was my chance and the only way out of this was to play him. I feigned merely bored. "Oh, Gary, very funny," I said. My heart was clamping fast, in tight little squeezes like from the bubble of a bicycle pump, but my voice drawled.

"Okay, now, let's do something else. I'm hungry. Let's go out for some food."

"You're not mad?" he asked. He sounded disappointed. But he was moving closer.

"Well, of course I'm mad," I said. "You scared the shit out of me. But mostly I'm tired and I have an itch and I'm starved." Gary looked at me, and it was the single, scariest moment of my life. I knew he was debating whether to head deeper into the darkness

or move toward the light. I assumed my most moderately exasperated expression. I had the sense that my ability to pretend that this
was no big deal would determine my fate. A moment passed, then
two. I sighed, as if a naked, tied-up me was mostly uninterested. I
think the sigh did it. Gary just walked over to the bed, untied my
feet, and then my arms. I couldn't believe it. I wanted to race to the
front door and run out, but I stayed cool. Slowly, I wrapped my
quilt around me and walked normally to the speaker by my door.
He didn't even follow me, just plopped on the bed as if we were
going to plan the next activity. I pressed the intercom. When the
doorman answered, I spoke slowly.

"Hi, Bill, it's Bitsy in 16-D. There's a guy coming down right
now in the elevator. If you don't see him in two minutes, then I'm
in trouble and need help, okay?"

I opened the door for Gary. I was shaking then. The physical,
adrenaline-based, released-from-the-freezer kind of shaking; I
couldn't make it stop. He smiled as if he was resigned, got up, and
walked toward me. On his way out the door, he kissed my cheek.
"Get out." I said, wiping my face. And he did. I closed the door,
and as he walked down the hall toward the elevator, I heard him
singing. It was the song "Daisy Bell," only instead of "Daisy," he
was singing, "Bitsy, Bitsy . . . I'm half crazy . . ."

". . . SOME SORT OF DAZE. Mrs. Lerner. Ma'am!" I opened
my eyes, having forgotten for a moment that I was in my own
bedroom and not that New York City apartment of years ago.
Someone was speaking to me, touching my shoulder. It was the
one female paramedic. It took me a minute to focus. "Are you
all right?" she asked. "Sorry," I said, and stood up straighter.
Then she turned back to Alan in the bed, and as I gathered

myself, I shook Gary off, and with his memory also some of the fear. I watched the paramedic. She was a wholly foreign creature to me, a different species from the women I knew: large and dressed identically to the men. She wore a white shirt with a GV/EMS Rescue emblem across the pocket and loose, black uniform slacks. Her dark hair was chopped short and her massive chest strained against the buttons of her blouse in one great undefined mass. Despite the *size* of her chest, it could never have been construed as provocative. Her breasts were not flirtatious; instead, their girth seemed a warning to steer clear. I was fascinated by them. Working breasts, I thought; not for nurture or for teasing but to add bulk and heft. Perhaps even to menace. Her stomach spilled over the belt of her pants. She conveyed a sturdy, industrial strength, as masculine as she could be and still have ovaries. I found her slightly repulsive, which was strange, since it is usually Alan who is repulsed and me who says, "Oh really, Alan, be nice." But this was not the first time I'd subconsciously adopted Alan's view as my own. After so many years of marriage, it was impossible to experience anything solely with my own antennae, and I often found myself registering Alan's opinion, even when he wasn't there.

It was this woman who was in charge, barking directions at the men, stopping only to speak into her walkie-talkie or ask questions of me.

"When was the last time you spoke to your husband? What medications is he taking? Is he allergic to anything?"

I answered her calmly, all the time wondering what she was like at home. Did she fix her own plumbing? Watch wrestling as she guzzled beer? Ride a motorcycle whose license plate said LIVIN' LARGE? When she put the plastic mask over Alan's face and leaned down to within an inch of him, I thought, *Now*.

Now is when the director will yell "Cut" and Alan will sit up. Alan would never tolerate being touched by this mountainous woman. In fact, he's quite fatophobic. He is so disgusted by fat people that he avoids sitting near them in public places. He gets pained whenever I make dinner plans with a couple in which either the husband or the wife is overweight. Of course, in our circle, that isn't often.

T W O

I t's no accident that I ended up in my Colonial, cul-de-sac life, with a husband, two kids, and a bright red SUV; I have always been the ultimate suburban girl, full-fledged, card-carrying, right down to my Tuesday tennis game, my invisibly fenced golden retriever puppy, and my secret shortcut from Nordstrom's to Neiman Marcus at the Garden State Mall. (Do not ask me about the shortcut; I'm not sharing.) Here's the thing: I was born to suburbia the way some are born to royalty or a particular caste. I have the DNA, maybe the gene. One day, they'll identify it: number 517B, the marker for domesticity, a cluster of chromosomes responsible for taking reasonable, college-educated women and turning them into obsessive zombies who become paralyzed for hours at Home Depot or Linens 'n Things, paralyzed because they are desperate to get it right.

Sea foam or pale mint? Cotton or sateen? Round evergreens or conical? And this is just the decorating. Wait a few years and the parenting and marital dilemmas take center stage: Which kindergarten teacher will be the best fit for your five-year-old future Bill Gates? What summer camp will nurture the inner Chris Evert in your slightly uncoordinated, undersized darling? Must you really get a Brazilian wax to keep your sex life interesting? Well, scratch that last one; I mean, that's not much of a dilemma at all. What woman wouldn't be willing to spice up her marriage by having thin muslin strips coated in hot wax applied to and then ripped off her labia?

AS A YOUNG GIRL on Long Island, way before I was old enough to contemplate sacrifice, labial or otherwise, I took comfort in the rituals that have become the very clichés of suburbia. My attraction to these rituals mystified my mother and now bore my own children to death, furthering my theory that domestic bliss is a trait, in this case one that skips a generation. I loved climbing the massive willow tree that sheltered our yard. I loved Sunday barbecues, Girl Scout meetings, and the Good Humor man who came weekly during the summer with our regular delivery of chocolate éclairs and strawberry sundaes. Surely there was no joy so deeply stimulating, so primitive and visceral, as the joy triggered by the bells of that ice cream truck. At age ten, that was as good as it got.

Since she was hardly domestic and rarely at home, my mother's official title of housewife was just one of the many misnomers with which I grew up. We had the same live-in housekeeper from the time I was three until I turned fourteen, at which time, after more than ten years in our house, she went home for an ordinary weekend off and mysteriously never returned. I tried to call Vajay at her house in Queens, but the number was disconnected. My mother never even tried. I thought it all came back to her name, Vajay, pronounced "Va-gi"—like the beginning of the word "vagina." My mother had been trying to get her to change it for years, even put the emphasis on the first syllable, "*Va*-gi," like "Magi," but it never stuck. This

West Indian woman soothed my earliest skinned knees, upset stomachs, and broken hearts. She lit a candle at my bat mitzvah. But when Vajay left, my mother expressed only relief. "Well," she announced that night, over takeout from LaTosca Pizza, "at least there'll be no more saying '*Vaji.*' At least we're done with *that.*"

SO, MANY OF *our* suburban rituals were courtesy of others: barbecues were primarily at the neighbors, and gardening was done by landscapers. I had to beg to become a Brownie because it involved a parental (read "maternal") *commitment,* and there was no chance my mom would even consider being a troop leader, not even a coleader. An afternoon of brown-uniformed eight-year-olds reciting poetry and making S'mores could not compete with her regular routine: lobster salad at Millie's, an afternoon of shopping on the Miracle Mile, and then a quick change before dinner out at Peter Luger's with my father. So while the other girls complained about the ugliness of the faded brown uniform and orange tie, I was grateful to have one. But even at eight or nine, I knew the difference between my mom and other moms. Jan's mom showed us how to make candy apples in the fall, and Jody's mom taught us how to mold papier-mâché, and Robin's mom had a basement crammed with every item you might need for an art project or science report.

On the other hand, my mother had wonderful closets. Rows and rows of pressed, color-coded suits, each hanging in its own niche, some covered in plastic from the cleaners, others in sheaths opaque and padded and zipped. In my house, it seemed as if "mother" was more of an honorary title. I mean, she was there: I had new school clothes; and my tests got signed; and I got all my shots, just like our miniature schnauzer, Mary Elizabeth. It's just that it was all one-dimensional; she could have phoned it in.

This is why I treat my own children to every experience suburbia has to offer, why I inject myself into their childhood like Doris Day on steroids. I slip Hershey's Kisses into their lunch boxes, bake cookies from scratch, and ply them with holiday stickers and excessive decorations, and keep hoping they'll warm to the lifestyle. I'm just so afraid that despite my efforts they will never truly take to it, that scorn, too, is a trait, like long legs or curly hair, a trait passed down to them from their grandparents: genetic disdain. Still, I think I'm making progress. My kids don't exactly set up lemonade stands or swing from tires or ride their bikes through the neighborhood; and at twelve, Lauren wouldn't think of joining the Girl Scouts, but she does want a cell phone, mostly so she can call me and ask permission to overspend at the mall. Evan is nine and a baseball addict, which puts him squarely in the hub of the community. In Glen Vale, baseball is air, and Evan is currently on not one but three different baseball teams; Rec, All-star, and Elite.

PERHAPS THEIR RELUCTANCE to embrace the neighborhood simply has to do with the times. What with after-preschool activities, then all-day kindergarten and soccer and T-ball starting practically in the womb, there doesn't seem to be much time to explore the interesting creek behind the house two yards down. For me, it was so different—the neighborhood was a constant adventure, a roaring rapids of a ride. There were skateboard disasters, random games of capture the flag and ghost, spontaneous hopscotch tournaments, feuds settled by once, twice, three times—shoot. I craved our pickup softball games the most, not because I loved to play or was any good but because the game drew all the older boys in the neighborhood and I'd had a crush on Sandy Littman since I was eleven, from the first time I saw him remove his white, Fruit of the Loom T-shirt to reveal his seriously sculpted and tan fourteen-year-old chest. Sandy never noticed me, not with Joanie Schecter and Marsha Kon around. They were his age and had breasts, so I didn't have a chance, but I liked to fantasize that he recognized my incredible intelligence and great potential and secretly loved me. This required a certain amount of resilience on my part, based on the extent of our conversation over three years.

> SANDY: Beberman, ya wanna play?
> ME: Uh-huh.
> SANDY: You better go to Right.
> ME: Okay.

I was always in the outfield, but I never protested. I was happy to watch Sandy and his brown chest. Occasionally, a ball would come to me, and that was almost always a disaster, but since we never had enough kids to field an entire team, there were no long-term consequences. Years later, when Sandy was in college and I was a sophomore in high school, we actually dated and remarkably the conversations were not that different from the ones of years before. Instead of his backyard, we were on the bed in his room, but we were still playing ball, in a way, and we had moved from second base to third, an event which was less thrilling than it was . . . sloshy.

> ANDY: Beberman, ya wanna ball?
> ME: Nuh-unh.
> ANDY: You better go home.
> ME: Okay.

I danced to the rhythms and the rumors of the neighborhood. I even cherished the nasty, hunchbacked woman who lived in the decrepit house on the hill. Well, that's not exactly right. I didn't cherish *her;* I never even met her, couldn't really say she even existed, but I relished the lore of her. Every year at Halloween, it was rumored that she gave out jagged pieces of glass dipped in chocolate, but no one knew anyone who had actually gotten this chocolate. For that matter, no one knew anyone who had actually rung her bell, either, not even the boys who made brave threats that never materialized.

By junior high school, it became clear to me that I was different, that my Ozzie-and-Harriet identity was both dated and extreme. Like good, progressive, upper-middle-class daughters of the day, my girlfriends were already planning their careers. I had two friends, Fern Nudelman and Lydia Golden, who were both semi-misfits. Fern was tall and broad and athletic, except she had a mild case of scoliosis, so her posture was awkward and her gait lopsided. When she walked, she led with her left arm and hip; her right side caught up a full beat later. Fern's mother used to call attention to it, bringing home brochures about full body braces that Fern would literally shred into perfect, minuscule bits; too perfect, if you ask me. Fern's mom didn't have a clue about how she made her daughter feel. She'd say things like

"Girls, believe me, Mr. Nudelman and I have to take out a mortgage just to pay the seamstress so Fern can appear *level*." I can tell you how much Fern loved that. By the summer of tenth grade, Fern wouldn't be able to enter her own house unless she'd smoked some grass. Years later, I heard that she even did some time in a fancy rehab.

Physically, Lydia was the opposite: a round butterball, five feet two inches in all directions, and a brain as big as her belly. While Fern wanted to be a doctor, a pediatrician, Lydia was going to be the next F. Lee Bailey. I wanted to be Samantha on *Bewitched* and make a nice home for Darrin.

"A WIFE AND mother . . . ," I announced breathlessly, as we gorged ourselves on chocolate cream pie at the newest restaurant in town, a chain called 4 and 20 Pies. It was the summer before we were to start tenth grade at Great Neck North senior high.

". . . maybe a Brownie troop leader and definitely class mother," I added with a proud smile. This was met first with stunned silence and then outright indignation.

"You can't," Fern said, with dramatic teenage deadpan, "be serious."

When I nodded, she cried out as if I'd declared that I was entering a convent.

"But that's practically medieval! Oh no, absolutely not. I won't let you!"

"Really, Bitsy," Lydia patronized, "you aren't seriously thinking of depending on a *man* your whole life, are you?" She and Fern had a good laugh, and although I wanted to defend myself, I suddenly felt the way I had two years before at my slumber birthday party when it seemed like every thirteen-year-old but me had gotten their period and they all just happened to be having it *that* night. "Oh, the cramps," they commiserated, and then said sympathetically to me, "You're lucky you haven't gotten it yet, it's such a pain." As a late bloomer, I wanted that pain more than anything in the world. And now, I *wanted* to feel what Fern and Lydia felt, a desire to do something, achieve something, and be something, but I didn't. When given the choices, it seemed pretty simple to me.

Choice A: *Get a job, wake up early every day, put on stockings, and haul yourself to a place where someone tells you when to arrive and when you can leave and what to do while you're there,* Or Choice B: *Wake up, make some cereal for your kids, throw a coat on over your pajamas and drive them to school, and then have the rest of the day to do whatever you want, and occasionally you might have to clean something.* This was a no-brainer. I couldn't understand why everything had to change before I got a chance to set up house, but high school is about fitting in and keeping what few friends you may have, so I pretended to be swayed by their passion.

IF MY FRIENDS were important to me, they were less so to my mother. She was never thrilled with my choices; she thought I could do better.

"I saw Kimmie Kaitz and her mother in Jildor's this afternoon. She's awfully pretty. Why don't you have her over for a sleepover?"

Why? Why? How much time do you have, Mom? Because the reasons are endless. Because every single boy at Great Neck North is in love with Kimmie and probably most of the girls, too. Because Kimmie has perfect blond hair styled into an elegant graduated pageboy by Donnie, the hottest stylist at Peter's Place, which is the hippest salon in town. Because she buys size 26 jeans at Great Neck Department Store and pairs them with perfect pastel angora sweaters from Junior Fair that cling to her modest but perky 34-B chest. But mostly because Kimmie Kaitz hasn't spoken to me since the first grade.

As if any fifteen-year-old would just randomly invite a girl in her grade over for a sleepover, let alone one with a popularity quotient that was not even within striking distance of mine. I fantasized about possible responses. "Oh, Kim asks me over all the time," I could say, "but we're both just so busy." Or "Oh, Kim asked me to go on a ski trip next month. We'll plan the details soon." Finally, I just opted for the spiteful.

"Kimmie Kaitz is a big slut," I say sweetly, "who does drugs with her boyfriend before school." Sorry, Kim. It wasn't your fault that you were so perfect, but those were desperate times, and I sacrificed you to the gods of "getting Evelyn off my back," and I'd do it again.

Maybe, in some convoluted way, my mother did make me feel confident, because when it came to Fern and Lydia, I imagined myself as the cool member of our little threesome, a swing friend, really, because I did in fact have some contact with the popular girls; I was *their* borderline friend. They would occasionally include me, though I suspected it was more out of desperation than desire: when they absolutely could not find a fourth for hearts or spades, or no one's mother could drive them home from the movies and mine might.

Still, I didn't want to jeopardize my standing in the threesome, so before long I proclaimed that my destiny was to be a great artist, a destiny that was accepted unquestionably since

I was the only one of my friends who could actually draw a face that looked like a face. Also, I had the kind of penmanship that other girls envied: neat, compact, curvy. I easily drew block letters and bubble letters, and I was the one who was asked to make the posters and scenery for events at Great Neck North High School. So it was assumed that I would paint or sculpt great works of art in the future, and thus even my course of study at college was preordained.

Don't get me wrong. I loved drawing and sculpting, especially at the new community center in town that offered after-school classes in ceramics and pottery design, and even more so in the studios and workshops at college. Plus, artists got to wear large, shapeless smocks that cover what my mother referred to as "a multitude of sins." Many afternoons, lost in the cold but sensual sensations of wet clay, I might have glimpsed self-worth and joy, but none of it matched the excitement I felt when my mother prodded me to consider what color dresses my brides-maids would wear or what music would be played when I walked down the aisle. A deliberation over dripped or poured glaze was no match for the captivating debate my mom and I had over just how many pieces of a dining room set could match before it was overkill. I was going to college to find the perfect husband, with whom I would eventually live in the perfect house with our perfect children.

In 1980, graduating from high school, I kept it to myself. And in college, when most young women were seriously begin-ning to contemplate the myriad choices available to them, I hid behind my oversized, regulation-black artist's briefcase, wedged it between my politically correct opinions and growing intel-lect. My intellect was real; it grew in spite of me, but at home this became a betrayal of the family dynamic. In psych class

I learned about family systems theory, which says that if one person changes, the whole system is put under stress. I was not ignorant to the fact that latent academic excellence was a textbook case on how to upend the family equilibrium.

Occasionally, at the dinner table, I might offer up an opinion; this was met with silence, and then my mother would look sympathetically at me, as if I were making a mistake so grave I couldn't possibly understand. There was an unspoken agreement in our home: The boys were smart and the girls were pleasant, and throughout my childhood we maintained that myth no matter how many As I racked up or how many courses Eddie had to repeat over the summer or how many math tutors Mitch had to endure. Even today, when I forget the rules, and offer an informed opinion, my brothers quickly find a reason to change the subject.

THREE

ome on Alan, I will silently. We are civilized people who Recover. Rebound. We do not put in hysterical calls to 911 in the middle of the morning. After answering questions, I have again taken up my safe place against the blush-colored wall. The wall is my friend. I allow my head to lean back and rest for just a moment while I take a really deep breath, the kind that seems to come from way down deep in my groin and makes me shudder just a bit.

The past year has been a strain on both of us. It's true I've played around with those unthinkable words "separation," "divorce." I've let them linger in my head, imagining a life without "us" and a "me" all alone. But not with any sort of plan; just a few "what ifs" to soothe myself after Alan's increasingly frequent complaints and to occupy some of the evenings when he stormed out to "be alone and think." And these fantasies never took on a shape, I never saw an actual house with just me and the kids in it, not a different yard or a different car; it was more a state of mind, a sense of imagined peace. Not unlike a feature in *Architectural Digest:* the suggestion of an English garden; a palette of stone and great purple wildflowers; or perhaps a hint of the dunes on Long Island, gently sloping mounds covered in sea grass. Occasionally, there might have been a figure, fuzzy, indistinct, an outline of someone solid, strong, and gentle, but only an insinuation and only in the background. A very pleasant insinuation, for sure, free of tension and criticism, free of icy silences and unspoken offenses, but just for play.

Nor did I ever go so far as to contemplate attorneys, although I did read an article in the dentist's office about how some men hide their assets and you need a forensic accountant to figure things out and this is certainly something to keep in mind. If one should need it. Which I don't.

But Alan is unaware of this, and I'm sure a little harmless imagining had no part in this physical event. Still, looking over at him, the guilt floods through me just as I am running out of techniques to cope. So, on the off chance that I actually have some sort of secret powers by which my thoughts affect the future, I begin to concentrate on healing Alan. It's the least I can do. I know this is ludicrous and yet . . . once I have the thought, I can not make it go away. If only I concentrate, think hard enough, focus, I might be able to influence something, some energy vibe or magnetic field. I try my hardest. I visualize Alan sitting up, taking off the mask, holding it out dramatically, and making one of his obnoxious comments, something like "Ahh, 1992—an excellent year for pure oxygen. Bold, assertive bouquet, just a subtle hint of methane, but I think I'll pass."

Instead, Alan just lies there. The only sounds are from the medics as they hoist him onto the stretcher and not without difficulty, due to the fact that he already has *two broken legs*. There are raised eyebrows as the casts are discovered, but nobody comes right out and complains about the extra weight or even asks me how it happened. I observe, jarringly, that they are moving fast, this emergency medical team; they are purposeful and still methodical, but they've definitely upped the pace. They work well together; their movements are orchestrated and in sync. I have an image of the Harvard crew team, forty-eight men and one captain, rowing in perfect cadence, their boat eating up meters of the Charles like a smooth, preppie Pac-Man machine.

TOGETHER, THIS MASSIVE bulk of a group, now a sweating cadre of white uniforms and black equipment, so incongruent among the sea foam greens and tea rose pinks of our bedroom, descends down our front stairs and rolls out the door. And I'm still thinking, although a bit shakily, that this *could* turn out okay. I mean, the house is still standing and the children are at school, thank God, and there is a lovely breeze and it doesn't seem as if a single leaf or piece of mulch is out of place. The outside world hasn't changed a bit, so maybe the neighbors haven't even noticed the black-and-white circus in our drive. This could all be one big misunderstanding. Just like an episode of *ER* I saw a few months ago in which the evidence pointed to one thing but the resolution was quite different. By the end of this hour, there will be an explanation, a perfectly good one that will clear everything up, connect all the dots. There will be no fault with Alan or myself. His condition will be the result of some highly unusual, rare event; perhaps a strain of Ebola or the bird flu. An especially vigilant emergency room doctor will pick up on it.

"Good thing you smelled that faint odor of burned cotton, Doc," someone will say.

"Aw, it was nothing, just something I picked up in the service."

AS THE FLEET of emergency vehicles begin to disperse, a sergeant gives me directions to the hospital, then takes my elbow and asks if I am all right, and I am thinking that he's awfully nice but surely he's overreacting, making this such a drama. Before I can answer, the stillness of the early spring morning is shattered by the piercing whine of the siren as the ambulance pulls away. So much for not alerting the neighbors. Reflexively, I begin to concoct a plausible response to the influx of phone calls which are sure to come; maybe a vague implication about E. coli?

STANDING ON THE front steps, formulating potential explanations, my hands over my ears, my eyes follow the tire tracks in the grass, then a clump of squashed purple and yellow pansies that look strikingly like one of my son's spin-art paintings. As the police cars back out and as the ambulance with its flashing lights turns the corner from Autumn Court onto Autumn Hill, it occurs to me that maybe, just maybe, this is a slightly bigger deal than I'd hoped. It may be that the noise of the siren has punched a hole in my thick, emotional bubble wrap. It may also be the bluish white pallor of Alan's face, which I glimpsed as the stretcher slid noisily into the van. Or the grim faces of the various technicians who possibly avoided my glance. And, of course, it quite logically could be the empty vial that I have never seen before and which the paramedics found in the bed with Alan and have confiscated. Standing on my front steps, on this otherwise perfect April day, I begin to realize that we have crossed a line, and that my clearly defined picture of the perfect life in the perfect house is becoming fuzzy. Blurry. Hazy. A little less Lichtenstein, a little more Monet.

I suppose another girl might have seen the signs, recognized the bumps for what they were: precursors to a veritable minefield of troubles. Another girl might have at least made a stab at being prepared. But this never occurred to me. No more than having a nervous breakdown would have. I, Bitsy Beberman Lerner, have no need for an escape hatch, no Plan B waiting in the wings. My intentions have created a map as indelible as a permanent tattoo or a signed painting.

Since the bondage incident with Gary, I can *physically* slip into recovery mode, and I do so now; my breath begins to slow, and my lungs inhale more deeply and evenly. My hands loosen, unclench, and smooth down my black J.Crew slacks, unwrinkled though they are. By the time my spine begins to raise itself just a bit higher and stiffer, I am imbued with new confidence and a carriage so imposing that Diana Vreeland would be impressed.

Now my mind can follow suit. I bathe myself in rational thoughts and anesthetizing mantras; I will not panic or rush to judgment; I will not overreact. Surely other women have gone to wake up their husbands and found them unresponsive, with an empty vial in the bed.

Well, I will not ask for a show of hands.

as a fine arts major at American University, where the criticism was more sophisticated, my teachers sensed something was missing and labored to inspire me. They said that I had talent, that I had mastered form, but that my work lacked a certain spark. I knew why. I really didn't care. No matter how wonderful it felt to lose myself in acrylics, no matter how many times I looked up at the clock amazed that whole hours had gone by, I knew that my love for paint, clay, and charcoal could only confuse me, divert me from the road to happiness.

Certainly my mother had told me enough times to "concentrate on finding the right man first. Get your life set—husband, kids. Then you can worry about what you like to do."

An hour with my brushes and the university's incredible kiln was as soothing as drugs or chocolate were to other girls, but ultimately it was deception, not aspiration, that brought me to the studio, deception spawned in high school while sprawled on trundle beds or squished into hard, orange, curve-backed booths at the local pizza parlor. Deception by pink Princess phone, which merely morphed into deception by dorm-room phone. Late at night, "attached," as my mother would say, to these phones, we wowed each other with our career plans, and once I committed to the lie, I never missed a step.

As girls coming of age in the late seventies we were unsure, displaced a bit, caught between the lingering righteous passions of the late sixties and the looming decadence of the eighties, but one message was clear: Amount to something. Otherwise, the efforts and strife of those that came before us would have been for nothing. We had new role models, Gloria Steinem and Margaret Mead and Billie Jean King.

I continued to try to ignore the truth that I was not embracing my new freedoms and possibilities. I hid my shame, joining in as wholeheartedly as possible in the renouncement and disdain of our mothers; how could they have blindly continued to spend hours curling their hair or baking bread when the real heroes were eschewing makeup and their aprons? True, my mother was not much of a baker, more of a Sara Lee Pound Cake buyer, but I had to offer her up as a sacrifice to help allay the guilt I felt for harboring my secret desire to marry and breed. At times, even the art I loved seemed a betrayer of sorts: confusing me, pulling me, teasing me with the idea of a life spent teaching, exploring, creating. Don't listen, I told myself. You have your plan. Stick to it.

The result of this inner deception was that it became an essential part of who I was, the little black dress in my emotional wardrobe. "Our next contestant is Bitsy. Bitsy is wearing a long sheath from Cacharel, which gives the illusion that she does not have a new and embarrassingly large bosom. She's perky, upbeat, likes puppies, and walks in the rain, and excels at lying to most everyone about everything. *Thank you*, Bitsy."

I WONDER NOW if my deception is similar to what people endure who hide the fact that they're gay. Everyone *assumes* that you're just like them but deep down inside you know that in One Big Way you're different. It's a wonder all the people with secrets don't simply combust and explode in random bursts all across the country from all the pressure. Like an egg in the microwave. You'd be sitting next to someone on the subway when suddenly there is this little pop and a whoosh and the person just vaporizes in front of you. And in their seat, which is red hot, there are just some mutated cells, some damaged DNA, maybe just enough to regenerate and possibly get it right this time.

AFTER ONE OF our frustrating (for me) and satisfying (for everyone else) family dinners, I was told to do the sensible thing and switch from a fine arts degree to a BA in education with a *minor* in art, so I could teach. I wanted to rebel, but my family was so pleased by the idea and I didn't really care one way or the other, so after college I ended up just the way my family imagined. I lived in the city for "a bit" (translation: till you get married) while teaching art to elementary school kids at a private school on the Upper East Side.

The thing is, I loved it. Just a little too much. The kids were so incredibly open and creative, and the art room was like one huge, award-winning children's book, a rainbow of warmth and joy. I sometimes had to remind myself that I was still pretending to enjoy this life of a modern city girl. This wasn't me. I was simply doing "suburban girl does obligatory stint in the city after school and prior to marriage," which ultimately is an extremely suburban rite of passage. I decided to renew my vow to get Alan to commit.

Of course, when the school offered me the top salary allowed by the teacher's pay scale, begged me to come back, and dangled tenure as a prize, I may have faltered. Luckily, my mother reminded me that it was a lot easier to get a teaching job these days than a husband, so I was able to snap out of it and refocus. I told Alan it was either make a commitment or we were through, and I watched as he mentally weighed his options. His eyes ended up on my chest, which was where most parts of him ended up on any given night. As his eyes settled on my breasts, I was confident we'd soon be engaged, and I was right about that. I had a ring by Valentine's Day, and we were married that fall. From that day on, I expected everything else simply to fall into place. And for a time it did. But a family is a living thing, and like most living things, no matter how impeccable the surface appears, the inner workings are a completely different matter.

b y the time I grab my bag and ease the Land Rover out of the garage, I have firm resolve. Just then, I catch sight of my neighbor, Peg, in the window across the street, and my confidence dissolves. She is my "Mrs. Kravitz"; my nosy, nightmare neighbor from hell. And she is trouble. By the time I clear the driveway, she'll be on speed dial to the neighborhood if not the county. I make a mental note: damage control. I pretend not to notice Peg and stare straight ahead, gripping the wheel as I learned to do so many years ago in driver's ed, with hands at ten and two o'clock. I thought I'd actually outgrown some of the pretense, but lately I've been doing so much of it: pretending not to notice, pretending not to care, staring straight ahead. I don't blame the neighbors or anyone else. I should have known better.

Life in the suburbs is not all flower beds and carpools; there are rules. And even though I am somewhat of an expert, it doesn't translate into much of an edge. It doesn't help me get Evan on the right baseball team, the one he really wants to be on, which is not the one where the coach is a father who is nice and fair and believes in giving the boys equal playing time. The team he wants to be on is the one with the psycho competitive father who plays favorites, loads the kids with sugar, and mysteriously leaves every draft with an inordinate number of "A" players and thereby wins the championship each year. My knowledge of the suburbs will also not help whitewash a sullied reputation. Sure, anyone can *live* here, but flourishing is another matter. Break the rules and you're likely to get thrown out of the game. And believe me, every sweet little town from Sausalito to Saddle River has rules. *Not* having financial problems is just one of them—quite a big one, in fact, and one that we broke. Unfortunately, this year we broke quite a few more.

AS I APPROACH the emergency entrance to Bergen General, I suddenly feel dizzy and have to pull over to the side of the road. I am not falling apart; I just need to catch my breath, which is perfectly understandable considering the circumstances. In a minute, I'll be fine. I put the car in park, lean back, and close my eyes, and despite my usual ability to see the sunny side, for the second time in less than half an hour I begin to entertain just the teeniest, tiniest possibility that we, Alan and I, the Lerner family, won't ever be the same again.

When you grow up with a name like Bitsy, there are presumptions. When your name is Bitsy, the outside world wants you to be a cute little popcorn-shrimp-of-a-girl. Otherwise, you are a human oxymoron and way too confusing for them, let alone yourself. My preemie weight inspired the name and caused my parents to abandon the innocuous Barbara they had picked out; by the time I was a teenager, the nickname had reached a laughable plateau. I'd gone from "perky" in fourth grade to "bubbly" in seventh, only to wind up in high school with still-developing size C breasts that made everyone feel uncomfortable and me feel guilty. What was I supposed to be now, bouncy? In true irony my "little" name had inspired me to become my own version of one of the Seven Dwarfs!

So there I was wearing tube tops that were a size too small under my shirt so my friends wouldn't feel jealous of my breasts and awkward about their own. And if they were feeling awkward, it was nothing compared to how I felt, which was something between mortified and betrayed. Factor in the shameful ache of noticing how my own father didn't know where to look when he spoke to me, which was frighteningly less and less, perhaps in direct proportion to the way my cup size increased, until finally our conversations became just fragments of information or instructions. "Bitsy, wash up for dinner." "Bitsy, turn out the light." "Bitsy, phone's for you." *Bitsy, take out the trash, and while you're there, please return to age nine.*

A part of me wanted to confront him, to walk right up to him and say, "Yep, here they are, my big bazumbas. Let's all take a long, hard look, so maybe things can get back to normal." But I would no sooner have done that than bomb Teen Scene, the hip clothing store on Middle Neck Road where I could no longer find anything among the Nik-Nik's and Baby Jane's to fit over my chest.

I was confused. On one hand, I was embarrassed about becoming a woman, but also secretly thrilled. If my father didn't know where to look, the boys at school did. It was like they had X-ray vision, and every effort on my part to hide my breasts had failed. If I was walking down the hall between classes, they would pass me, unable to pull their eyes from my chest, sometimes never even once looking up into my eyes. Before long I could pick out just the moment when one boy in a group might nudge the others to look up because I was coming their way. I was embarrassed, but I liked the attention, too, and a part of me even wanted to flaunt what I had, but I didn't have the confidence. Instead, I did the opposite, employing even more creative minimizers: oversized shirts and undersized bras and muumuus shortened and hemmed into smocks. And I slumped. I was so intent on rounding out all protrusions that I began to look deformed, lumbering around all hunched over like a big letter C. At fifteen, I spent so much time trying to be invisible that eventually I had no clue who the hell I was. And when you aren't sure, one thing is—the world will tell you.

BITSYS DON'T GET the romantic lead in the school play; they get the part of the baby sister. Or the troll. When our senior class did *Oklahoma!* they came and found me in the art room and asked me if I would play a Tumbleweed; the new drama teacher, who was universally worshipped because he looked like a hippie (he wore jeans and told us to call him by his first name, Dusty), was directing an experimental version of the Rodgers and Hammerstein classic, and he wanted some sort of symbol of the Heartland. I agreed, because school plays were cool at Great Neck North and I was desperate to be in the mainstream, but at the first rehearsal I regretted it. I had to somersault across the stage three times during the show like a dust ball, which took about fifteen somersaults, and by the fifth and last (finally!) performance had to have my back taped with gauze to cover the skin on the bony parts that had completely peeled off.

All the kids hated the production. It *was* ridiculous—I mean, why mess with "The Surrey with the Fringe on Top" by adding a *guitar* solo—but they loved me tumbling across the stage because it was so stupid it provided much-needed comic relief. Every night I got the most applause. As for symbolizing the heartland, the only thing I thought it was symbolic of was Dusty's obvious drug experimentation. Still, I craved his approval as much as the other kids, and when he patted me on the back and said, "Cool rolls, man," I beamed, despite the searing pain.

In school, I tried not to disappoint anyone. But by this time I was so unsure of myself; I thought there was no telling when I might be seen for the freak I was, so I tried to anticipate what others wanted me to be and create a personality to match. I thought a good idea would be to stay upbeat and unchanged, so I made up my mind to seem that way. I would "see" their cheerful, and "raise" them a perky. I wore pigtails long after fashion and age dictated otherwise. I suppose I thought the pigtails might counteract the large breasts, neutralize them. If I dressed and moved like a little girl, maybe no one would notice. Bouncy? No problem. Sparkly? I can sing that in four notes. Each time I heard the remark "Oh, that Bitsy is soo adorable," I felt a sense of accomplishment. I wanted it to be the mantra of my adolescence, spoken by teachers and peers alike.

Alhough I was not unpopular; I was never especially included. Even with Fern and Lydia, there was a sense of detachment, something unspoken but clear; we shared activities, but not souls. I was just bouncing too fast. I guess when you're trying so hard to be an adjective it's not that easy to be a friend. I told myself that it didn't matter, that being popular or connected was not a requirement for happiness; that one's friends could be something of a trail mix, a snack to reach for now and then. And that's exactly what I was, a little bit of a friend. A Bitsy. The power of it still astounds me.

MY PARENTS AND I tag-teamed this dynamic, I see that now. Unwittingly, perhaps, they gave their largest dollops of approval when I was quiet, unassuming, and in the background, and I wanted their approval badly. This was a challenge, morphing from one role to the next, overtly schizophrenic, but I was determined. It took some practice turning on and off again, and it wasn't unusual to see me walking home from school, taking deep breaths and talking myself down. "That's it," I'd whisper, modulating my tempo. "School was fine, just fine." Just a half hour earlier I'd been waving frantically to Lydia through the window of her bus, jumping up and down and signaling for her to call me on the phone. "Call me, okay? Are you going to the library tonight? Talk to you later! Okay, bye! Bye!" It was exhausting but strangely satisfying; at the root was an element of control similar to that in an eating disorder. On some level, you know that what you're doing isn't healthy, but the ability to do it is so intoxicating that you can't stop. Besides, you don't know any other way to feel good.

One day, years later, I was watching the movie *Mrs. Doubt-fire* with the kids, and there was a scene when Robin Williams had to keep dashing in and out of a restaurant restroom to change not just clothes but genders. At one table he was the family nanny, an elderly Englishwoman. Every few minutes he had to become his actual self, a thirtysomething young man and step out of the restroom and go to a different table at the same restaurant for a business dinner. Impressing the people at both tables was equally important to him. And so it was with me. I was in desperate pursuit of acceptance, acceptance that seemed absolutely crucial and was so pathetically tenuous, at both school and home, that my transformations were just as deliberate and just as frenzied. Eventually, Mrs. Doubtfire got caught. She was lucky. I never got to give up the facade and just relax into being myself. I'm still playing to sold-out crowds, and the result is that I am often left wondering if I'm me, or just someone who resembles me.

When I think about the name, it seems like a prophecy. Bitsy. Could there be a more limiting and obvious mandate? I didn't actually know this as a child; it's not the kind of thing that a young mind crystallizes, more of a vague notion, like a smell you can't quite identify but you know you've smelled before, lingering, daring you to recognize it. It hangs unspoken when a young girl cartwheels, not perfectly but proudly, and looking to her mother for applause is met with a bland "Very nice, Bitsy." It's the slight twitch felt in the neck of a seventh grader, who slides expectantly into her older brother's car when he picks her up from school; she is desperate for his praise, and he looks past her toward a group of eighth graders, and in particular, at Jill Corwin, who is not only the prettiest girl in the school but the meanest and asks lustily, "Who's that?"

There are no grand statements, no abuses, just an absence of expectation and challenge, and a cumulative family implication not to try too hard. What would be the point? Probably, it was the real reason I was content with the notion of motherhood, the reason Lydia Golden eventually smelled a rat and cut me loose, the very tangible lack of a sense that I could and should accomplish. My role model was my mother, and my memory of her is a string of material objects: her Pucci scarves, her perfume, Casaque by Jean D'Albret, and a collection of soft, crinkly, vinyl boots she'd slide up her legs all the way to the knee. Sometimes I'd sneak into her closet, step into the boots, and stand straight up into her mink coat, burying my face in her smells. It was the closest I ever felt to her, even closer than when we'd actually hug, which was a stiff affair. My mother is a perfect size 8, her chest a 34-B. I am like a great mutation of her; the resemblance is there, but not the elegance. Her face is all angles, and she has the smoothest skin I've ever seen. My face is round, my skin more like oatmeal than cream of wheat. Where my mother has cheekbones, I have skin, and my eyes never quite curved into the distinct almond shape of hers. My mother always looks like she's wearing an illuminating foundation. Her complexion is the palest shade of coffee, and the texture is so fluid; to this day, whenever anyone orders a coffee milk shake, I think of her face. People always tell her she looks like Lee Remick, the actress who played the mother in *The Omen*. People tell me I look like the actress who played the mother in *Home Alone*. We are different types. I got my boobs from my grandmother, who died when I was a baby.

Now my mother is obsessed with going to doctors and getting checkups. Every week she has at least two appointments. "Monday afternoon is my full body check with Dr. Waldorf and Thursday afternoon I have a dental cleaning with Dr. Gould." After she gets through with the traditional appointments, she finds alternative ways to screen. Last week she went for a consult on how to "eat right for your blood type." Because my dad is an ophthalmologist, she always requests "professional courtesy," so I guess she gets enough of a discount to justify all the extra appointments that no insurance company in the world would cover.

MY BROTHERS, who were five and seven years old when I was born, leaked their resentment of my birth like a constant morphine drip. To them, I was a silly result of their usually levelheaded parents' flawed behavior. Inconvenienced by my arrival and insecure enough about their own capabilities, Mitch and Eddie eagerly embraced the idea of me as background noise, human Muzak. Sort of a mild headache, although one for which they just couldn't find the Tylenol. On some level, I understood that my mother felt guilty about having me; she saw my birth as something she'd done to the boys. Her penance required that I remain as inconsequential as possible.

If this bothered me, I don't remember knowing it consciously. Eddie, the oldest, now lives in Florida. He is a physician like our dad, though not an ophthalmologist. Ed is a podiatrist, and he went to medical school at Howard University, which is primarily African American, a subject that is *never* broached. I was only ten when Ed went to college, and I vaguely remember a series of loud arguments and slamming doors before he finally ended up at Ramapo College. I may have been young, but believe me, it wasn't his first choice. You only have to listen to him aggressively describe Ramapo today as the most under-rated four-year college in the Northeast to know that the podia-trist doth protest too much. I was, however, fourteen when Ed went to medical school, and I don't want to say Howard was his only choice, but let's put it this way: It was either that or develop a taste for tequila and tacos.

Ed's wife, Brenda, is a nurse, and together, they are the most sensible couple in the Southeast. Seriously, if there were such a contest, they would own it. After lengthy research, they determined that Florida, full of senior citizens, was the final frontier in which to live long and prosper, if you'll pardon the mixed *Star Trek* metaphor. They have two teenage sons, both of whom are serious, bespectacled, polite young men who attend private school and appear to be on track for similarly stable, respectably boring lives. There is the little matter of the boys rejecting Judaism and practicing Scientology, but my brother and sister-in-law, naturally, avoid this topic. Eddie and Brenda have serious doubts about me. They always appear to be trying very hard not to judge me; this is evidenced by their sincerely curious questions. Usually, Brenda starts.

"So Bitsy, what exactly do you *do* all day? I mean, besides shopping and all." (Sneaks a grin at Ed.) Then Eddie will jump in. "She's not begrudging you the ring or the fancy car, Bits, she's just *sincerely curious* about how you fill your day."

Usually, I dress down when I'm going to see them; it seems to provoke them less if I don't wear jewelry. Sometimes, I fantasize about accidentally stumbling onto a cure for cancer, maybe while planting pansies or separating eggs for double-fudge brownies from scratch. It will be a miraculous accident that I notice only when I wipe my hands of soil or batter and my wrinkles or freckles go completely away and I realize I've discovered a nutrient or compound that reverses age or mutations. Then, when Brenda and Ed ask me what I do, instead of mumbling something about the kids and the house and volunteering I can tell them I received the Nobel Prize for Medicine.

My other brother, Mitchell, with whom I vaguely remember sharing a brief part of my childhood, is a software engineer. This despite the fact that his math tutor practically lived in our house when Mitch was in high school. I don't know much about computers, but it seems to me that boys who need that much help in math shouldn't go in for computer programming. Yet he makes an apparently decent living working for a pharmaceutical company that sends him worldwide approximately three weeks out of every month, so even if you wanted to have a relationship with him, you couldn't. Two years ago, Mitch married a Taiwanese girl, Celeste, who smiles a lot and accompanies him dutifully wherever he goes. He also changed his name after 9/11. Because of his work and the places he goes, he didn't think having a Jewish name like Beberman was very smart, so he completely dropped the "Beber" and now calls himself Mitchell Mann. Very nice. Personally, I think it was also because Celeste had trouble saying Beberman. It always came out like a baby blowing air bubbles. "Hello!" she'd say, with lots of smiling. "Nice meet you, Missis Bu-bu-mum."

I thought the name change might upset my parents, but they used to cringe when Celeste made the motor bubbles, so I think they were relieved. Instead of excommunicating Mitch, they processed his departure from the family name and norm as his "indefatigable ability to adapt to a changing society." That's what my dad said. For a while, I thought Mitch and I had a chance—he's a little looser than Ed, and a little younger—but it was not to be. By the time I entered high school, Mitch was lost to foreign worlds, speaking languages I'd never heard of like COBOL and FORTRAN and DOS.

SO HERE I AM, married, Jewish, with kids who can recite the Boray and the Motzi, practicing a Conservative Judaism that closely mirrors my parents' and the only child who hasn't moved far away from Sid and Evelyn, either physically or spiritually, and the stench of dissatisfaction is as sharp as ever.

Halfway through my teens, I realized that being Bitsy was a kind of okay destiny. Whether through sheer chance or pointed prophecy, I was merely one of millions of ordinary souls who quite nicely peppered the world, and this did not cause me great disappointment. Besides, there is an upside to being average: no great achievements, but no great downfalls, either. That was an okay trade-off. I never once thought of giving up my nickname or insisting that I be called by the name on my birth certificate, like the Dickies who later demand to be called Richard, the Bobbys who convert to Robert. I saw nothing to rail against, nothing so mammoth as to need a fight.

NOW, LEANING BACK in the SUV, trying to will my hands to stop shaking and the dizziness to ease, I wonder. And wondering is not like me, not like me at all. But neither is being paralyzed and unable to drive. I guess when your husband is unconscious and an empty bottle of pills is found at the scene, a burst of sudden introspection is to be expected. Like people who find God just before the ship goes down. I must be in shock. Why else would I be sitting here, head back, eyes closed, entertaining thoughts of transgenders, those souls who are trapped in the wrong sex. Only for me, it's not my sex in question, it's my whole self. For me, it's the notion that all this time I've been living as a Bitsy when I might just be a Barbara after all.

know I have to actually go into the hospital; there's no getting around it. I am the Wife, after all. But it feels so strange, like someone handed me a script and pushed me out onto the stage, and not only haven't I studied for this role, I've never even seen it. In my mental handbook, I have whole gigabytes of advice for surviving suburbia, nuances only an insider would know: How to Lobby Your Child's Elementary School for the Best Teacher, Choosing a Summer Camp That Attracts Prestigious Families for Future Networking, the Art of Phone Messages with Your New, Non-English-speaking, Live-in House-keeper. But nowhere, no matter how I mentally Google, can I locate the chapter on Accompanying Your Overdosed Husband to the Hospital.

I force myself to turn in and park in one of four designated spots across from the emergency entrance. The ambulance that brought Alan is still parked in front, its rear doors open. I walk through the automatic double doors and announce myself at the front desk, but even as I say the words "Mrs. Lerner," I have doubts about what that means. I am given four pages of papers to fill out and asked for my insurance card and then told to wait, and that a doctor will be with me shortly. I briefly debate insisting to the receptionist that I get some information right now, but that would cause a scene, and I have already over-drawn that account. Besides, the emptiness of the waiting room is comforting, the stillness is nice. The very *lack* of a scene seems promising. If there are no rushing interns and crashing carts, then maybe Alan is okay? It is 10:45 in the morning, and I am supposed to be at Happy Nails, halfway through my IOB light-sensitive gels fill-in. Instead, I am biting off what is left of one cracked, French-manicured pinkie and sitting stiffly in a hard plastic seat. I stare at the TV; a young girl I have never seen is singing. She looks just a few years older than Lauren. I think of Lauren and Evan, each safely tucked away, Ev in third grade at Cherry Lane and Lauren in her first year at Glen Vale Middle. Can it really be eight years ago that we moved into our first home? Eight years since we had such high hopes?

It didn't start out badly for us at all. In the summer of 1992, Alan and I were house hunting. We'd successfully nar-rowed it down to two: the black-and-white Colonial with the pretty landscaping and the Tudor with the circular drive, both in Woodcliff Lake, a semirural suburban township in northeast Bergen County, New Jersey, fifteen miles from Manhattan. Undecided as to the better buy, we made offers on both. I didn't even know which one to root for, but it didn't matter since we lost them both.

"Indians with a bag full of cash," said our broker, Phyllis, about the Tudor. "And the other people took the Colonial off the market, just changed their minds." I was devastated. I'd already played house in both.

"Something else just came on, though." Phyllis's voice was thoughtful, as if she wasn't sure whether to tell us or not. I waited.

"It's really perfect, actually. Great street, big house, the cul-de-sac is only four years old." I waited some more.

"I saw it this morning and loved it. The only thing is . . ." As she trailed off, I thought, Okay, here it comes, this is the part where she tells us about the triple murder that was committed and how even though they've washed away almost every single speck of blood she feels morally bound to mention that they never did find the youngest son's left thumb.

"It's in the next town over, Glen Vale." Oh that figures, I thought. Since it only took Alan and me about a *year* to decide on Woodcliff Lake, naturally the Perfect House was in another town.

"I don't know, Phyl . . ." My turn to trail off.

Glen Vale. I'd certainly been through it a number of times in the past year as I traversed Bergen County looking at houses. Tenafly, Ridgewood, Upper Saddle River, Franklin Lakes—I was like a Fodor's guide to the local residential real-estate market. Weren't there a lot of *horses* in Glen Vale? And barns and things? I'd learned to be careful in New Jersey. It was nothing like Long Island, where you know what you're getting. In New Jersey, it can look like the Gold Coast one minute and Tobacco Road the next. Just yesterday, we'd passed a house (I hoped it wasn't in Glen Vale) and I'd remarked to Alan that it looked like the kind of place a kidnapper could hide a child for years and no one would know.

But Phyllis had become something of a demigod to me; she was older, assured, a recent refugee of the Manhattan real-estate game, maybe slightly past her most hip prime, but in her hunter green Donna Karan suit and ivory Charles Jourdan pumps she was impressive, and fast becoming a tour de force in the suburban real-estate game. I wanted to please her and sensed that becoming her client would have its own status. (I was right: Just two years later Phyllis opened her own agency on the border of

Cresskill and Alpine and became the number one agent for the multimillion set.) Besides, I'd imbued Phyllis with maternal qualities, which had much more to do with my needs than her attributes, and there was safety in letting her steer us; it was a vulnerable time. My own mother, being perpetually detached, regarded everything west of Manhattan as "out there."

I needed to roost, to build my little suburban nest, and I was tired of looking. So within twenty-four hours we met the asking price and three days later had a closing date and by November we were the proud owners of 17 Autumn Court in the desirable Autumn Hill section of historic Glen Vale. And since it was the Perfect House, neither one of us mentioned the rumble of cars on Route 17, nor did we comment on the fact that our neighbors to the side had an elaborate tower of wires set up, purportedly for their ham radio, but which looked (and hummed) as if their real mission was to detect life on Mars. We were happy. We were home.

O n our second day in our new house, we meet the neighbors. Lauren is just four years old, and she and I are pouring sand into the green turtle sandbox in the backyard while Evan naps in his stroller. Lauren is just ecstatic. We have come from an apartment in Fort Lee, and she has talked about nothing else but this sandbox for weeks. I am so pleased that my little girl is so placid; this is not her natural state. No matter how Alan and I try to sugarcoat it (Oh she's just high-strung!), Lauren has been difficult to raise. If there is a "stage" (translation: problem) that a child might go through, Lauren has. At one month old, it was colic. But not your ordinary run of the mill colic; I called it colic on crack. Seriously, I know that babies who are born addicted to drugs are sheer hell to calm, but pacifying them can't possibly be worse than what I went through with Lauren. One particular day, she had been crying for forty-eight hours, and neither of us had slept in as long. Alan called to ask if he could bring anything home, and I told him to pick up an Uzi and a full round of ammo. While I waited, I called the pediatrician for the sixth time in two days, having tried the swaddling, the rocking, and even the Levsin drops, which must have been pure barbiturate, and which, the nurse assured me, *had* to work, but hadn't. I put the baby in the center of our bed, and when the very prominent, very busy doctor finally came to the phone I laid the receiver down next to her and said, "Here. You listen to her for a while," and I left the room. Not my finest moment.

At three months old, Lauren developed stranger anxiety. Naturally. She was in her stroller and we were in the lobby of our building when the loveliest of old ladies bent down to coo at the precious bundle. Lauren's screams were so piercing that I thought the lady might need medical attention. By the time she was two years old, I'd already had a lifetime of apologizing to strangers, doctors, salesmen, and even relatives. My own mother, not overflowing with maternal stirrings to begin with, took to eyeing her cranky grandbaby with mistrust, raising her glasses and taking a few steps backward, searching for diplomatic immunity. The implied request was that we bring her back when she was pleasant or thirty-two, whichever came first. So today, on this milestone of a first day in our wide open backyard, this new easygoing, giggling, four-year-old is a welcome and deserved surprise.

As we smooth our sand with plastic shovels and rakes and prepare to make pies, we are interrupted by a "Hello!" and I turn to see a woman and two girls approaching. I stand up, and within seconds my little girl launches herself back into the womb, or at least as close as she can get, which is behind my back, face pressed completely into my butt, hands clenching the extra material of my pants around the sides of her face and over her ears. She refuses to come out and say hello. In addition to the awkwardness of trying to greet someone with a Small Child Wedgie, I am quite embarrassed, a feeling which is compounded when, after a few seconds, my new neighbor asks, "How old did you say she was?"

Of course, *her* perfect angels have both introduced themselves and cheerfully told me their names (Kaley and Kendra), and their ages (eight and five). Their mother, whose name, I learn, is Gerry Sloan, informs me proudly that she and her husband, Andrew, were the very first owners on our fourteen-house cul-de-sac. She waits for me to respond, and although I say, "Oh, I see. That's nice," I have the feeling that I, like Lauren, have failed a test. I wonder if I've missed something impressive. Does being first on the block entitle them to some sort of leadership badge? A title? I am tempted to ask, but instead keep the thought to myself. I may not know all the rules of my new neighborhood, but I know enough not to be offensive.

Over the next few weeks, Gerry establishes herself as a prime source of information, a role she relishes, and, I suspect, manipulates, depending on what it is she wants me to know. For example, she does not mind telling me that the best butcher is up at the farm, but conveniently forgets to mention that I have to request a spot on the private school bus for Lauren by January. (I am late, and we end up on a waiting list.) Little Kendra is already in kindergarten and is clearly the king of the younger kids in the neighborhood, and while Lauren eventually does speak to her, their friendship will always be tenuous. Kendra likes control and Lauren, despite her shyness, has a problem with that, even though it will be years before she has the confidence to say so.

One thing Gerry does warn me about is the family to the left, the family with the wires.

"Sooo strange," she whispers, her hand covering her mouth, although there isn't anyone within earshot. She leans in conspiratorially.

"We practically never even see the son, and I would keep Lauren away from the girls, they're filthy! And those names! Flaming fire and something! I can't even pronounce them!"

As it turns out, neither of the Rabinowitz girls is named Flame or Fire, but Gerry's not far off. The older girl, who is almost ten, is named Ezora Blaise, and the younger one, the baby, who is close to Evan's age, is Magenta Skye. They definitely are weird names. In fact, when I first heard them, I thought they sounded like superheroes from a comic book, something like *The Adventures of Ezora Blaise and Her Faithful Sidekick, Magenta Skye.* Alan thinks they sound like porn stars, and I guess he has a point. But when I finally meet Susan Rabinowitz, she turns out to be pretty interesting, in a kooky sort of way, and she's actually a lot nicer than Gerry Sloan, or Madam Mayor, as I like to call her in private. Their son is six, right in the middle of his sisters and about a year older than Lauren, and his name is Ross, which is thankfully normal, but based on Ross's vocabulary, I believe he's in Gifted and Talented Everything. The first time I met him, Susan was struggling to put little Magenta in the car seat, and six-year-old Ross bent down and said evenly to his baby sister, "You must be restrained. It's the law."

A few days later, despite Gerry's warning, I invited Susan and the kids over for lunch. Zory had already eaten, so she sat and read a book, and the little ones went in the playpen. I sat Ross and Lauren at the Little Tikes picnic bench and served them grilled cheese sandwiches that I had cut into fours. I gave them juice boxes, cups of carrots, and boxes of raisins on the side. After a minute, Ross asked me what type of cheese I had used. Amused, I answered, "American," and asked if that was all right. He said it was fine, but that he preferred Asagio. *Asagio.* I laughed out loud and Susan started to apologize, but I told her that wasn't necessary. Still smiling, I asked Ross if he had a favorite food. He looked me dead in the face and said he couldn't decide between lobster Vesuvio and chicken saté. Then he proceeded to eat his lunch while reading a book about Abraham Lincoln. It was a child's book, but still. While Ross *dined* and *perused* a biography, Lauren made lovely little balls out of her bread and cheese and sang "Row, Row, Row, Your Boat" over and over—and not too well, either. She insisted on singing it her own special way.

> *Whoa, whoa, whoa your boat,*
> *Gently down the stream.*
> *Merrily, berrily, ferrily, perrily,*
> *Gently down the stream.*

I had to give Ross credit. Only once did he look up at her and shake his head as if to say *crazy kid.* Ross is certainly eccentric (from time to time, there is an actual explosion next door), but through the years I've decided that he's actually quite charming, if a little brighter than most. The girls *are* kind of dirty, but that's because Susan spends most of her time doing weird projects with them and doesn't seem to care whether they have papier-mâché on their clothes or chocolate fudge in their hair. As it turns out, Susan has homeschooled the kids, and because of that, as well as the fact that we have very little in common, we've seen little of each other over the years. Ezora, now eighteen, has been accepted at Brown University. Ross is fourteen, and he and his little sister, Magenta, who is nine, continue to learn at home. Every once in a while, I see them studying in their backyard—*together.* No fighting or name-calling; in fact, they actually seem to get along.

Despite their quirks, and despite Gerry's admonitions, the Rabinowitzes are not nearly the weirdest neighbors on the block. That distinction belongs to the family directly across the street from me in the redbrick Georgian, and the reason they're so weird is because they are wound so tight. We are talking type A wired, competitive squared. The Winstons, Peter and Peggy, have four children. The oldest, Trevor, was thirteen when we moved in and was going to boarding school for ice hockey, somewhere in Connecticut or Massachusetts. Now he's a senior in college at Colorado State and rumor has it that his career as a goalie for the New Jersey Devils remains a part of his father's elaborate delusion fantasy. The next boy, Darren, was ten, and his nickname was Bubba and still is, because he's enormous. Darren has some sort of social or emotional problem and attends a special school in Westchester. A few years ago, they tried to bring him back and mainstream him, but he brought a blowtorch to school and set the Glen Vale Schools municipal sign on fire. These boys look just like their father: broad, bullish, very macho.

Peter Winston is a self-made businessman (as he is happy to tell anyone at any time—after two vodkas, he will even relate the whole uncut version, plus you can get his "how I lost my virginity" story for free) who bought gold or something at the right time and went from being a rather crude, working-class guy to a rather crude, working-class, self-impressed jerk. The license plate on his red Porsche Carrera reads SHLONG. Enough said? He is on the borough's rec commission and is in charge of the baseball program, which in Glen Vale means he carries more clout than George Bush. Peg is a rather quiet type who has done her best to rectify her physical deficits with several plastic surgeries and frequent visits to Neiman Marcus. She is one of those women who never had any confidence and was never very pretty in high school, but now, with a wealthy husband, expensive jewelry, and a closet full of designer handbags, suddenly thinks she's gorgeous and has developed the superior attitude to carry it off.

Their third son, Keith, almost seven back then and now fourteen, looks more like his mother, fair and slender, and I always felt he was the best-looking, and the nicest, although he would certainly prove me wrong. And then there is the Winstons' daughter, eight years old when we moved in; her name is Cartier. That's right, Cartier Winston. When Gerry told me, I thought she was kidding. We were standing at my front door and she was pointing to each house and rattling off names and biographies. She had just done three painful minutes on the eyesore of the Lewises' front yard and was beginning to tell me about the Winstons when a car emerged from the Georgian's three-car garage.

"Oh, there goes Peg with little Carty!"

Gerry waved furiously at the silver Jaguar.

"Carty?"

"Yes, it's short for Cartier."

"Cartier? Like the jeweler?"

"Mm-hmm." Gerry's voice was wistful, reverent.

"And their last name is Winston?"

I looked at Gerry, to see if she thought this was as absurd as I did, but she was staring, clearly impressed.

"Gerry, you do realize that the child's name is like two jewelers?"

"What's your point?"

I couldn't believe that. Wait till I tell Alan, I thought. I decided to try again.

"Well, it's like naming her Mercedes Ferrari," I said, "or how about Mink Sable?" Gerry gave me a blank stare. Then she said, "Ooh, I like that, Mink Sable. Too bad I'm done," she added, rubbing her belly. "Well, gotta go, hon."

Later, I relayed the conversation to Alan, expecting a conspiratorial laugh or at least a shared chuckle.

"So? So they like fancy names. How are you ever going to make friends if you judge everybody?"

Turning away from Alan, I suddenly felt smaller, with a little lump lodged right in my heart. Was I crazy? Was this not funny? Now I realize Alan used to do that all the time; say something unexpected and send me off to question myself and my own sense of things. On that day, he'd touched a nerve, so I was especially vulnerable; I was a stay-at-home mom with a toddler and newborn in a new town, and I wasn't exactly overflowing with friends.

By chance, a few days later I was getting the mail and ran into Susan Rabinowitz doing the same. In a moment of abandon, I decided to share my take on the Winstons and was rewarded with the conversation I'd wanted from the start. She rolled her eyes, shook her head, and lowered her voice. "Over here, we call them Stereotypes on Ice." I laughed out loud. I wanted to hug Susan and launch into a hundred other topics. But Alan's words had lingered more than I'd expected and my confidence was diminished. Would I spoil it by taking it further? Would Alan even approve of my first friend being Susan? So I just collected the mail and went in.

One thing I do remember was feeling positive that the pretentious Winstons had doomed their daughter to a life of hurtful teasing and superficial slurs with that name. So naturally, at fifteen and now in high school, Carty Winston, as Lauren tells me frequently, is the prettiest and most popular girl in the tenth grade.

THE MEMORY IS diverting, but ethereal. It quickly dissolves with the entrance of a doctor in green surgical scrubs and mask. His face is drawn and white. I stand up, upsetting my purse, and its contents spill out onto the floor. I must look panicked, because immediately he holds up both palms as if to say *It's okay,* but instead he says, "He's sleeping. In fact, he's still quite sedated, although we pumped his stomach. But we think he's stable for now."

I open my mouth to speak, but I don't know what to say. I have just gone through this two months ago, this shocking, larger-than-life blitzkrieg of an event, only the hospital was smaller and the drive longer. It had been surreal, driving upstate to the country hospital and later to the gas station where Alan's car had been towed. Alan clearly did better than the car, even with his broken legs and contusions. The car was a cartoon version of itself; crunched-up blue metal and black leather, silver chrome. An X something or other. I can never keep them straight. Alan collects cars with attitude, edgy cars, cars that have something to prove. They all have letters that cut, like X and K, serious numbers like 911, and names like Viper. The blue one was one of his favorites, I knew, although I couldn't remember which one it was, and there was certainly nothing left on the car that would identify it. Later, Alan said it was the BMW.

"Is he going to be all right, Doctor?" Even to myself, I sound far away, removed. Like a Lifetime TV movie.

"We'll know more in a few hours" is the stilted reply. "We're going to admit him." A bad soap opera, I think, with bad acting. This doctor speaks in a solemn voice laden with drama that rings false, obligatory. He sounds like Joey on

Friends. Any minute now he will tell me that he is the famous brain surgeon Dr. Drake Ramore and a team of transplant experts are standing by to assist him as he performs a delicate, dangerous operation to save my husband's life. What would Samantha do? I find myself thinking. But this just wouldn't happen to Darrin Stephens. Bumbling human that he was, Darrin always knew where to draw the line.

Even as I have the thought I also know there's something wrong with me. I'm speaking with an emergency-room physician and yet I'm thinking about soaps and sitcoms. I physically shake my head to clear it and bend to collect the items from my purse, not so much because I care about the loose change and lipstick but because I need a distraction, a moment to think clearly. The doctor waits. I gather my things. Even though we've had a tragedy and even though this man is a doctor, I'm still embarrassed for him to see the Tampax that has rolled out onto the floor.* (See "pain you can relate to.") I quickly shove it back in, pretend that neither one of us has seen it, stand back up, and ask him what happens now. He explains that Alan's vital signs appear to be on the low end of the normal range, and since they are not sure just how long the drugs were in his system, they can't know whether there will be any long-term effects.

"The drugs?" I ask.

"Vicodin," he responds, shifting uncomfortably from side to side, "perhaps more than half of a bottle."

I take this in. The doctor clears his throat, and then speaks.

"May I ask what happened to his legs?"

IT TAKES ME a few minutes, but I manage to mumble something about a car accident, and I almost work up to regaining some composure when I am distracted by some movement behind the doctor. Coming toward us are two uniformed police officers. The doctor is trying to explain something to me, something about controlled substances and the law, and I am trying to listen, but there is something more important pulling me away, something even more pressing than the approaching policemen. It is like a rumbling tremor of an idea that picks up steam and turns into one big boulder of a thought followed by an avalanche of others and it is that Alan did not break both his legs in a car accident, no, it was not an accident, my God how is it possible that I couldn't have known that and isn't that something I learned in school, that there are no accidents . . .

". . . in cases such as these we have to file a report. Mrs. Lerner, do you understand?" I know that I have been asked a question and I do have an answer, but it is to something else.

"Freud." I smile slightly, proud to be able to recall.

"Pardon?"

"Freud said there are no accidents." I look up at the little group of three. There is an uncomfortable silence. An exchange of looks. One policeman coughs. The doctor suggests that I should probably go home and get some rest. The second policeman says that we can talk later and asks if there is someone I can call. And then I deflate. Oh God. Alan is in the hospital. He is lying in the emergency room, where he may have actually been inches from death for the second time in as many months. Quite possibly, he is there by his own hand. Still, I won't fall apart. At least not right now. Right now, there is something I must do, something much harder than falling apart, something that scares me almost more than the events of the morning. Right now, I have to call Alan's mother.

many of my fellow graduates took a year off after college to pursue a passion or simply search their souls in Europe. For me, this was never on the table. I knew the sooner I graduated and got a job, the sooner Alan would ask me to marry him, which he did. To the friends who wondered why I was in such a rush, I explained that Alan and I were too much in love to be apart. At age twenty-two, survivors of a liberal four years marked by Quaaludes, cocaine, multiple sexual partners, and an overall sense of undetermined malaise, many of my fellow *female* graduates found this explanation not just acceptable but enviable. For the first time, I wasn't completely out of vogue.

I met Alan Dean Lerner, four years my senior, during my sophomore year. He was in his last year of business school at George Washington University and had a house in McLean, Virginia, just over the Potomac, with six other guys. I loved going to that house, straightening, cleaning, domesticating. I was a regular, attending to them with unreasonable attention, cheerfully assuming the role of Wendy to their Peter Pans. There was a house dog, a mutt named Paco, whose ownership was under debate and therefore the associated responsibility of taking him out. I would often arrive to find several piles of Paco's petrified waste in corners, the result of standoffs over whose turn it was to walk him. Cleaning up after Paco made me feel strangely righteous and lofty. In a twisted way, it made me feel important.

In my spare time, I made ceramic plates, drew pictures and framed them, even carved their frat letters and other slogans du jour, like LSD, into various pieces of wood for decoration. Despite this, or perhaps because of this, I was occasionally the butt of Alan's housemates' crude and obnoxious jokes.

I was a good sport. It helped to think that they were only teasing me the way they would a sister, and since my relationship with my own two brothers was fairly nonexistent, I had no measure of a positive sibling relationship.

Alan is an entrepreneur. I realize this is a fancy word for what some might call a wheeler-dealer. Even in college, he always had some profitable venture going, whether it was scalping tickets to a Hall and Oates concert or selling wholesale designer clothes out of a suitcase (during my sophomore year, Alan scored a cache of butter-soft angora sweaters in pastels of lavender, yellow, and pink, two of which are still in my closet today). It was always a mystery how he managed to get involved in these schemes.

When he couldn't earn quick cash, he'd take odd jobs— driving a pastry truck, parking cars at a hotel, house-sitting. More than once, he had turned these jobs into connections; the bakery owner would provide free bread and cakes for a party or the hotel manager would make a suite available for a weekend. You'd think this would be a commendable personality trait, something others would admire, not to mention a surefire attribute for financial success. I certainly did. But you'd be surprised at the number of people who look down on Alan's background, how it pales when compared to an MBA from

Wharton or a law degree from Penn. The disdain is not overt. Nobody actually says that they're uncomfortable, not in words; at a cocktail party, the message registers in prolonged silences and quick exits. Other times, it's the absence of an invitation to the Simon wedding or a phone call for a birthday lunch that never comes.

The same up-from-the-bootstraps style that was so enviable in the 1950s is subtly déclassé today; it would be preferable to come from old family money than to actually come from nothing and make good. Most of the time, people don't really know what Alan does and they don't come right out and ask, which is good, since I don't really know myself, but for the longest time it's been okay not to know. Then, a few months ago at the club, doubling back to go to the ladies' room, I overheard two men talking as Alan passed by. "All flash and no cash," one said. I never liked the club all that much anyway, so I guess it's no big deal if we have to drop out.

Alan's father, the late Phil Lerner, who everyone called "Pally," had a string of businesses, never settling on one, so I guess Alan comes by his style honestly. First, Pally Lerner owned a sports bar, then an amusement center, then a nursing home. Alan remembers it as feast or famine. Before he died, at age forty-nine, just months after Alan and I married, he'd made two fortunes and lost them both. Unfortunately, he'd bankrupted his marriage just as completely. When Alan was fifteen, the year his dad purchased the nursing home, he also purchased a little duplex in lower Manhattan to cavort with the wife of the nursing home's previous owner, a flamboyant, unstable redhead who was as indiscreet as she was starved for affection.

Marian Lerner, already martyred by having to endure her husband's first and second financial collapses, received a chatty, deranged call from the woman and promptly took her son and left with not much else, except an apparently endless supply of righteous indignation. Later, when Alan's dad contracted colon cancer, his mother felt smugly vindicated. It was the only time I ever saw Alan come close to objecting to anything his mother said, and ultimately, even then, he backed off. At the funeral home, before the mourners showed up, Alan was asked to view the body. He came back from the task clearly shaken. As he wiped the perspiration from his forehead, his mother remarked, "Not such a big shot now, is he?"

I stared in horror as Alan took a menacing step toward his mother, a look on his face that I had never seen there before. His mom noticed it, too, and quickly backed away just as one of the funeral directors came over to steer us into the chapel. The moment passed, but I was never able to reconcile what Alan's dad had seen in Marian. He'd been a warm, affectionate, funny man who was sweet to me even though he was already feeling the effects of his illness when we met. And though I didn't condone his excesses or sanction his affair, as I got to know Alan's mom, it was not hard to imagine why Pally Lerner had sought warmer arms.

That was fourteen years ago, and since then, when it came to his mother, Alan led two lives. She thought him a devoted son, which he was, and a solid businessman, which he was not. He appeased her fears by telling her what she wanted to hear, spinning his story in such a way as to give the impression that he had a secure, salaried income. The first time I met Marian, I saw Alan deftly switch personas in her presence. Perhaps it should have been a red flag, but at the time I saw it as adaptability. After all, it was something we had in common; we were two chameleons doing what they did best.

In real life, Alan was, if not his father's son, than an homage to him. Phillip Lerner had earned the nickname Pally for his friendliness, his ability to make everyone feel as if they were a part of his inner circle, and Alan seemed to have inherited the gift, if not quite as naturally, than purposefully enough. His mother, on the other hand, if not exactly stoic, was stiff, contained. Our first meeting took place at a restaurant. I'd been dating Alan for close to two years, was about to graduate, and thought I'd done a marvelous job of exorcising some of the inadequacies I'd adopted at home. Perhaps I wasn't exactly confident and self-possessed, but neither was I shrunken.

"So this is *Betsy* . . ." She let her words trail as she looked me up and down, not frowning, exactly, but not smiling, either. I had been her son's girlfriend for two years and she got my name wrong. But worse still was the way she looked at me, appraising, the way one eyes a dress, wondering if it will do or if you'll need a seamstress to correct the flaws.

"It's B*i*tsy," I replied. "So nice to finally meet you." All of my old insecurities bobbed to the surface and some new ones to boot. I wondered why *I* had to correct her, not Alan. She made some sort of sound, like "Mmm," nothing revealing and certainly nothing like "Nice to meet you, too." And then she turned to her son.

"Alan, darling, you're looking thin. I hope you're going to order a hearty meal. You look like you could use a nice prime rib." Her comment felt like a direct stab at me. Back then, there was still an unwritten mandate floating about: woven into the fabric of being a real woman was the responsibility of keeping your man well fed. This was way before cholesterol and quiche consciousness. I'd felt the subtle dig: I was not woman enough to take care of my man.

My future mother-in-law barely spoke to me the entire night. I spent the whole meal alternately trying to get her to like me and worrying that in my tan slacks and purple sweater I was underdressed next to her slim gray suit, white pleated shirt, and cameo brooch. It didn't help that she spoke for several minutes about one of her all-time pet peeves: how it was a huge mistake when girls were given the right to wear slacks in school. This had been one of the true joys of my childhood, liberation of celebratory status in second grade, the chance to wear a drawer full of Danskin pants outfits to school, but, of course, I didn't say so. I endured a long diatribe about how pants had given way to miniskirts and "those provocative white boots from France" and in general had precipitated the "egregious decline in young girl's morals," and guess who she looked pointedly at when she finished.

By dessert, I'd decided she probably had X-ray vision and could even see my beige rubber diaphragm. In my cervix. Alan, who had been trying to get me into bed since our first date and had used every trick in the book for six months before I finally gave in, and who actually had quite a few little fetishes, including a distinct fascination with panty hose, didn't argue with her about anything. He just nodded and ate.

It didn't surprise me to learn that Marion Lerner was a ninth-grade math teacher. I'd needed a tutor to get through ninth-grade algebra. I had never fully mastered percentages or the plotting of coordinates, and I lived in fear of my teacher, a sour-faced disciplinarian named Mrs. Yablenski, who shared a similar countenance with Mrs. Lerner. I spent at least ten minutes doing the math in my head to determine if it was possible that they were twin sisters or, at the very least, college roommates. Not that anyone noticed my silence as I added the numbers, since neither Alan nor his mother included me in the conversation. Later, I wondered aloud if it was me, specifically, that she didn't like.

"Don't be so sensitive," Alan chided. "She's just afraid you'll take me away from her." I think that was supposed to comfort me.

MY PARENTS WEREN'T wholly in favor of Alan or the marriage. My father, Dr. Sid Beberman, is seriously old school, and Alan's wild schemes and proclivity for high-profile and risky projects made him nervous. If you held a parade of all the people who might be suspicious of an entrepreneur, my dad would have been named grand marshal. Of course, Dr. Sid would have objected to anyone I brought home who wasn't terminally boring. I suspect a nice rocket scientist or biological research engineer might have pleased him.

As an ophthalmologist, my dad has almost zero knowledge of finance and loans, and to this day keeps strict, orderly accounts, safely pocketing enough money for a comfortable if modest retirement, rarely splurging on purchases likes jewelry or vacations. He's never understood Alan's energy, distrusts his taste for luxury, and thinks him frivolous, immature, not solid or stable enough. But he's had to bite his tongue, which always makes me smile just a little. No matter how skeptical, it was hard to argue with Alan's quick success after school, evidenced by the two-thousand-square-foot condo or Mercedes SL convertible or the sparkly surprises he'd leave on my pillow and which I have no problem showing off to my parents to this day.

When I insisted on marrying Alan, my mother, Evelyn, who has always gone along with my father about everything

(I mean that literally; I don't once ever remember her having a single difference of opinion with him, let alone an argument), supported me. We have never been close, not in the real way that I see when I watch other daughters and mothers. And while I don't think my mother means any harm and while I don't take it personally (she doesn't seem able to connect with anyone), there are moments when I miss the bond, any bond, to the point of physical ache. Her support always surprises me.

My mother thought marriage was a sensible move. Not that she necessarily approved of Alan, he was secondary; she approved of me being settled. "Glazing ashtrays" (which was what she called my painting and pottery) was a nice hobby, she stated, but not a life. When we were first married, and I was waiting to get pregnant; we moved to Fort Lee, New Jersey. I didn't know I was waiting to get pregnant; that seems to be something I see in retrospect, or maybe I did, it's just that every time I look back on those days I have this vision of myself ghostlike and drifting in slow motion with feet a foot off the ground through some self-induced emotional coma. I continued to teach art at a local elementary school, learned to shop at the butcher and cook for two, and we got a dog (more approval from mom—dog = domesticity; more thin lips from dad—I guess he was just staying toned), but I remember feeling as if I was going through the motions. I remember feeling *indefinite.* Was I Bitsy, or was I Mrs. Lerner, a graduate, a teacher? The only role I felt clearly was that of dog owner, and that was because of the negative impact.

Our dog turned out to be a major mental case; the result, we later found out from the breeder, of incest. Our adorable puppy grew into the canine equivalent of Jeffrey Dahmer. My parents believed Alan and I made the dog neurotic by our parenting. (Fast forward to having a child with several neuroses. Can you spell "therapy"?)

Peaches was a purebred, fifteen-pound Lhasa apso that thought she was a Saint Bernard. And she had a mean streak. It seemed her raison d'être was to terrorize the other dogs in our building—the larger, the better. When Alan would lift her up to keep her from other dogs, she would attempt to bite him. Once she turned her head right into his stomach and took out a chunk. Most of the other dog-owning tenants quickly learned to avoid her. One man on our floor was afraid to walk out of his apartment with his 130-pound Newfoundland on the off chance that Peaches might be playing in the hall. He called me twice a day to let me know that Astro was going out to tinkle and to please keep Peaches inside. Eventually, we had to face the fact that Peaches was too much for us to handle. After a series of false pregnancies, during which the dog would actually lactate, we were exploring the options and coming to terms with the fact that we'd have to give her up or put her down, but were not quite there. Then, shortly after I discovered I was pregnant, I broke a glass while doing the dishes and the pieces shattered on the floor. Peaches had come to regard most of what fell on the floor as hers, and this was no different. She clamped onto a jagged piece of glass and refused to let it go, even as the glass cut into her gums and blood dripped from her mouth. It took us four hours to finally distract her with a fully cooked rib steak. In the morning, Alan took her to our vet, who assured us he knew a nice old lady who lived alone in a large house who could handle the dog. I was very upset, but I did realize how much stress Peaches was causing, and also that there was no way this dog could coexist with an actual human baby, so I let her go.

My fellow tenants were ecstatic. When they learned that Peaches was gone, they couldn't hide their smiles. Suddenly, people would get on the elevator with me, ask about my due date, and how I was feeling. They tried to show sympathy, too, for my grief at having to give up Peaches, but their glee was ill-concealed. I think there must have been a lot of high-fiving going on behind my back, probably little dinner parties to celebrate. For me, it became the reason to quit my job, though I'm not exactly sure why. Both Alan and my mother thought I was under too much stress for a second trimester pregnant woman, and I never thought to question it.

When I think back, teaching was actually the more enjoyable part of my life as a "young married," yet I became convinced that the best thing for me would be to relax and focus on the coming baby, and that was that. It was a time of vulnerability, a time when that vulnerability was stoked like a constant fire, not just by a husband who fervently needed to direct but by my own desire to fervently please. I was convinced by Alan to have natural childbirth and to breast-feed. He felt strongly about this, of course; men always do. And it was the right move, medically, I'll give him that, but isn't it amazing how many men are so sure of the right things to do when they don't have to do them? Years later, I admitted, though only to myself, just how much I hadn't wanted to do either. And my resentment about those decisions has festered for years. With all the talk about the mind-body connection, if, God forbid, a doctor told me today that an X-ray revealed two big black cancer balls in my stomach, I would say that I know exactly when I got them, and you could name one Natural Childbirth and the other Breast-feeding. And I even enjoyed breast-feeding. It's just that I didn't choose it.

When Lauren was two, I became pregnant with Evan. Soon after Evan was born (can you guess how?), we bought the house on Autumn Court. My mother grandly announced that my "real life" had begun. By then, I was completely guilt-free about the life I'd chosen. I'd long since outgrown Lydia Golden and Fern Nudelman, although I may have momentarily been stunned to hear through the grapevine that Lydia, who was in fact an attorney, had bought a Manhattan condo on her own. Still, if I'd had even a glimmer of fear that I was a fossil for choosing to become a stay-at-home mom, I don't remember it. I really don't.

Somehow I convince the doctor that I'm fine, that I can drive myself home and that I don't need any drugs for myself. Funny, in all the years we've been together I don't think Alan or I have taken anything stronger than Tylenol with Codeine. I guess that's another reason the idea of Vicodin is so stunning. Vicodin. Jesus, isn't that the drug that's been on the news, the one that has some sort of a street value?

All along Ridgewood Avenue there are neat, well-kept little houses. They look so sane. Is it possible that there are child molesters and wife beaters and Vicodin abusers just beyond the manicured patches of grass and rustic stone walks? I pass a school, a darling little preschool; it looks like the predecessor to a fancy private school, all ivy and cobblestone with dark-green canvas awnings. I dial the number for Alan's mother's school, one I haven't seen, but one I imagine as infinitely more institutional. It is surprisingly difficult to convince the secretary that it is a true emergency and yes, I need to interrupt her in the middle of class.

"Are you sure?" she asks me three times. Finally, Mrs. Lerner, none too pleased, comes to the phone. When I tell her the situation, she is not only shocked, she is angry. That is her main emotion, I would say. I do my best to deflect, to explain how little I know of his condition, but finally I give up and just tell her the doctor's name and the hospital.

"That's all I know. Feel free to call them yourself." As I continue driving, the tears begin to spill out and roll down my face.

"How could this happen?" Marian kept demanding. And the implication was clear. How could I have let this happen? What tremendous flaw in *me* is responsible for the fact that her perfect son is lying in a hospital? What did I do to force Alan to ingest the remains of a bottle of painkillers that I guess had been prescribed for his leg pain. This leg pain that was the result of not one but two broken legs caused by a terrible accident. Alan's car had veered off a mountain road and crashed into the embankment of an overpass. There was no documentation of skidding or braking or tire marks to be found. How could this happen, indeed?

WIPING THE TEARS away so I can at least see, I think about who else I should call. The doctor said there is nothing I can do for Alan, that the next forty-eight hours are the most critical. I should get some rest, he said, and yet I am really not tired, since I am ashamed to say that I slept perfectly soundly through the night, without the slightest sense that Alan was in distress. Caring only that his incessant tossing hadn't disturbed me, I didn't realize that anything was wrong until almost 9:00 a.m., when I suddenly realized that he hadn't phoned me down in the kitchen to say that he was ready for me to bring up his coffee and the paper. So I am going home, not to sleep, but to be there for the children. I will call my parents later when they get home from work, a phrase I am still not used to using in reference to *both* my parents.

My dad retired from his eye practice a few years ago, and about the same time my mother, who never worked a day in her life, sort of fell into her own business, and now my dad is helping her with that. It's almost unimaginable but it's true.

My mom's housekeeper, Veronica, who replaced Vajay, is from Martinique and had a steady stream of cousins and friends who would come into the country from the Caribbean looking for domestic work. My mother had her own steady stream of Long Island matrons who were continually losing or firing their help, and before she knew it, she had an informal kind of referral service going. My dad, being a stickler for the law and having way too much time on his hands, decided that they should open a little business in the old section of Great Neck, down on Middle Neck Road near Steamboat, where the rents were cheaper. After he investigated, insured, and filed all the proper forms, Evelyn's Eminent Helpers was born.

Turns out, my mother is really good at this.

"I do have a knack for making the right fit," she says. "You can't send a country girl from the Dominican when it's an older Polish lady that will fit the bill." Go figure. Evelyn Zacher Beberman, currently of Kings Point, formerly of Franklin Square by way of the Grand Concourse, whose greatest claim to fame was her stellar play in the finals of the Nassau County regional duplicate bridge tournament of 1986 that resulted in the two-foot-high gold trophy prominently displayed on the mantel in the den, now knows the difference between patois and Farci, most legal loopholes pertaining to visas and residency requirements, and even the approximate time it takes to get from the Port Authority Bus Terminal or the Grand Central subway station to every community on Long Island's north and south shores. This business acumen does not preclude her from the occasional faux pas.

At Mitchell's wedding, she managed to take her new Taiwanese daughter-in-law's family aside and tap them as a source for housekeepers.

"Hello, Celeste, dear, I'm just asking your mother and aunties if they have any friends who are looking for work."

Luckily, my dad was able to cut her off before she explained why she was asking and before Celeste focused in. Celeste's family is not wealthy, but they are educated. Her father works for the government and her brother is in the import-export business, plus two or three aunts or uncles have PhD's and are teachers. Thankfully, they hadn't made the connection, and Mitchell, who had turned a nice tomato red, managed not to explode. I guess you can take the housewife into the business world, but you can't make her politically correct.

Other than troubleshooting my mother's possible gaffes, my dad organizes the books, check references and visas, and makes my mother swear not to deal with any illegal immigrants. How that can possibly be achieved in that business is beyond me. Anyway, I will not call them now. They will handle it better later, at home, and it will be nighttime, so they won't feel compelled to come all the way out here, and they will be relieved about that.

I guess I should call one of my friends, but I can't exactly say who my friends are these days. There is Mara, of course. Her husband, Joel, is a psychiatrist, so she thinks that makes her one, too. We've been friends since I moved into town, but "Dr. Mara" has three children who are perfect in every way, and I'm in no mood to hear her reframe all their weird quirks as "gifts." I swear, her kids could rob the grocery store for crack money and she'd say, "My kids really work together to get what they want." That's how she talks, too. It's always "my Sasha this and my Alex that." Last year, she had some problems with her middle son, and she went around saying, "My Ricky is the creative type." That meant he was able to total their brand-new Lexus without leaving the garage. If anyone could reframe my problems, it would be Mara. "Perhaps Alan is acting out latent anger issues with drama and strength as a gift to you so you can challenge yourself to grow as a person?" Still, what if my situation is too depressing for even Mara to spin? I just can't take the chance. Besides, come to think of it, I haven't heard from Mara in a while.

I guess I could call Susie Lippman. She's a longtime friend. Not that I trust her. Susie is interested in one thing—furthering her husband Arnie's career. Arnie is one of Alan's business partners. Unlike my husband, Arnie has made and kept a ton of money, and Susie has decided she's now a decorator. Her main objective before she became a decorator was to associate with as many wealthy families as possible so they would invest with Arnie, thereby bolstering his already impressive portfolio and keeping Susie in Loro Piana and Chanel. Now her main objective is to decorate for them.

Susie's chief qualifications as a decorator are that Arnie's family had enough money so that she was able to hire Mario Buatta to consult on their Saddle River home, and because her house is now a drop-dead-gorgeous study in chintz and Italian marble, she thinks she has a gift for design. She seems to have conveniently forgotten that she paid 35 percent on every last hand towel to Mr. Buatta for that "estate look," but there she is with her own name in raised gold letters on beige business cards: *Susie Lippman, design consultant.* Now she even talks like a decorator.

"Now this table," she says, running her hands along the top of a low wood oval as we stroll through an antiques market, "this table is trying to say 'use me.' Can you hear it?" I look around. Is she serious? Um, no, Susie, I want to respond, I don't speak table. I do hear every normal person in America groaning, but no, no table. Instead I murmur "Mmmm . . ." Scratch Susie.

There are girls I could call from various segments of my life: tennis league, Hebrew car pool, the school. I could list them: Wendy, Leslie, Rona. But for some reason, not one of them feels right. Wendy is too harried with her own life all the time, and Leslie's husband is playing around whether she knows it or not, and the last time we went to Rona's for dinner she reached into the top of a closet the minute the guys pulled out of the driveway to get the Chinese takeout and produced a bottle of Grey Goose vodka.

"Don't tell Marc," she whispered. "He thinks I have a problem."

Ya think?

Funny thing is, since Alan's first accident, I haven't heard from Wendy or Leslie, either, and Rona's only called once, and that was to see if she could borrow some wine "for a recipe." I really haven't heard much from anyone lately, but I guess I've been so preoccupied I haven't noticed.

I suppose the most logical choice is my best friend of sorts, Diana Gilbert, who lives around the corner. Her kids are exactly the same age as mine, only in reverse: Victoria is nine, and Stevie is twelve.

Diana and I don't really bond, not in the way I imagine real girlfriends do, but our lives throw us together a lot. The kids often have the same teacher or after-school event and we're a natural car pool, so I guess she's my best friend by default: friendship by geography and frequency. Her husband is a researcher with a pharmaceutical corporation, several years older, not into any sports, and, like his wife, overweight, so he's Alan's least favorite kind of guy. They don't have much to talk about, but occasionally we get together as couples and it's . . . well, civil. My one big problem with Diana is her unwillingness to commit to anything. Let me rephrase, to commit to anything that might help anyone out. She's happy to commit to fun, especially food related, but just try and nail her down for a committee or even just to do a small favor, and forget it, out come the stall tactics and the excuses. I think she's almost pathologically afraid to say yes. You could ask her if she'd like to receive a million dollars on Friday and she'd probably say, "Friday? Gee . . . I'm not sure."

I first learned about this quirk when I needed a semi-emergency root canal. We'd lived on Autumn Court for a year, and Diana and I had been friendly for about four months. I called to ask for her help.

"Hi, Di, I need to ask a favor. Do you think you could bring Lauren home from school tomorrow? I wouldn't ask but I'm having a root canal."

"Ooh, root canal, poor you."

"Tell me about it."

"So what happened?"

What happened? I just told her what happened. Does she want the details of my dead tooth? Maybe so.

"Well, I had all this pain and I couldn't drink anything cold or hot and I finally went to the dentist today and the root is exposed so it has to be done."

"Wow. Yuck." Uh-huh.

"So, do you think you can just bring Lauren home when you get Steve?"

"When is it again?"

"Um, tomorrow."

"Welll . . ." This, I will come to learn, is Diana's signature "Welll . . ." It serves two purposes. First, it gives her time to think of a good reason she can't commit. Second, the pause might make you feel so awkward that you voluntarily withdraw your question. I don't. I wait.

"You know, it *might* be fine, but you know me, I can't even tell you where I'll be this morning!" Another of Diana's tactics is to characterize herself as scattered and disorganized. She hopes you'll decide you'd be better off asking a more competent friend. This directly contradicts Diana's actual skills; she could unionize the squirrels in her backyard to stop collecting acorns if she so desired.

"What time is your appointment?" This one throws me. What's the difference when my appointment is? I need her to pick up Lauren at three.

"Um, it's at noon."

"Oh great! Then if something comes up, I mean worst case, I could let you know in the morning, right?"

Much of the time, Diana actually does come through, but first she wears you out with her waffling, and ultimately it has the desired effect: You hesitate to ask her for anything because it is such a painful experience. I always wonder what she'd say if there was a real emergency.

"Hello, Di? I've been hit by a bus. I'm paralyzed from the neck down. Could you watch the kids for an hour?"

"Welll . . ."

In actuality, being hit by a bus is possibly no worse than what's happened to me today, and certainly I'm paralyzed, at least emotionally, so perhaps I should give her a call and find out the answer.

ELEVEN

It's single-lane traffic through Ridgewood, where the houses look so homey and darling. They cost maybe one-fourth of the houses on my own street, but they look so much more inviting, as if each is as snuggly and comforting as a womb. As if, instead of a plasma TV and a Sub-Zero refrigerator, inside each is the soft thump of a beating heart. These are real people, with real friends. I want to pull into the drive of one of the little cottages, walk up the stone-lined path, and knock on the red, arched front door and tell my story to the kindly, grandmotherly type who answers. Then we will sip hot tea and nibble on freshly baked buns at her small kitchen table. Because she is lonely, she welcomes the company and offers me the extra bedroom at the top of the stairs that used to be her daughter's because she hasn't heard from her daughter in some months. It will have a full-sized canopy bed covered in a Danish blue-and-white quilt, sheer white ruffled curtains, and round braided rope rugs on the hardwood floor. I will just lose myself in another life, a different life; start completely over.

Reluctantly, I turn north on Maple, head out of Ridgewood, and try to get a picture of Alan in my head—not the way I last saw him, limp and hooked up to tubes, but when we first met. I want to remember why it was, exactly, that I chose him. On the outside, there's nothing blatantly wrong with Alan. He's been a good provider, and he's handsome enough. He didn't take to parenting quite the way I'd hoped, and his relationship with the kids is more functional than affectionate, but even though sometimes it's been exhausting trying to make up for his aloofness with them, overall we haven't argued much. Through the years, certain traits revealed themselves that I was unaware of—Alan's need to impress people, for one. He hates that we have a dog, but as soon as he's with someone he admires who *has* a dog, he talks about Casey as if the retriever was his idea, like the two of them are best buddies, when in truth he hasn't even once thrown Casey so much as a twig. In addition to his phobia about fat people, Alan likes to carve people up, to dissect them and find disease. Many times, after what I think has been a perfectly lovely dinner, we get in the car and he starts: "What an asshole." This will be followed by lengthy, passionate, verbal surgery, during which Alan will reveal all the husband's flaws or the wife's manipulations, all of which I have invariably missed.

While I imagine most married couples come to find areas of discord, I wonder if perhaps I was so committed to the plan that I gave little thought to its components. Why Alan? Certainly, I was intrigued by his persona; he was the total opposite of my father, the slow-moving, pinched-lipped, sternly authoritative Dr. Beberman. He had no plan past business school, and barely made it through that. Having had no formal internships or summer jobs, he graduated without offers from any firms, but he was always busy working on some sort of financial or real-estate deal and immediately began acquiring high-ticket items; he painted an intoxicating picture of what life could be like. He was a natural salesman. But was there a moment, an instant, when I knew without question that he was the one? There must have been qualities, characteristics that I adored. Why can't I think of them? Was he incredibly witty or funny or overwhelmingly sexy? Did I even think about it? Could it be that he was just there? Like a husband *unit,* the right age, shape, and persuasion? For that matter, why me? What drew Alan in such a way that for two years until I finally graduated and joined him in the real world he stayed faithful (at least as far as I know) and committed to me? I wonder if he has a clue. Through the years, we've used the word "love" liberally, casually, the way we use cream in our coffee, out of habit and without thought. But I don't remember the push of it, the power of it. So if it wasn't love, the only thing I can remotely imagine is that it was the sex.

I had a slow start with sex. I showed a complete lack of judgment with Gary and my one attempt to experiment, I think, because of this. There was Sandy Littman and the petting sessions in high school, and during my senior year there was a fellow artist, as we precociously called ourselves, with a penchant for black turtlenecks and black jeans, named Glenn. Glenn was almost my first. We certainly came close. It was a time when Warhol and Lichtenstein were in the foreground, when the frenzy over Jasper Johns was practically sexual (and to me, still is). Between hormones and all that glorious discord, it was hard not to get carried away. But as with Sandy, I never did go all the way with Glenn; it took me long enough to work up the courage to give him a hand job, and that didn't go well at all.

During my first attempt, I was completely thrown to find something sticking up out of the top of those tight black jeans and had to consult Lydia for a lesson in male anatomy. I mean,

I knew that guys got hard; I just thought when they did, it made their thing hang straight down. I couldn't fathom why in the world it would be pointing up! That first time with Glenn I thought I'd missed something in health class about the male body or possibly that Glenn had a horrible deformity. Seriously. When Lydia finally explained everything, I felt so stupid that I made her tell me exactly how to give a hand job so I could make it up to Glenn. She did so, with feigned superiority and impatience, on the leg of my stuffed bear, stressing grip and speed, lots of speed. So it gave me a bit of pleasure when I finally did do it and Glenn said, "Whoa, take it easy, it's not a race." Not because I wanted to be a bad hand-job giver, but I did want Lydia to be.

For some reason, after that I was never uptight about sex, just blasé. I held back from Sandy and Glenn only because I wasn't that interested in having some guy just plunge himself in and out of me. I mean, based on how it felt when they did it with their fingers, there was really no rush. By the time I was thirteen, I knew how to make myself come. I'd spent all that time alone in my room, after all, and the guys could never make it happen better than I could myself; they didn't even get me to stage two, preorgasmic excitement. There were a few escapades in college—those breasts really drew them in—but nothing felt right until the day a handsome, smiling, perfectly groomed graduate student in The Tavern, AU's campus bar, offered to buy me a beer.

Alan turned out to be really uninhibited and curious, even a little kinky. After the first couple of times, I started to figure out how to move and position my body so I could actually have an orgasm with him. Not to say that Alan was always concerned with this; he touched me everywhere, but it sometimes seemed self-serving, a prelude to getting me ready for what he needed. There were more than a few times when I found myself in the bathroom finishing what he started, but even so, sex was never an inconvenience or an imposition; in fact, it was my pleasure, especially when I decided that Alan was going to be the one. After that, I would have done anything he wanted.

I know I am in the minority about liking sex now—one lunch with Gerry Sloan or Diana is enough to remind me of that—but the fact remains that as I get older, I've begun to feel blissfully liberated when I'm naked, even in bright light, and unself-conscious when entwined in any number of sexual positions, and believe me, through the years Alan and I have attempted a bunch. It is not because I am so gorgeous naked. I mean, I'm not terrible. My butt's all right and my hips are fairly slim, but after all, I've nursed two kids with this oversized chest, and I wouldn't exactly have a fit if someone offered me a free breast lift and a tummy tuck to boot. It's not that I get off on the sight of my body; it has more to do with the feel. Years ago, when we were potty training Evan, he'd sometimes take his diaper off himself and run through the house like a liberated prisoner; it became a game, he purposefully being mischievous because he knew I'd chase him through the house to get it back on. But now I realize that was only part of it; naked felt free to him, natural. And naked makes me playful, sensuous, and feline; I turn into a piece of taffy, wanting to be smoothed and stretched, massaged like the very clay I used to sculpt with— who knows, maybe there is a little artiste in me after all? Or maybe it's the only time I'm really sure that I'm not an exact duplicate of my mother, not properly composed and laminated like Evelyn. Eminent Evelyn. I can't ever imagine my mother experiencing abandon, let alone sexual passion; in fact, I can't even use the words "abandon" and "my mother" in the same sentence, unless it is to say that "All natural expressions of emotion or displays of spontaneity were *abandoned* by *my mother* long before I entered the world."

So then, sex it must have been. That is as good an explanation as any for why twenty-four-year-old Alan Lerner wanted to marry me. I mean, let's face it, in terms of sex, I was a young man's dream: always ready, always willing—to be blunt, always wet—which didn't stop him from using it against me through the years, as an insult, a dig, as if I should feel ashamed. The last time was about a year ago, when my credit card maxed out for the second time at the A & P, when I yelled at Alan for what I thought was irresponsible bill paying.

"Do you have any idea how humiliating it was to have my card turned down? Twice? I wanted to die. I can't take this anymore, Alan, I just can't." And then he just exploded.

"You think I like it? Maybe if you spent a little less time thinking about shopping and getting your nails done"—and then the clincher—"shoving something between your legs, you'd see things are tough out there and all the pressure's on me to handle our money issues." He said "issues," but it was clear that he meant "problems."

I felt really ashamed when he said that, and dirty, as if suddenly my father was standing right there, just outside our bedroom door, nursing that sour look and nodding knowingly at my impurity. I also felt incredibly stupid. I thought that we were dropping out of the golf club because he really was too busy and really had developed tendonitis in his right elbow. Looking back, I wonder if it was Alan's attempt to shield me or to save face. I'm not sure. When he suggested we take a family trip instead of sending the kids to summer camp, I waved him off as if he was being ridiculous. And when he systematically unloaded all but one of the sports cars, I believed that he really had lost interest. His last exchange had been a Porsche for a Ford Explorer, and I was definitely surprised by that. But Alan claimed he needed a four-wheel-drive truck for navigating rural and rocky real-estate sites, and why would I think differently? After the confrontation, he came clean. He said we would have to curb our lifestyle, and I confess that I cried. This was so unexpected. I didn't want to believe it, and I didn't know how to cope. This was not *the plan.*

Alan offered sketchy explanations: money was tight, banks were not lending, one deal fell through because a lawyer had absconded with funds. Whatever he told me, it still came down to the same mandate—we had to make changes. First, we cut back on cleaning help, firing our live-in, five-day housekeeper in favor of a cleaning lady who came three days, then two, and finally we were down to a service once a week. Next, we changed landscapers three times, finally settling on a young kid who merely mowed our acre of lawn. The country club followed, not that this was such a devastating loss; as everywhere, I had made only superficial friendships in the three years that we'd been members, and I had no interest in smacking some microscopic little ball around for four hours a day—it was just the *giving back* that was such torment. I'd rather never own a thing than have to give something back. And it was all so confusing! Just a year before, it seemed that we were doing remarkably well, but since Alan handles all the finances, I guess I can't be sure. Since he wasn't offering any concrete details, I decided not to ask and to just hope for the best. I was so embarrassed. I thought about telling my parents, but only for a second. It would be preferable to have my organs removed while still alive than to see my father smug and self-righteous, so I'd decided to just pretend as much as possible until Alan turned things around. And he would turn things around. What other choice was there?

Since I was fierce about protecting our image, I took to the pretending like an all-star. I'd convinced myself that this was only a temporary setback, and I was desperate to maintain appearances. If people called to make dinner plans, I implied a lingering stomach flu. If I had no new clothes, handbags, or shoes to sport, I lamented this season's uninspiring styles. Probably there were those that guessed at the real reason, probably some who actually recognized what was happening sooner than I did; these would be people who *called* their problems "problems," and maybe even faced them. But as we began to withdraw from our former lifestyle, I told myself that no one knew what was what.

The involuntary physical effects began within months. I started to grind my teeth at night, had frequent indigestion, and developed a slight twitch in my left eye. Since then, Alan and I have talked less and less and he hardly sleeps, which I know because I feel every small turn or shallow sigh, thanks to the softness of our luxury pillow-top mattress, which we bought in exactly twenty minutes at Sleepy's barely a year ago for almost $2,000, a sum that did not seem extravagant at the time. This, not just because I was blissfully unaware of any financial *issues,* but because the mattress's springy softness was incredibly arousing, tantalizingly soft, an aphrodisiac for an already varied repertoire of lovemaking; it created new sensations during sex, sensations that are now but a mere memory since we haven't even kissed, let alone made love, in months.

And then, about six months ago, just before Halloween, Alan said things were looking up. He said there were plenty of coals on the fire, that it was only a matter of time before one of his deals came through. I relied on his words as if I'd been lost and wandering in the desert and he was dripping ice water into my parched, thirsty mouth. With hope, I could manage. But then, on Halloween, something happened that I didn't expect and nobody could have been prepared for, something awful. And right after that, everything seemed to go very bad very fast, like we pressed fast-forward and it got stuck. Then Alan had his accident. After that, he didn't even seem to be trying to manage his business, and it was hard enough to run the house and raise the kids with him in two casts and barely able to get out of bed, and now this.

let myself into the house. Casey is bouncing up and down to greet me. He doesn't know we have problems; it's not like his life has changed at all. He still gets his rawhide chips and Iams puppy chow and all the hugs and kisses any golden retriever could ever want. Even more from Lauren these days. Since Halloween, she's taken to lying down on the rug with Case and holding on to him the way she used to hold her giant Hello Kitty when she was three. "Oh, Alan," I say mournfully to Casey as I bend down, take his soft face in my hands, and look into his brown eyes, "what is going on?" Casey, of course, thinks I said something in doggy that means he might be getting a porterhouse steak and simply cannot contain his tongue, and for once I do not back away but let him cover me in wet licks because wet licks wipe away tears even better than tissues. Of course, the main reason Casey is covering me in kisses is because he has to go outside and not because he understands my need for love. Not wanting to be so pathetic that I milk the dog for affection, I reluctantly stand up and let him out the back door.

We have a perfect setup for our pup, a fenced-in area off the back door just big enough for him to play, with a corner covered in pachysandra, his personal favorite for doing his business.

Outside the fence is the remainder of the yard, lots of perfect sod, a large wooden swing set with a yellow canvas-covered slide, plus a trampoline and a soccer goal and a badminton net that has seen better days. Casey is allowed in the rest of the yard, which has the Invisible Fence, only after he goes to the bathroom in his section. I spent many nights planning the logistics of this, and it was a major consideration when we looked for a house, as were all the little details. They seemed so important at the time. Looking out the back door at Casey, I wonder if perhaps I had my priorities skewed. I did spend an awful lot of time planning out the poop.

I check the clock and see I've got an hour before the kids come home. I have to think of what I'm going to say, and instantly I decide to lie. There's no way they can handle this, not after the accident two months ago. Sadly, I don't think that Alan's *absence* will have that much of an impact on their lives, but scandal will. I don't think they can handle any more turbulence or trauma. I am going to tell them that daddy wasn't feeling well and he's going to be in the hospital getting checked out and because both his legs are in casts, they had to send an ambulance to take him there.

As usual, I am especially worried about Lauren. Her difficulties as a toddler gave way to other anxieties in preschool, and each age has brought newer and increasingly complicated woes. She is stubborn. Also anxious. Often needy. The girl has a lot of fears. From ages five to eight, those fears and phobias absolutely dictated how we lived our lives. In order to get her hair cut, I had to drive a half hour to Fair Lawn to a children's salon that had seats shaped like fire engines and ponies. Even this only helped a little, and she cried through the entire five-minute ordeal. She was afraid of the shoe store, afraid of the hard silver measurer. I toyed with the idea of drugs. "I think you're coming down with a cold, honey. Let's just give you a little of this decongestant." Not a chance I could ever do it. When it was time for a visit to the doctor and, God forbid, a vaccination, I almost brought the cough syrup, but for me! The staff was all very familiar with Lauren; they came into the examining room en masse, two nurses and the doctor, insisting that I hand her off like some kind of pediatric version of the scene in *Sophie's Choice*. It was a nightmare.

By the time Lauren turned nine, we had consulted a therapist, who supported our decision to send her to summer sleepaway camp, as an extreme intervention. She went kicking and screaming onto the camp bus, completely unashamed of making a scene in front of the other campers.

Camp Robinwood had a rule that no phone calls were allowed for two weeks so the kids could adjust. Three days into the summer, the phone rang; it was Dotty and Gene, the owners. I think they wanted me to come and take *them* home. Since entering the Knotty Pine bunk, she'd gotten her bunkmates to help her make a calendar entitled "Days Left in This Stinky Place" and taught them a song whose refrain was "Dotty, you're the biggest dot I ever saw." But the biggest problem was medical. Lauren had declared a hunger strike, and the camp nurse had never seen any child so resolute. Since she'd left home, Lauren had eaten only Jolly Ranchers, and Dotty and Gene were breaking the no-phone rule so Alan and I could convince her to eat. Somehow, we managed to get through to her that she was not coming home and better eat, and, eventually, she did, but she made me pay by writing me sad letters that cut right to the heart.

Dear Bitsy, I will not call you mother because no mother would ever put her child in such a terrible place.

Thanks to you I am filled with anxiety and frustration. I know you won't bring me home because then you will be embarrassed because everyone will know that your daughter didn't make it at sleep-away camp. I hope someday someone sends you to a horrible prison so you know what I'm going through. Your miserable daughter ["daughter" was crossed out] Lauren Lerner

Lauren made it through the summer, but I didn't have the heart to send her back, and she's been going to summer *day* camp ever since. I thought that would make her worse, more attached and unwilling to venture out, but, in fact, it's had the opposite effect. It's as if she wants to show me that she knows best, and she's been more social and less anxious than ever before. She even goes to the doctor without threatening to vomit.

And yet, despite the maturation, since last Halloween she hasn't been the same. Maybe it also has to do with turning twelve and being in middle school, but my daughter is definitely changing again. Her best friend forever is Allison, who lives down the block at the end of Autumn Court. Allison is even quieter than Lauren, and extremely mature. She is an only child whose parents both work, and she is responsible for many chores around the house. Her parents are very strict, but they've always allowed her to come to our house to play, which she used to do almost every day after school, but not lately. Now she goes home to an empty house and does her homework and then helps to prepare dinner before her parents come home. At least that's what Lauren says when I ask her why Aly doesn't come around much. I have a feeling that the girls are drifting apart, mostly because of the changes in my own daughter, but also because many days I drive past Aly's house and she is sitting on a lawn chair doing nothing much at all.

Meanwhile, Lauren has discovered the phone, and I see her line constantly lit up and hear Alicia Keys blasting from her room, which makes me wonder how she can possibly *hear* to have a conversation. She's been asking for a cell phone, too, and experimenting with makeup. Because of all that's happened to her, I've been pretty lenient, giving in on just about anything she wants. I can't stand the thought of her being unhappy or not fitting in. I also feel a little guilty about everything that's happened since it was my decision to let her go out alone with her friends on Halloween after all. Not that Alan disagreed; he doesn't get involved with the decisions about what the kids are allowed to do.

I wasn't really worried because Halloween in Glen Vale is pretty safe. Almost all the little kids are followed around by groups of parents, and each year it gets earlier and earlier so that half the time the trick or treating starts by three o'clock, practically the minute the kids get home from school. But this year Lauren begged to go alone with her friends, and she had all her arguments ready. She was eleven, *almost twelve,* for God's sake, and in *middle school.* She said *middle school* in such a way that apparently it was supposed to sound as grown-up as *law school.* All the girls were going alone, and Kendra across the street had been doing it for two years already. She ticked off a list of kids she'd be with, all on the Autumn Hill side of town, and all, I took note, in what I knew was the popular group, the group Lauren craved to be a part of and was on the fringe of at best: the group of Cassie and Stacey and Felicia. Lauren pleaded. They had invited her to come.

"Pleeasse."

"Oh well, fine," I'd said, secretly pleased that she was being included, and added, "Home by seven because it gets dark."

"But Stacey's mom is having pizza after—everyone's staying!"

"Okay, stay for pizza, then right home after that."

Halloween night was freezing, and Lauren wore her ski jacket and one of her brother's scary masks. No costumes. Later I found out that Cassie, Stacey, and Felicia went as Me, Myself, and I (they had planned it already), and Lauren was still the odd man out.

LOOKING BACK, I wonder if I'd been less enamored of Phyllis the realtor and more assertive, holding out for Woodcliff Lake, we'd have gone so wrong. Perhaps our problems began because we landed in the wrong town. Sometimes living in the wrong place is like watching a movie in another language without the benefit of subtitles. You keep trying to figure out what's going on by concentrating on body language and visual clues because you know you don't have a clear understanding of the dialogue. Did you ever spend an evening with someone from another country who spoke English but with such a heavy accent that it took you an extra minute to process what she said? By the time you figure out what she's saying, she's finished laughing and on to the next joke and you are always too late. That's what it's like when you have the wrong upbringing or background for your town. You are thrust into a society in which most of the people are foreign to you and the messages are mixed. You might as well move to France or Bolivia. Your reactions are on delay. You second-guess everything you do and say. Sadly, you are destined to screw up. I guess that's what happened on Halloween.

I didn't really know the culture, didn't know about how middle and high school kids rove around in bands after six o'clock.

When I think about that night, I catch myself using my Lamaze breathing, even though Evan, my baby, is almost nine years old. First, the short breaths come, then an inner voice instructing me to *slow down, take it easy.* This is why I can only think about Halloween at the exact right time, and this is certainly not it. The kids will be home soon, and it will not do for me to be deep breathing and imagining I'm in "my special place." Would Samantha fall apart right before Tabitha came home? No, she would not. She'd figure out a plan. Well, in all fairness to me, she might just wiggle her nose and make someone disappear. But I will function because I have to, because that is what a normal person does. Perhaps I embrace normal and average a little too zealously, as if they are states that do not naturally occur, but rather goals or achievements. Perhaps I will just water the plants.

THIRTEEN

t he school bus from Cherry Lane also stops at the middle school, so both kids are on the same bus, although they sit in very different sections. Evan sits up front, against the window, and Lauren at the back, in the long bench seat against the emergency back door. The older kids commandeer the back of the bus, and I suspect that on class trips, Lauren would likely be precluded from the very coolest seat, the last, but on the school bus home the popularity quotient is diluted and her status rises. From my house, I can't see them until they've disembarked and turned the corner, unless I'm waiting in the car to pick them up for a haircut or a doctor's appointment. Today, I decide to take Casey out and walk toward the bus stop.

The first thing I notice when I see the group of kids is that Evan and Lauren are walking together, and behind them, straggling, is Allison. In the light of day, I do see startling differences. Lauren is dressed in low-rise jeans, a white Juicy Couture cropped T-shirt and clunky black Steve Madden platform shoes. She has a shoulder bag whose strap goes across her body and her long brown hair is parted down the middle and loose. At age twelve, she is developing early, and already has the beginnings of a woman's body—nothing major, just some curving at her waist and the beginning buds of a chest. Allison is also wearing jeans, but they are slim-fit and less stylish, probably Levi's. She has on white sneakers, a loose-fitting lavender T-shirt with no writing on it, and a backpack that says JanSport. Her hair is held in place with a white headband. Despite the fact that Allison is taller, she is skinny, boyish, and Lauren looks like the stylish older sister.

"Hi, guys!" I call and wave.

"Casey! C'mere, boy! Mom, let him off the leash!" Lauren bends down as she calls to the dog. Casey is straining and whining. I realize that he might take off, but there is no way I can keep him restrained. I bend down to release him, which is no easy task.

"Casey, sit! Hold still." Finally, we are disengaged, and the dog sprints toward the kids, who squeal and cover their eyes as Casey jumps up and tries to lick their faces off. By the time I reach them, the dog has knocked poor Allison down and is straddling her, licking any open skin he can find. Lauren and Evan are hysterical. Allison less so.

"Casey! Stop that!" I shoot Lauren a look that says, *You're a big help,* but she shrugs and continues to giggle. Allison is not scared, but she does look uncomfortable.

"Don't worry, Aly," I say, pulling Casey off by his collar, "Casey would never hurt you; he likes to *lick* his victims to death." As soon as Allison stands up and brushes off her clothes, Casey forces his big, black wet nose right into her crotch, which sends my two kids into hysterics again. Finally, Aly retreats to her yard, and I hook the dog back to the leash as we head toward home. I look over at the kids and see Lauren laughing with Evan, making a big L out of her left thumb and forefinger, placing it on her forehead, and tipping her head in the direction of Aly's house. I'm horrified. I know this is the sign for Loser. But when did my daughter get so mean? When we are out of earshot, I probe.

"So you two don't have that much in common anymore, huh?"

At least Lauren softens a little. She says quite evenly, with a little bit of exaggerated patience, as if I am the child, "Mom, she's a little bit like a baby, you know, she's kind of a goody-goody." Well. This is revealing. My little bookworm, a former champion goody-goody herself, values something else? Like what, exactly?

It's so hard to be a parent when it comes to the social stuff. You want your child to be popular, but you also like a slow crowd because that's usually a safer crowd; softer, too. You want them to find that perfect balance of confident independence and group acceptance. It's a huge dilemma, the only saving grace being that how you feel or what you want will not matter anyway. I take another look at Lauren. I notice she is wearing hoop earrings and lip gloss; funny, I hadn't noticed that before. Well. Girls will be girls. There are more important matters. I take a deep breath.

"Listen guys, I have to tell you something. Daddy is back in the hospital."

"What?" My little bejeweled, lip-tinted sophisticate suddenly crumples and cries out like she is four years old. "What happened?"

I look over at Evan; as usual, a little man of few words. Evan is not nearly as emotional as Lauren, nor as neurotic. Basically, he's everyone's favorite play date: agreeable, good at sports, gentle, and soft-spoken. With his sandy hair and blue eyes, his looks are as easy on the eyes as his personality is on the psyche. Where Lauren is full of fire and mixed messages, with

Evan, what you see is what you get. But even he has stiffened and is waiting for an answer, too.

"Well"—here goes the big lie—"something related to the car accident I think, maybe something they missed that got hurt inside, but they don't really know"—I sort of rush the words out—"so they have to watch him for a while."

"Is he gonna be okay?" Lauren asks. No wonder Ev doesn't speak; when Lauren is around, he doesn't need to.

"Oh, I'm pretty sure he's going to be just fine, honey, but we might have to be a little patient." I hesitate. "He could be there for a few days." We are walking and stopping and walking as we have this conversation. I feel like I'm botching it, but I don't know what to say. I don't want to scare them, but I don't want to make like everything will be all right because, well, enough said. As I grab the mail from the box, Evan opens the front door and without turning around heads upstairs to his room.

"Evan," I call out, "how about a snack?"

"Nah."

That's it. Nah. Then a door closing. Lauren has unleashed Casey, dropped her shoulder bag on the first stair, and curled up on the landing with the dog, molding her body to his so they form a perfect semicircle. Casey has rolled onto his back and she is rubbing his belly, cooing, "Ooh. I love you, Case. Ssh."

Unconsciously, I find myself rubbing my neck, trying to release the tension of this day, perhaps of this year. I thought I had put Halloween behind me, but now, looking at Lauren as she absorbs another shock, I can't get it out of my mind. Lauren has become such a study in extremes, and how much of it is due to the detours we throw her, I can't say. One minute she is whiny and immature, the next she is secretive and snotty. I've been telling myself that it will all blow over, that it's just normal preadolescence, but I'm not so sure.

AT SOME POINT after trick or treating, Lauren decided she did not want to go to Stacey's house for pizza. I don't know if she felt left out or if she was just uncomfortable; the one thing she never shared was exactly what made her leave the other girls and head home. Although they were still in the Autumn Hill vicinity, the girls finished up well down the hill and several blocks over, so Lauren was pretty tired by the time she turned onto Autumn Court. Suddenly, also turning onto Autumn from the other direction was a group of older boys, five or six of them, all eighth graders at the middle school where Lauren is only in sixth. At first, they were whispering among themselves, laughing out loud and shoving each other around as they walked. Lauren thought she heard them arguing, with a series of "No, you's," "I dare you's," and "Go ahead's." Then they started whistling at her. And calling out. "Hey honey, how 'bout a kiss?" More laughter. Then "Hey, do you go to high school?" She knew it was a joke, that they were teasing her, but she started to get scared when they crossed the street and walked right behind her and the taunting continued. She recognized Keith Winston, who lives across the street, and she thought she knew the other boys from school, although not too well because the middle school keeps the fifth and sixth graders in their own wing, separate from the seventh and eighth grades. She tried to go a little faster, but when she did, they laughed even harder and said, "What's your rush? Don't you want to stay out and play? Are you trying out for the track team?"

Finally, she could see the lights of our house and broke into a run, but that seemed to incite them. They easily sprinted in front and blocked her way. She started to cry and looked right at Keith. They don't really know each other, but she knew he knew her and thought maybe he would help, and for a second he almost did.

"Hey, it's my neighbor, she's a baby, let her go."

"No way, man, she's no baby, look at her." Then another boy said, "It's too dark to see anything, maybe we ought to have a feel." He went to grab her.

"Let me go!" Lauren struggled, tried to kick them and wrench herself away, but one boy, a huge, wrestler-looking brute who already had a mustache, held her arms behind her back.

"C'mon Winston, you always back out, man. It's your turn." Keith Winston came toward her. She started to scream. The big one hooked her arms behind her with one of his arms, then used his other hand to cover her mouth. It happened really fast. Suddenly, she felt a pair of cold hands reach up under her ski jacket, under her blouse, and grab her bare chest. She gave one last jerk, and the boys must have gotten tangled up because she broke free, fell down, and skinned one knee, but managed to race off before any of them could grab her again. Apparently, at that point they were laughing and didn't even try to follow. As she ran toward the house, she heard one of the boys ask how it was and Keith Winston answer.

"Pretty flat for a sixth grader."

Later, despite the helplessness of being outnumbered or the humiliation of having her arms held behind her back, or the actual touching, Lauren said it was those words that actually made her feel the worst.

Lauren had come in crying, panicked, bleeding from the knee, and she spilled the entire story immediately. Alan went crazy. He just snapped. He grabbed his jacket and started to go out and find the boys himself, but Lauren got hysterical.

"What's with her?" he asked me. "Does she think we're going to do nothing?" Lauren was a mess and Alan was practically irrational.

"Just wait a minute," I told him. "Hold on. Let her calm down a little."

When Lauren stopped crying, Alan told her that we at least had to call the cops, but she began crying again and said that she would never go back to school if he did, and she would rather just die if anyone found out.

"Let's just forget it, please, Daddy. *Please.*" She was begging. She looked totally pitiful, with red eyes and her little shaking body, and I just hugged her until finally Alan gave in, but he said he was at least going over to talk to Peter Winston, man to man. Lauren started to protest again, but Alan said he'd be damned if he was going to let that little perverted punk just get away with this, and then he stormed out the door.

I don't know exactly what happened at the Winston's, but it wasn't good. Alan returned in a foul mood and accused me of having no clue about life and how things worked, and on that point he was right because I couldn't imagine what he was talking about. Lauren just sat there through it all, watching us fight, miserable, until Alan actually turned to her and yelled "Stop crying, okay? What the hell were you doing out alone after dark anyway?" To which Lauren responded with a new round of tears as she flew out of the room and to which I responded by fighting with him over his insensitivity for the next hour.

WE DIDN'T TALK much about Halloween after that, not because I didn't try, but I was torn. Lauren seemed so miserable and embarrassed every time I tried to bring it up that I just stopped. Also, every time I thought about my poor baby being felt up by those boys, I wanted to get in my car and drive to the school and wait for them to come out and then run them down. I also thought about my own seedy past, about Gary and being tied up in my own apartment. I told Lauren many things: that she would survive what happened, despite the embarrassment and sense of vulnerability; that the boy may have briefly touched her outside, but he could never touch who she was inside; and that he was obviously sick and needed help. I had a sense that I could've been more convincing if I'd told her that something similar had happened to me, but I couldn't exactly share a bondage story with my preteen.

I decided that Lauren would have talk to someone. Maybe I was overreacting, as she kept insisting, but I wasn't about to let a twelve-year-old dictate what she thought was best. I spoke with the pediatrician and he gave me a name, but he also suggested the guidance counselor at school. "They deal with this stuff all the time." He sounded soothing. Really? His tone might be comforting, but the information was exactly the opposite. Still, someone on the middle school front lines might be just the thing.

"Absolutely no way, not in a hundred, million years, not in a thousand million, mega eons will I talk to weird Mrs. Williams."

"Okay, but tell me how you really feel."

"You think I'm crazy. You think I have mental problems."

"Will you stop being so dramatic? You've had a trauma, whether you know it or not"—oh, that made a lot of sense— "and when that happens, smart people talk it out."

"We talked it out! I'm fine!"

"Lauren, I think you're fine, too. But I love you too much not to make sure you get everything you need. You'll just have to think of it like when you get an ear infection. You feel better before all of the infection is really gone. But you have to finish the antibiotic to make sure it doesn't come back. Well, this is like that. We talked and you're healing, and we're going to do everything to make sure that continues." I was really proud of that one. Not that it worked. Lauren threw herself across the room, stamped her foot like she was five, and declared that she would go but wouldn't say a word while she was there.

"By the way," I said, "the pediatrician said this kind of stuff happens all the time." That stopped her.

"It does?" she asked.

"Mm-hmm. That's what he said."

The following week, Lauren saw Mrs. Williams, and they met informally over the next few months. I spoke with her once, and she remarked that Lauren was a very nervous child (tell me something I don't know), but that she didn't think the incident had left any scars. Once I heard that, I relaxed somewhat, and after a few weeks we stopped talking about it. The weeks became a month, then two, and suddenly Alan had his car accident and Lauren's problems were no longer front seat, and if Evan had any problems at all they were so far down on the family agenda that they were in the trunk.

There's no way I can let that happen now. Evan will resist, but I know he needs to talk about Alan. Although he's the silent type, he's usually the *happy* silent type, but lately I've seen a lot more silence and a lot less happiness. They both probably have a lot of questions, and I think a mom should have some answers, but I don't. Still, not talking would be worse, so I'll do my best. I have to at least address the instability that has crept into our lives, instability that once was episodic and is now chronic. I take the mail, walk into Alan's office, stand there for a minute, and then plop it all on his desk. It can wait. Perhaps he'll be home soon, and he can deal with it himself.

FOURTEEN

What's amazing is how even when the unthinkable happens, the days actually do go by and the most mundane tasks, like feeding the dog and watering the plants and chauffeuring the kids, get done. Alan's "accident" was four days ago, on Tuesday, and yet it seems like just this morning the house was filled with paramedics. It's the weekend already and almost nothing has changed. I go to the hospital every day. I receive icy stares and clipped greetings from my mother-in-law, sympathetic smiles from the ICU nurses, and a sketchy prognosis from Alan's doctors. Meanwhile, Alan is primarily still. His vitals have improved, but only slightly, and not as much as the doctors would like. He's low on hemoglobin and high on platelets, and every day they decide to run more tests; and while they assure me that recovering from an overdose takes time, I sense a growing concern. There should be more and more lucid moments. Whenever I am there, Alan sleeps; and when he does wake up, he seems disoriented and exhausted and unable to converse. Almost as soon as he sees me, he turns over and goes back to sleep. Yesterday I brought some pictures of the kids we'd taken last summer at the club. We all look so healthy and tan and happy. I'd wanted to show them to Alan—I thought they might cheer him up—but he barely glanced at me in his stupor, and I ended up leaving them on the windowsill. The nurses say that his time clock is all screwed up and he is much more awake at night, but you'd think I would have been able to have at least one decent conversation with him by now.

I've slipped into an increasingly robotic routine. Each morning, after the kids leave for school, I shower and dress and drive to the hospital. I know my way around now, where to park and how to circumvent the traffic, avoid the front entrance, and slip through emergency and up to ICU. I stay for about three hours and barely overlap with Marian at all because even though she's taken sick leave, she arrives later. By noon, I usually leave to get ready for the kids. They aren't allowed in ICU, so I haven't had to bring them, which is good. Our conversations about "Dad" follow a familiar script.

"Do you guys have anything you want to ask?"

"Will Daddy be home by Passover?" This from Lauren.

"I don't know, sweetheart. We'll have to be patient."

"Is it like he had a heart attack?" Lauren again. "Josh Danziger's dad had a heart attack, but he's fine."

"I suppose it is a little like that."

Total silence from Evan.

"Ev, do you have anything you want to know?"

"Nope."

I try again. "Honey, I know this is a little scary. You can ask me anything you want."

Whenever I broach this subject, Evan gets very busy fiddling with something. If we are at the kitchen table, he twirls his fork. If we are in the family room, the TV remote does back flips. And in the car, he kicks the seat. But so far no actual discussion occurs, and all of his communication is nonverbal. I try another tactic.

"Are you worried that baseball is starting and Dad isn't around to take you?

"He didn't take me last year. You did."

"Really? I didn't remember that." Well, maybe I did. I suppose that's when everything started to go bad. And in the last few months it's accelerated dramatically; Alan's been especially strained, quicker than ever to lose patience, and they've had to more or less navigate around him like he was a land mine.

"Mom, can I go watch TV now?"

"Sure, Ev. I love you, baby."

"Me, too." I get a little smile as he ambles out. Then Lauren looks at me sympathetically, as if we're *peers,* as if to say, *Poor kid just can't express himself; we'll have to watch him.* But all she actually says is "I'm going to do my homework." I can't decide if this is good or bad, Lauren being sensitive enough to see her brother's struggle or being burdened with the emotional weight. Watching them go, one thing strikes me, and that is that they don't actually miss Alan even though they're worried about him.

I lean my head back and realize that I am bone tired. A deep, headachy kind of tired, like when I was pregnant. Just like then, I want to take a nap every afternoon. Instead, I force myself to make dinner and clean the house, but no matter how hard I try to keep up a good front, I fear the kids must notice the difference. Along with the usual baked chicken and grilled lamb chops, I've thrown in a night of nuked chicken nuggets and cold cereal. Maybe next week, if Alan is still here, I will do better. Marian has to go back to work, so at least I won't have to sit with her and her tight lips. Maybe that's what wears me out. I swear that if she could figure out a way to eat and drink with her lips pulled into a stiff little line, she would. I will definitely visit Alan during school hours so I won't have to see her at all.

My parents are coming today for the first time. They offered to come during the week, but I know they were relieved when I told them there was really nothing they could do, that Alan would hardly know if they were there. So it's Saturday, and they're coming here to the house and taking the kids and me out to dinner. I know they've arrived when Casey starts barking like crazy and I hear my mother's voice as she enters the kitchen.

"Was there a monsoon in here?"

I know I haven't exactly been Martha Stewart this past week, but you'd think she'd give me a little slack, considering. But Eminent Evelyn is aghast.

"Bitsy, my God, when was the last time anyone cleaned?" I look around. I honestly don't think it's that bad. Messy, yes, but in a lived-in kind of way, certainly not in the disease-ridden way her tone implies. I am about to protest, but luckily the kids come in. Not bounding in or tumbling in, or entering in any way that might suggest excitement at seeing their grandparents. They enter casually, sedately, one after another, as if in line to get a form. Their greetings are reserved.

"Hi, Grandma." Lauren looks like she's in pain.

"Hello, dear." Chaste kisses.

"Why, Evan, hello there. I think you've grown. Hasn't he, Sid?"

"What? I suppose so, yes. Hello, Evan." Handshakes.

"Uh, Lauren. Hello." First a handshake then a stiff, awkward kiss, made especially awkward by the fact that Lauren is wearing a cropped belly shirt and jean capris, and my father seems stunned by her recent maturation. He doesn't seem to know where to look, and the flashback to my childhood is so vivid that I'm sure everyone must be blinded by it. Nobody says a word, and my dad turns away quickly, his attention to his grandchildren complete, and then settles into his usual form of conversing with me, which is not conversing at all but pronouncing.

"Cross-Bronx was a parking lot. Always is. Don't know how you take it."

I digest this. Somehow, I am responsible for the Cross-Bronx Expressway being the always-congested route to New Jersey. Never mind the fact that I am not the one who has to use it to go everywhere, that I am not the one trapped on Long Island, and that I, believe it or not, had nothing to do with the long-range transportation planning for the tristate area back in 1892 or whenever they built the bridges and tunnels. Still, I always take the bait.

"How about the Triboro?"

"Ach." He waves me away with his hand. "On a Saturday afternoon? Do I look crazy?" I don't touch that. I look at the kids with sympathy. They certainly got cheated in the grandparents department. No warm cheek pinches or hair ruffling, no foil-wrapped homemade goodies or secret slips of $10 bills. Nada. Nothing. Just an elegant-looking couple in good linen and designer cologne called Grandma and Grandpa.

"Bitsy, is this how the children plan on going to dinner? Dad and I made reservations at Pescadoros." I look at the kids, who roll their eyes. Lauren makes an especially cranky face at me that my parents do not see. Pescadoros is the kids' least favorite restaurant. Not just because they only serve seafood, but because it's old and musty, and the average age of the waiters is dead. Which is just slightly older than the clientele. Men need a jacket, and women are not admitted unless they have covered themselves in pancake makeup that is one shade too dark or overlined their lips in red pencil that seeps nicely into the lip lines like a child's drawing of sunshine rays. When Alan and I first moved here, someone suggested that it was a nice place to take our parents, and they were right. The Bebermans were at home with the menu and its familiar, unchanging offerings of sole Florentine, shrimp scampi, and stuffed lobster. The thing is, since then, my parents have become more adventurous. I know that they experiment with nouvelle cuisine with their friends on Long Island and occasionally in Manhattan. Yet every time Alan and I suggest one of the trendier restaurants that are surprisingly plentiful in New Jersey, they wrinkle their noses.

"No, no, let's go back to Pescadoros. Our treat." That is my father's rule. When they come for dinner, he will not let Alan pay, but he gets to pick the restaurant, and it is always Pescadoros. Perhaps he is punishing us, I don't know, for moving to New Jersey, to a state where he is not an expert on traffic patterns.

"I'll fix them," I imagine him saying as he is stuck in traffic on the LIE. "Whenever we visit, we're going for fried fish and bad service." Although why he should care that we moved away, I couldn't say, since whenever we are together his face is frozen in a permanent scowl, as if he's wedged a piece of lemon in his cheek like chewing tobacco, keeping up a constant squeeze of bitter distaste. I know the kids want me to object. They would rather have another bowl of Cheerios for dinner than have to figure out what to eat at Pescadoros. It has an obligatory children's menu ("For Our Little Skippers") but as I remember, it only features a choice of fried fish sticks or spaghetti.

"Oh . . ." is all I can manage to say. And even worse, "We'll all change." Lauren's body language lets me know that I will pay later. Ev is compliant, as usual.

My father has gone from inspecting the hardware on my kitchen cabinets, presumably to find them inferior, to scraping off dried paint from the panes of the French door on Alan's office with his thumbnail. He notices the stack of mail on Alan's desk and asks if I need help with the accounting. Actually, he says, "Looks like you need help with the accounting. I haven't seen this much mail since I was on mail duty in the service. You've got to get on the stick, girl."

I'm not sure how to answer him. He's dying to get in there and have a look. It's tempting. I haven't dealt with the bills at all this week because I've never dealt with the bills. Alan always did that. I guess I could use some help, but I don't relish the idea of my dad being the helper. I can just imagine his comments when it comes to our purchases. He still thinks everyone should buy sneakers at the five-and-dime. On the other hand, there have been several calls this week from people looking for money. Apparently, Alan hasn't gotten around to mailing all our checks this month. Some of the people were not so sympathetic, even when I explained Alan's state. Some of them said that they'd been waiting for months. I wouldn't even know where to start, and my dad *is* handling the books for my mother's business, so maybe it wouldn't be so bad to let him get us a bit organized.

"You can have a look if you want. I think we're a little behind, what with everything that's going on."

At this moment, we hear a loud cracking sound, followed by two short pops that sound like firecrackers. Everyone looks up and then outside, but before we can react there is suddenly the most vile, noxious smell, like sulphur and vomit, pouring in through the screen door.

"Oh, gross!" Lauren is writhing and holding her nose. Evan is making vomiting sounds.

"Oh! Oh my!" My usually composed mother is having trouble remaining so and my eyes are starting to burn. My dad begins to say, "What in the wo——"

Suddenly, a tall lanky boy with red hair comes bounding up the deck stairs, waving a towel and searching for something. He reaches down, and we all crowd toward the sliding glass doors to the deck, where we see an unusual object. It is a white plastic ball with a red rag hanging out and what looks like plastic wings on the side. As he picks it up, he notices us all, standing in a row, looking out and covering our noses and mouths.

"Oh! Oh my gosh, sorry, it was our stinkaroo!" He seems to think better of the explanation. "Our—my sister's science project," he says, then, fumbling for words while backing up, "It was a little off—sorry, really—didn't mean to disturb—sorry." And then he is gone.

"Who in the world was that strange young man?" my mother whines, fingers pinching her nose.

"It's a Rabinowitz!" Lauren says. "Ugh."

"That's Ross," offers Evan. "He's not so bad."

"Oh, right. If you want to smell like fart."

"Lauren!" I shout.

My mother raises her eyebrows. My father turns away.

"C'mon." I herd the kids away from the screen door. "Lets all go get dressed."

"And Bitsy, honey." I turn back to my mother, who lowers her voice. "When you talk to Lauren about her language, could you also ask her to wear something less revealing?"

WE ALMOST DON'T make it to dinner. We're all dressed and ready to go, but my father emerges from Alan's office looking grim.

"Bitsy, come in here."

I am seven years old, and I am in trouble. The boy next door, Mark Berlin, has talked me into throwing eggs onto the roof. He says the roof tiles are made of rubber and the eggs won't break if I do it right. I believe him. Even after the seventh smash. He is older and he is paying attention to me, and even though I'm only seven I know how cool this is. Four years later, he will kiss me in practically this same spot and thereby occupy two very important files in my memory bank. Like a top-forty song, my father's voice brings me right back to my childhood, but unlike when I hear "Hey Jude" or "Cherish," "Bitsy, come in here" makes me shake. I tell the children to go watch TV or play Sega, and my mother and I follow him back into the office. He looks at me. He shakes his head. Then he smiles—I swear, he actually smiles. But it is a twisted, painful, Dr. Evil smile.

"What?" I ask. "What? Do we owe a lot? What is it?"

"What is it? Do you owe a lot?" His voice is sneering, imitating me. "Bitsy, you don't just owe a lot. You owe a fortune. I've never seen anything like this. Cars, mortgages, credit cards—the whole thing is all paper. You owe more money than some people make in a lifetime. And your assets?" He sort of laughs. "Basically, I don't think you have any. Unless that idiot husband of yours has some secret stash somewhere. I've looked in your savings and checking accounts, and for some reason there are about twelve of them, all basically empty, of course, and . . . and . . . I'm no expert, in fact, I can't make heads or tails of most of this . . . I mean, do you know you have six different American Express cards and—" I am starting to get dizzy at this point, really dizzy. Like I-don't-think-I-can-stand-up dizzy. I grab the back of a chair. But he keeps going. "And all of them have balances. Jesus." He throws some papers in the air.

"There are Platinums and Optimas and Starwoods, and I haven't even told you about the bank loans!"

He looks up at this point and stops. I'd like to think he realizes that I am not feeling well, that some fatherly sensitivity has emerged and he stopped himself before he hurts me too much, but, in fact, he is just momentarily choking on his own saliva. And disgust. My mother, hovering just outside the door, flies in and past me to assist him with his coughing fit. She tries to pat his back, but he waves her away. When he recovers, he walks away from the desk and says to me, without actually looking at me, "You better get some help. I'm not the one to sort through this. You have to get a financial guy, but I'm pretty sure you'll have to sell the house. By the looks of things, you might have to file for bankruptcy." As he walks out of the room, he has one last cough, then tucks in his shirt and straightens his collar. "Now, let's go have some dinner. I've had about as much of this as I can take."

I make it through dinner somehow. When they drop us home and the kids run into the house, finally free, my father hands me a check for $500 (he barely touches the check as he drops it in my hand. It's as if the check is part of a disease called Bitsy syndrome and he might catch it) and tells me I better get started on cleaning up "that mess" as soon as possible or I'm going to find myself without lights, phones, and who knows what else. I don't know where to start, how to find a "financial guy." I say this as I get out of the car. I am pathetic.

"What about your neighbor, the guy on the the cul-de-sac?"

He means Andrew Sloan, Gerry's husband. And although I cringe a little, I guess he does have a point. Andrew is solid, older, and has been working at some financial firm for like a hundred years; he would probably be able to help. I don't dislike Andrew, not the way I dislike Gerry, but there's nothing very appealing about him, either. He is of average height, with a round gut, puffy cheeks, and small eyes. He wears wire-rimmed glasses and has thinning brown hair. Gerry is not much more attractive—her skin is seriously starting to sag, and the fact that she starves herself to stay under a hundred pounds doesn't exactly help her skin—but at least she tries to be stylish. Andrew falls into that group of men who wear their belts too high. Still, these may actually be desirable traits in an accountant, and he's always been very nice to me. I think he might even be a little embarrassed by his wife, her affectations and social climbing. I bet he even has some sort of confidentiality code, and would keep our secrets. So even though Gerry will know I need help, she won't necessarily know the scope of our problems, and if Alan is embarrassed by this—which, of course, he will be—well, he should have thought about that before he abandoned us and plunged into this half-catatonic state.

Tomorrow, I will suck it up with Gerry and call. I tell my father that I'll get on it right away, and instead of responding he shifts the car into drive and pulls away. I think my mother sort of puts up her hand and waves. Either that, or she is fixing her hair.

FIFTEEN

"Oh, Bitsy, hang on a minute, I'm so glad you called. I've just been dying to talk to you, but I didn't want to intrude. You know, I'm not one to go in for gossip, but the rumors, my God, they've been flying. Now don't you go anywhere, just hold on." I hear her speak to someone.

"Kaley, I'm not going to tell you again. First learn the words, and then I'll test you, not before." Then back to me.

"Okay, I'm back. Honestly, these kids, if it's not one thing—but then I don't have to tell you, you've certainly had your hands full. How *is* Lauren doing these days? And you? And Alan, of course? Okay, you go. Better start from the beginning."

I hold my breath. It's possible I want to die. If that's what it takes to escape Gerry Sloan. But the bills and my father's warning force me to continue. This is the worst of all possible scenarios; I need Gerry's help.

"Oh, well, we're all doing fine," I offer, unconvincingly, "but I am a bit overwhelmed. It seems that Alan's had a . . . a . . . complication. From his accident. Some neurological damage that was missed. So he hasn't been able to, um, keep up with things, and I'm just terribly confused by all these numbers and dollars and I was wondering if Andrew might be able to take a look, you know, help me sort things out?" There is a pause; perhaps Gerry is thinking. More likely she is jumping up and down with ecstasy, unable to control her excitement. Although I haven't directly imparted any tidbits, no cries of woe or admissions of shame, the fact that Andrew will have access to our financial statements will be an unexpected treat of huge proportions. I think about Casey when he knows he's about to get a treat. This is like holding out a T-bone. I can already hear Gerry at the next meeting of the Junior Women's Club.

"Well, you know, they needed Andrew's help, and why they couldn't just hire someone to sort through it all, well enough said. But, of course, he couldn't say no, and let me tell you what he found . . ."

"Oh sweetie, of course Andrew will help. He can't make it tonight, though, since we're going out with the Schwartzbaums and Greens to celebrate Miriam's birthday, her fortieth, she says, but between you and me I know a friend of hers who she went to high school with and this girl is forty-three already. But whatever, I'm not one to gossip, so her fortieth it is. Anyway, tomorrow night we have the charity dinner at the club, but I think Tuesday might work for him. Do you want me to come along and keep you company?"

"NO!" Too loud. Soften it. "Uh, no, thanks, you stay with the kids. We'll be fine."

"Okay, hon, I've got to test Kaley on her vocab now. You take care." I wonder how long it will actually take her to get back on the phone. First, she will have to calm herself down, maybe breathe, maybe blot her chest, maybe just take the Valium early.

BY THE TIME the doorbell rings Tuesday night, I am beside myself. Alan has gotten slightly better, but not so much that he is actually coherent or available. The doctors say his vital signs are getting stronger and they have no explanation for his extreme lethargy. He is getting glucose and vitamins intravenously, but he is still sleeping and disoriented much of the time. At home, the pile of bills has grown into more of a mound. In case Andrew is prone to displays of outrage à la my father, I've farmed the kids out. Lauren went willingly to a friend's house, a new friend I do not know, named Cathy, and even more so after we had a major argument about what she was wearing (long hoop earrings and eye liner): an argument I lost. Evan has a baseball tryout. Even though he is only in third grade, baseball in this town is a religion, and the recreation season doesn't start until all the kids go through a series of drills in front of all the coaches. It takes three nights to complete, and they call it Baseball Skills Tune-up, which is the politically correct concession to sound less competitive, since a kid's father died in Connecticut last year as a result of a fight with the hockey coach. But everyone knows, especially the kids, that "Tune-up" is grown-up speak for "Tryouts."

Andrew Sloan smiles as I open the door, gives me a little kiss on the cheek, and holds my shoulders a little too long as he steps in. I back away, thank him for coming, and ask if he'd like anything to drink. He says yes and follows me into the kitchen. As I go through the choices—soda, juice, water—I decide that Andrew is one of those people for whom personal space is an issue. You know, they just don't get it—they stand too close, crowd you. Maybe it's the glasses. Again, I back away, but he inches forward, oblivious. He asks if I have anything fresh-squeezed. Can you imagine? I just laugh out loud.

"Let me think," I say, "was it ruby-red grapefruits I squeezed this morning or was it tangelos? Maybe papayas? Oh no, that must have been yesterday." By the time I finish, I am already sorry for the sarcasm. What am I doing, trying to sabotage the only help I might get? But incredibly, Andrew Sloan laughs, and for the first time in weeks so do I.

"I'm sorry," I offer, "I've been under a lot of stress."

"No, don't worry," he says, "I always liked that about you, your sense of humor."

"No," I reply, "it's not fair, you're being so nice to come over, and it's just that between running to the hospital and the kids and these bills, I just . . ." I don't even finish when the tears start to fall. Andrew moves closer and puts his arms around me in a hug.

"Please don't apologize," he says, "it's fine, really. You've been through a lot and I want to help." He pats my back. It's a nice gesture. I feel a little better. I reverse my initial feeling about Andrew. He is just a nice guy. I start to pull away, as much from embarrassment as awkwardness at being hugged with my arms hanging straight down at my sides. Andrew pulls me back.

"Sshh. There, there." And continues to rub my back. Only now it's weird, like the personal-space thing. And I've never actually heard anyone say "There, there" before, except in books. And then Andrew's hand is not just rubbing my back, it seems to be coming up my side, with the thumb splayed out suspiciously, so that if this hand continues upward the thumb will be on my—

"Okay," I say, breaking free and bringing my hands up. There is really no graceful way to do it. But even as I step back, precisely *as* I do, Andrew leans in and kisses me right on the mouth. It takes a nanosecond, that's all, and now I am really backing up, shaking, sputtering, "What?" and actually wiping my mouth with my hand.

"Bitsy, come on. Relax. Let's just go with this."

"What? No! Are you serious?"

"I just thought maybe you could use a little . . . you know . . . attention."

"You thought . . . Why? A-attention? Oh God. I don't believe this. Oh God!"

"Don't get so upset. It's no big deal. I know you and Alan have a lot of problems; everyone knows. I just figured maybe you might . . ." He lets this trail off.

"You need to go. You need to go right now." I am furious, almost hysterical.

"Don't you want me to look at your books?"

"I want you to leave. Right now." I walk toward the front door.

"Fine. Just relax, okay. This never happened. Okay?" He follows me, but when he gets to the door he turns. I back up about ten paces. You could drive a car between us.

"I mean it, Bitsy. This never happened." His voice is suddenly steely. "And if you say it did, I'll just deny it. In fact, I'll say *you* came on to *me.* And if you think nobody will believe me, think again. Everyone knows you guys are in trouble. And Gerry says your daughter already has a reputation. Like mother, like daughter, right?"

And with an awful lot of bravado for a wiry, nerdy, scummy son of a bitch, he slams the door. I am shaking. I wrap myself up with my own arms and pace. I really did misjudge Andrew Sloan. He is no inconsequential accountant. He is an evil, ugly, repulsive man. I only pray his threats were empty. I think he was just scared and winging it. I can't imagine that he will start something with Gerry. Probably he will just say I changed my mind or something like that. I can't believe some of the things he said. And Lauren? A reputation? God, what a vile thing to say! Five minutes go by. Then ten. I have been pacing, but at some point I've stopped thinking. When the doorbell rings, I jump. He wouldn't dare, I think, but I check the peephole anyway. It is not Andrew; it is a woman, one I don't know, but I am thrown nonetheless. I look again and decide she is no threat.

"Can I help you?" I open the door, but not all the way, and take a better look. She is about my age, coffee-skinned, simply dressed, cheaply even, but there is something about her carriage, the way she holds herself, that suggests breeding. Her wool coat is faded, her shoes scuffed, but her posture is almost regal, certainly self-possessed. When she speaks, she looks down, and I can barely hear her.

"I am Bhadra."

"Yes?"

"I am Bhadra. You must call me Bebe."

"Excuse me? Who are you?"

"I am from the agency."

"Oh, I think you have the wrong house. Are you looking for the Winston family? They live across the street."

"You are"—she consults a piece of paper—"Miss Barbara?"

"No. Well, yes. I mean, I am Barbara, but . . ." How would this person know my real name? "Who sent you here?"

"Miss Evelyn. She say to come here. To number seventeen Autumn Court. To daughter."

"She did? Oh, well, come in." I am wondering what is up. My mother is sending me a live-in? And referring to me as Barbara? How am I going to pay for a live-in?

"Let's get this straightened out. I will call my mother. Please sit down, um, Bebe, did you say? That's funny, that's almost like my name. It's Bitsy, by the way, not Barbara. You can call me Bitsy."

"Oh. Like this? Bitsy?" She holds her thumb and forefinger slightly apart, making the sign for something very, very small. Startled, I look back at her.

"Yes, I guess so."

"You like this name? Bitsy?"

"Well, I . . . you know, I don't know."

"Then I will call you Miss Barbara. Like famous saying goes: 'We cannot rise higher than our thoughts of ourselves.' "

"Oh." For a moment, the simple truth roots me. Then I think, Whatever. She can call me whatever she wants and quote Buddha or the Maharishi Maheeshiyogi for all I care since she's not going to be here long enough to matter. I dial my mom's cell.

"Evelyn's Eminent Helpers. This is Evelyn, may I help you?"

"Mom. What is going on? Did you send someone here?"

"Oh Bitsy"—she is whispering—"I forgot to call you. She is raw, from Guyana, no experience; I can't put her anywhere just yet, but I don't want to lose her, she's a gem. For now, she'll work for you."

"Mom, do you know anything about her?"

"Of course! She's a cousin of Ruby, one of my girls, I'm sure she's fine. The girls from Guyana always are. Ruby has a friend who runs a rooming house in Fair Lawn—that's near you, right? They have a large Indian community. I got her a room there for the weekends, and she'll live with you during the week."

"Mom, I can't pay her."

"I know, I know. This is just between us, okay? I'll just send her checks until you get organized and work things out."

"Mom, thank you, but—" But what? It couldn't hurt, and the truth was I could use the help. The house is a mess; hell, I am a mess. I just can't ever remember my mother doing anything this nurturing. In fact, there was only one other time, when I was thirteen, just after we lost Vajay, and that's only because she got drunk on the Passover wine. On that morning, the morning of the day of the first seder, a frozen can of orange juice had come flying out of the freezer onto her foot. The foot began to swell and turn purple immediately, and by afternoon my father thought it might be broken, so she had to keep it elevated and iced and couldn't serve the meal. Between Veronica, the new housekeeper, and me, we were doing fine, although we'd forgotten to make the charoset and started a small fire roasting the egg and shank bone for the seder plate. We were about two-thirds through the seder, at the part where you dip your little finger into the wine ten times to represent the ten plagues, and no one had noticed that Mom was actually drinking from her glass every time you were supposed to—in a seder, that can add up to four full glasses. My father was chanting and we were dipping.

"*Dom,*" he intoned. "Blood," we responded with the English translation.

"*Tzardaya,*" he said. "Frogs," we replied.

"*Keeneem,*" he chanted. And that's when I felt it. A little wet dart on my cheek.

I looked up and there was my mother, smiling mischievously, her still wine-stained finger poised in the air, aimed at me. I was shocked. I didn't know what to say. I couldn't reconcile the picture of my mother flicking her red wine at me like an ill-behaved little child. It was like seeing a space ship. Before I could react, she dipped her finger again.

"Awrov," my father's voice announced, and with a little flick, Mom sent a spray of wet red liquid toward my brother Ed.

"Whaa?" Ed grabbed his cheek, looked up, first at me, and then turned to see his mother joyously parading her wet finger in the air. Then she giggled. Ed's face looked like mine must have a minute ago.

"What's the commotion?" my father asked, breaking his concentration and looking up, annoyed.

Ed, in a daze, responded, "She flicked her wine at me."

My father turned to look at me before he realized that Ed meant my mother, and his expression changed from annoyance to confusion.

"Evelyn?" With this, my mother looked a little contrite. She tried to straighten her spine and stuck her finger in her mouth, presumably to erase the evidence. But she was still smiling.

"Ed, take your mother's wineglass away, she's had enough." Ed reached over, but my mother's hand shot out.

"NO! I need that!" She went to slap Eddie's hand like he was a two-year-old caught sneaking a cookie, and in doing so knocked the wineglass over.

"Now see what you've done. You bad boy!" But she was laughing and looking at my father. Then she belched. Really loudly.

"Pardon me!" she exclaimed. I began to laugh. I think even Mitch and Eddie were about to, but my father gave them a look. He put down the Haggadah and turned to me.

"Bitsy, help your mother up to bed." I got up, still smiling, and when my mother saw this, she tried to do the same. The ice pack fell down, and she grabbed hold of the tablecloth to get the leverage to get up, and then the seder plate began to slide off. Ed lunged and managed to catch it, but then the wine-glasses began to sway like bowling pins and topple, followed by the candles, which came out of their holders and fell, still lit, rolling in two opposite directions. Mitch grabbed one and I grabbed the other.

"Evelyn!" My dad was screaming now. "That's enough!" To me, he said, "Bitsy! Help your mother to bed!"

Then my mother started to imitate him.

"Bitsy," she said in a fake man's voice, slurring, too, "telp your bother to bed!" This made her laugh and belch again.

"I mean, Titsy, belp your mother!" Now she was hysterical, laughing.

"I said Titsy!" she roared. "Titsy! That's funny right?"

At this point, Veronica, who had just come through the doorway, murmured, "Lord have Mercy, she's three sheets gone."

"EVELYN!" My father was apoplectic. He turned to Veronica, called her Vajay, and ordered her to help me get my mother upstairs, and by this time my mother was leaning on the wall and holding her side from laughing or fatigue, I didn't know. Together, Veronica and I got her upstairs, and after, when Veronica went down to serve dinner, my mother called me over and asked me to sit with her, and she told me I was beautiful and strong and could do anything I wanted in life. She said that if I was ever afraid of anything or anyone, I should come and talk to her about it. She kind of mumbled most of it, but I hung on to every word as if they were drops from a hundred-year-old bottle of Château Lafite Rothschild. It was strange and wonderful and unexpected. My mother spent the next day in bed, in the dark, with a bottle of Bufferin, and when I went in to check on her she merely turned over and waved me away, and the day after that it was like nothing had happened at all. Evelyn, the future Eminent Evelyn, was back, possessed and controlled and stingy with affection—and nobody, not me or my brothers or my dad, ever mentioned Passover again.

The following year we had a large crowd of relatives for Passover and plenty of Kedem grape juice to supplement the Manischewitz wine for those who would "rather not drink"— which, of course, included my mom, not only that year, but in every other year to come.

So the fact that there is a live-in housekeeper sitting in my living room is as significant to me as if I'd seen another space-ship, and I thank my mother, hang up, and embrace the gesture, wondering, though, with just a tinge of resentment, if there had been more of them, more acts of support, I'd have needed this one.

Is it possible to press rewind, to see how exactly it happened that Alan and I got into this mess? Was there a way to avoid the demons, another way I didn't see? Was it my fault after all? There were so many pressures, right from the beginning; some material, some not. Lauren had to be put in the right kindergarten class; Evan had to make the right T-ball team. Our Audi had to become a BMW, and we absolutely had to put in a pool. Then it was the country club and the Falci bags and the Yurman jewelry and the vacations at the Cerromar in Puerto Rico. It all seemed to matter so much. There was a picture, a portrait, and a right way or wrong way to pose.

On my first birthday in our new house, Alan surprised me with a potter's wheel and kiln, and for a few months I'd taken so much pleasure in the luxury of having my own studio-quality equipment in the basement. But then there was Junior League to join and pizza lunches to serve at school and tennis teams to play for and charity luncheons to attend, and I hadn't even touched the wheel in years. I don't know exactly what I have to show for the last decade except a lifestyle that exceeds our income and a husband whom I've failed so completely that he apparently thinks his life isn't even worth living. How did we start out as one kind of family and turn into another? Alan and I used to laugh at people like Gerry Sloan and the Winstons, but then we suddenly began to covet everything they represented. Or maybe it was just me who was laughing and me who changed. Maybe Alan was never laughing; maybe he always wanted those things. Just because I've been thinking we've abandoned all our individual passions and quirks, like I abandoned the kiln, doesn't make it so.

And there's something else. I realize that I haven't managed to create one meaningful relationship as an adult, with the exception of the relationship with my kids. My parents don't seem to enjoy me, nor I them. I secretly think that the only reason we continue to celebrate holidays and get together with each other is because it would appear wrong not to. Basically, it's an existential act: We're here, therefore we convene.

My brothers have very little place in my life. Like my father, Eddie doesn't relate to Alan, his kids are older, and there is no benefit to any of us by getting together. Mitch I hardly know; he's never around long enough, and we've progressively become strangers. Before the fiasco with Andrew Sloan, Gerry was the most frequent figure in my life, and I like her about as much as a paper cut. Diana? Sure, if I always want to feel dissatisfied and wanting.

In truth, I am more like my mother than I want to admit, just as unable to connect with anyone. There are friends, acquaintance type of friends, people to have lunch with or carpool with or go to Nordstrom's anniversary sale with; just no friends to call when you happen to need help. I always thought that if I didn't want much, just a nice life with a nice family, everything would fall into place. I *am* a nice girl who doesn't hurt anyone. Doesn't that count for something? Where is the fairness? Where is God anyway? Is he slipping? Could he be suffering from some kind of celestial dementia?

I begin to feel something bilious building in my throat, something very close to anger, the really raw kind, in its most primitive form; the kind that builds at age four and is pushed down at age twelve and is denied at seventeen. It's ugly and bitter, but I embrace it. These things should be happening to someone else, someone like Gerry Sloan, the little bitch. Not to me. There, I've said it. I can't stand Gerry, and while we're on the subject I really don't like Diana Gilbert, either, and I definitely don't like Alan's mom, and one thing I would really like to do just one time would be to smack my own father in his pinched, judgmental mouth, and Jesus Christ, I wouldn't mind a backhand to Alan's face, too. I taste the resentment now; swallow it in whole vitriolic gulps. And instead of making me sick, I start to feel better; by drinking it in, I'm getting it out. Release through embrace.

I always thought that there was this unwritten pact, like a deal between some higher power and me. If I ignored the negative feelings, pushed away unhappy parts and stayed positive and pleasant, then bad stuff wouldn't happen to me. I remember a conversation I had with Gerry just a few months ago about Joanne Cannon, who used to be one of Gerry's best friends. Joanne divorced her husband after she found out he was having an affair and went from a beautiful four-bedroom contemporary in town to a run-down town house in Washington Township.

"I'm not saying it's right," Gerry shared, "it's just that had she listened to me, she'd still be driving her Lexus, having popovers at Neimans, and her kids would be right here in the Glen Vale schools.

"The thing is," she went on, "no matter how bad you think they are, the minute you toss them out there's always some witch waiting to take them right in." And Gerry was right. Hal Cannon had already moved in with a new girlfriend, and not the original one, either.

"But wait," I'd ventured, in a rare moment of abandon, "what if she was totally miserable? What if she just couldn't bear it a moment longer?"

Gerry sized me up and down, lifted up her glasses, and gave me one of her squinty, professional, social-expert looks. Then she shook her head.

"Oh, honey," she scoffed, and waved the thought away. "Don't you get it? Everyone's miserable."

So I guess I finally do. Only not the way Gerry means. You can't settle for feeling awful just because you're worried about what could be worse. Eleanor Roosevelt said that you might as well stand up for what you are passionate about because you'll be criticized no matter what you do. Bebe from Guyana says that if I call myself something so small, I may actually end up that way. Two women from completely different worlds, two women who are clearly more together than me, essentially say the same things.

Be yourself. Dream bigger.

But what if they happen to cancel each other out?

SIXTEEN

When the kids come home, their reactions to Bebe are mixed. Lauren borders on rude, rolling her eyes and dismissing Bebe as if she were an uninteresting shirt on a rack at The Gap. I am mortified. Judging by Bebe's reaction, a stiffening posture and raised eyebrows, the disdain is mutual. I am about to admonish my daughter when Bebe focuses on Evan, who warms to her immediately.

"What a handsome man." Bebe extends her hand. "How do you do, sir?"

"I'm good." Evan smiles, shaking Bebe's hand. "Do you like dogs?"

"Probably not, Ev," his sister answers, glaring at me. "They never like dogs." She turns to Bebe. "You probably eat them, though, right?"

"Lauren!" I'm so shocked and embarrassed. Who is this child? I turn to Bebe.

"I'm very sorry. Lauren, you will apologize right now."

"Never mind, please. It is late. Everyone is tired and young children must have bedtime." Lauren looks incensed.

"I'm twelve. And I don't go to bed at nine o'clock."

Bebe looks evenly at my daughter and replies, "Twelve, really?

In my country twelve different, more like grown-up. Sorry for my mistake." There is a tense silence, more like a standoff. Lauren glares at Bebe but Bebe doesn't flinch. Then Lauren just shrugs, walks away, and I let out a breath. It's been a long night.

In truth, I can't really fault Lauren for not embracing Bebe. We have quite a history with housekeepers and have been through so many it's staggering. When we first moved to Glen Vale, Alan suggested that we get live-in help immediately. Our first housekeeper was a young woman from Jamaica named Melrose. The kids loved her. She was five feet two inches, a size 2, had a huge smile, and looked like she was twelve, although her papers said she was twenty-one. Unfortunately, she acted more like how she looked. After two weeks, she still couldn't get that I wanted the kids to wash their faces and brush their teeth *every night*. It seemed like she thought it was okay if she remembered this *most* days. Alan and I would go out to dinner locally and come home to find Lauren in bed asleep, wearing only a pajama top, her face all covered in chocolate. The baby would be in his crib drinking forbidden apple juice and still be in the same diaper as when we left. Melrose let the kids watch MTV and eat everything they asked for; sort of like what a doting grandma might do. That is, I think that's what doting grandmas do.

After Melrose, I went for someone a bit older. Lulu was also from Jamaica, but she had about ten years on Melrose, plus she had children of her own. She didn't exactly have a huge IQ, and periodically put the oven on clean instead of bake, so we often started out roasting a chicken and ended up marveling over the cleanest pile of bones you ever saw. Say what you will about foreign manufacturing being superior to ours, but that General Electric Monogram oven could disintegrate every last bit of meat, grist, and grizzle on a three-pound Oven Stuffer Roaster.

We didn't actually get to view the superclean bones for four hours since that's how long it took for the self-cleaning cycle to cool down and the lock light to go off, but they say you can look at the bright side of anything, and the kids did eat more vegetables during that time.

Still, Lulu was aptly named. One time she was constipated, and having heard that fruit could be helpful, she proceeded to eat all the bananas in the house: seven, to be exact. We lost her for two days; she was too impacted to leave her room. Lulu was pleasant, though, and the kids liked her, so she lasted six months. It took me that long to trust her enough to leave her in charge of Evan's lunch. He was two at the time, and she had watched me make him his little sandwiches for half a year. I showed her how I used just two slices of deli meat or American cheese, pressed down on the white bread to hold it together, and then cut it into fours so he could pick it up. Not brain surgery. After seeing me do this more than a hundred times, I was confident that Lulu was up to the task. Evan was in his Sassy seat at the kitchen table when I came down, dressed and ready to go out. He was watching TV, halfway through what I thought was a turkey sandwich, happy and smiling and eating with pleasure. I bent down to kiss him good-bye, and as I turned to go, a faint smell stopped me. I couldn't quite place it, but it was familiar.

"Lulu . . ." I hesitated. "Is the baby eating turkey?"

Lulu turned and shrugged. "I don't know, miss, I give him like you do."

Slowly, I inched back to Evan. There was only one and a half squares of sandwich left. I took the one whole square and peeled back the bread. Then I almost fainted. My baby was devouring, and happily, a lovely little sandwich of raw bacon.

I decided to try the agencies, explaining that I wanted someone who was smart and a take-charge type. They told me they had a very competent woman from Ecuador. When Maria entered the house, she circled the foyer, did not make eye contact, and seemed to be inspecting.

"How many betrooms?"

"Uh, four."

"Bats?"

"Three and a half."

"You espect I am cooking?"

"Well, sometimes, for the kids, yes."

"How much you pay?"

Although Maria scared me almost as much as she scared the children, I decided to give her a shot. It would be nice to have someone who knew how to run a house for a change. She started on a Tuesday. That afternoon while Evan was napping, I asked her to take Lauren out on the cul-de-sac to play. Not that Lauren wanted to go—she started whining immediately and tried to slink behind me—but I wanted them to get to know each other. Maria put her hands on her hips.

"I have down thee stairs to vacuum yet."

"That's okay, don't worry about that today, you can vacuum tomorrow."

Maria sighed, as if I were an unfortunate nuisance, and made some sort of huffing sound.

"Come on, girl, don't be such thee baby." This is what she said to Lauren.

"Just on the cul-de-sac, honey" is what *I* said. "You can see right into the kitchen where I am." Lauren wasn't having any of it. "You can ride your bike." I added. That was the tipping point. Lauren had a bike with training wheels, but our house was on a hill on the corner. At the back, on the cul-de-sac, it was flat, but in order to ride, someone had to accompany her. Since Alan was rarely in the mood, this usually fell to me, not so easy with Evan in a stroller, and so Lauren was extremely bike deprived. Sniffling, she agreed to go with Maria. "Please watch her closely in the street," I called out, and Maria turned around and gave me a look that said she would gladly sell me into slavery. Lovely.

After about five minutes, I peek out the kitchen window and see Lauren circling on her bike while Maria sits on the grass, reading. She does not look up at Lauren the entire time I watch. Then, after only ten more minutes, Maria gets up, goes to Lauren, and the next thing I know Lauren is getting off her bike and they are coming home. But they do not walk around in the street; they are cutting across the backyard, which has just been freshly sodded, and the bike is sinking in and making a visible groove. When they approach, I go out the back door to meet them.

"Back so soon?"

"She was hot." Lauren points to Maria. I pause. Maria offers no explanation. Instead, she says, "Where should I put thees?"

"That goes in the garage." I am a little agitated. "And Maria, in the future, please walk the bike or let Lauren ride it around on the *street*. I don't want it dragged across the lawn."

Without missing a beat, she asks, "What is big deeference?"

Unbelievable. I take a breath. "The difference"—I expel the breath—"is that the lawn is new. That is new sod," I say, pointing to the deep rut that now runs from the cul-de-sac to where we stand, "and the bike damages it." Maria looks at the rut. Then she looks back at me and says, "Oh, I think it weel be fine." And with that, she turns and steers the bike toward the garage, leaving Lauren and me standing alone, clearly and summarily dismissed.

That night I try to talk to Alan, who says I should do what I want, fire her or whatever. Maria scares me a little; I do want to get rid of her, but each time I hire someone new, it is exhausting. I have to teach them all about the house, the bus schedules, the appliances. Maybe she's just slow to warm up, I think. Maybe I should give her a little time. I am wrong again. Over the coming week, Maria manages to irritate or offend me several times each day. By the time Alan goes out of town on Thursday, I've had it, but once he leaves, I decide I don't want to fire her when I am home alone. In fact, after I ask her to use Clorox on some of the baby's whites, she makes a face like if she can't *sell* me, then she would be happy to murder me in my sleep, so not only do I *not* fire her, I sleep with a kitchen knife until she leaves on Sunday morning.

After she goes, I wander into her room. I had left her week's pay on the kitchen island the night before, since she wanted to make an early bus home. Thinking it was crass to just leave money out, I'd attached a small note: "Maria, have a nice weekend." Now, as I creep around her room, checking to see if she's left her clothes, which means she plans to return, I see the note sticking out from under the *TV Guide.* But it has been altered. The word "weekend" has been crossed out, and replaced with the words "Sunday and Monday." She changed the words. Can you spell resentment? I guess Maria feels pretty strongly that her Tuesday-through-Saturday job is a huge pain in the ass and under no circumstances should I label her two days off a "weekend." She has not written this for me to find, but only for herself. How scary is that? The thought of her angry little self scribbling on my note is the last straw. I call her at home and tell her it's not working out, and she tells me where to send her stuff. It takes less than a minute to end a toxic relationship that filled my every thought for a week.

After Maria there was Claudette, who read a pocket Bible in her spare time and hung not only crosses but pictures of the crucifixion all over her room. This was a little creepy, and I was not big on anyone who was overzealous about any religion, but the clincher was when Lauren crept into our room early one Sunday morning and asked, "Mommy, why did we kill the baby Jesus?"

After Claudette came Fifi, from Haiti, who was almost perfect. She was happy, and laughed a lot, and she loved the kids and they her. The problem was that Fifi hated housework, which is sort of a liability when you are a housekeeper. I held on to Fifi for a year, which was probably eleven and a half months too long. I even took her for driving lessons when she said she wanted to learn, figuring that if she drove, I could always let her do the errands while I did the cleaning, since she was already managing to sidestep most of the dirty work anyway, but she kept failing the motor vehicle test. After her third try and our third visit to the MVB in Ridgewood, a sweating, shaking driving inspector took me aside and whispered that I probably shouldn't bring her back.

"Never seen anything like it," he said. "Some sort of perceptual impairment. Don't waste your time, miss, it ain't never gonna happen."

Then there was Monica from Colombia, more of an au pair, who came with her own luxury SUV and wore diamonds. Even Alan took notice of her. He decided that she was probably a drug runner for some cartel, so she was gone after one week.

Monica was followed by Pearl, the fattest woman in the world. I don't even remember where she was from because Alan took one look at her and said that there was no way he could have someone so huge living with us. I thought about protesting; after all, it was me going through all the interviewing and training and firing, but Pearl broke into a sweat just walking up the two steps from our sunken living room to the kitchen, so how could she possibly handle a full flight of stairs?

After Pearl was Marina, a pale, fragile-looking girl from a small village in one of the Eastern bloc countries. I was really rooting for Marina; she had, after all, escaped a *revolution,* but she was also fairly clueless about everything. She said that the appliance she was most comfortable with was a hot plate and she found the toaster oven a constant source of delight. Every time its bell rang to signal that the toast was ready, Marina gave a little clap. I used to catch her playing with it, not toasting anything, just waiting for the little bell. She also gave Lauren an expired pink antibiotic that had been sitting at the back of the fridge because Lauren said that "she wanted some." But the real problem came two weeks in, when Alan and I returned home from a meeting with our lawyer to find Marina and the children coloring, not in the family room or at the kitchen table, but in the living room, sitting at the antique mahogany coffee table, on my imported Tabriz rug.

As I enter the room, in addition to the crayons, papers, and crayon marks that I can already see on the table, is an overturned cup of water lying on its side, a puddle from which is snaking through the green crayon mark and over the side and dripping onto the rug. I watch them, stunned, for several seconds, before they notice that I'm there.

"Hi, Mommy, look what I made!" I hear Lauren, I see her hold up the picture, but so many things are going through my mind that I am rendered speechless. I want to give Marina the benefit of the doubt. It's possible that she doesn't understand about formal living rooms, that I expect too much, despite the fact that she's never seen me take the children in there to *play* and despite the fact that she has specific dusting and polishing instructions for that room and despite the fact that I inadvertently *hover* over her when she cleans there. I would like to just be thrilled at this cozy domestic scene, but the dripping liquid is *green,* did I mention that? I take a deep breath, refrain from screaming "Oh My God!" and try to sound reasonable so I don't scare the children. "Marina," I say, with forced calm, as I point to the overturned cup, "were you planning to clean that up?" Marina looks up, and then points to five-year-old Lauren.

"She said to finish coloring first."

YOU'D THINK BY then I would've totally given it up, right? Oh, no.

Once again, the agency sends someone, since they still owe me a replacement for Maria. She is from Africa and looks lovely. I ask her name.

"Fatty."

"Fatty?"

"Yes, ma'am. Fatty."

"Oh, wait," I say, "you must mean Fati. Do you spell it, F-A-T-*I?*

"Yes, ma'am."

"Okay, and your last name is—?"

"Fati."

"No, hon, your *last* name."

"Fati."

"Fati Fati?" I begin to wonder if this is a cultural/language custom.

"Yes, ma'am. Fati Fati. But you can call me Ellen."

"Wait. Your name is Fati. Fati Fati, right? But I should call you Ellen?"

"Fati, Ellen." Oy. By this time, I'm so confused that I decide to call her "hon" until we can sort it out, but I feel good about her right from the start. Fati Ellen is so sweet and smiling and in addition to her gentle nature I am grateful for her perfect English. One day we are outside on the back lawn having a picnic: Fati Ellen, Baby Evan, and Mommy Bitsy. Because of Fati Ellen, I now think of everyone as having two names. Our new family includes Husband Alan and Sister Lauren, and we get our mail from Postman Jim.

At twenty-six months, Baby Evan thinks "pinkynik" is the best thing in the whole world. We put a blanket down on the lawn and he eats his grilled cheese sandwich and sips from a box of apple juice, and sometimes we blow bubbles or draw. On this particular day, I am working in the garden, and Fati Ellen and Baby Evan are on the blanket reading his favorite book, *Goodnight Moon,* when, suddenly, Fati Ellen turns pale (not an easy feat when you are from Nigeria), points hysterically, and at the top of her lungs yells, "LION!" With this, she flees, leaving Baby Evan (presumably to be devoured), and runs into the house. I look around for the wild beast that has caused the panic and see the Rabinowitzs' twelve-year-old overweight and arthritic golden retriever, Doggie Cooper, hobbling lazily near the edge of the property. He looks about as threatening as a goldfish.

That night I fire Fati Ellen, not because she is afraid of dogs, but because her first instinct in the face of danger is to save herself. Much as I liked her, it was a relief to go back to having only one name.

Luckily, after Fati Ellen, we found Jemmis, a young woman from Passaic, New Jersey. She had no husband or children; only a father and sisters who were thrilled to place her in a live-in job and called constantly to make sure she was doing a good job, which, unbelievably, she did, for about five years. Jemmis was a hard worker, never complained, seemed to enjoy all of the same programs as the kids, and would sit happily on the couch with them, be it Saturday morning or Friday night. Because of this, Alan insisted that "she must be retarded" and would find all sorts of things she did wrong to prove his point, but I ignored him. Jemmis was the best thing to happen to us; she was honest, I hardly knew she was there, the kids liked her, and the house was moderately clean. When we had to let her go, she had a little fit; I kept trying to explain that it had nothing to do with her, but she seemed unable to understand. I assured her family that it was our financial problems and not her competence that led to the firing. In the end, everyone looked at me with distrust: Jemmis, her family, and my kids.

Having survived the succession of strangers and the loss of familiar, comfortable Jemmis, my kids cannot be entirely blamed for their nonchalance or even mistrust of Bebe. I am sure they must be wondering, How long will we keep this one? Hopefully, by tomorrow, Lauren will remember her manners and at least be civil.

SEVENTEEN

In the morning, I come down to find Bebe already in the kitchen. I smell coffee, and something else, something forgotten: cooked breakfast food. Both kids are sitting at the kitchen table eating what appears to be Cream of Wheat and toast. The kids haven't complained about cold cereal or yogurt for breakfast every day, but the way they are lapping up the spread Bebe has laid out makes me feel guilty. It's a happy, domestic scene, no thanks to me. I don't say a word, but as I join them and bury my head in my coffee and the paper I think that maybe today I could at least try to sort out the bills on Alan's desk.

By midmorning, any hopes I had that we would be okay, are gone. Although the house is starting to look and smell clean again, I am feeling dirty, disorganized, and near tears. We have been getting final notices for months, on everything from insurance to cable to heat! As far as I can tell, none of the credit cards will work, and I have exactly $345 in the checking account plus the $500 from my father. I badly need to talk with Alan about all of this, but I don't see how I can go to the hospital and do that. If he is in the same state, it will be totally frustrating; and if he is more alert, I will have to control myself and not bombard him with all of my rage and anxiety. He is, after all, recovering. It's simply a lose-lose.

I walk outside onto the deck in a daze, thinking I will just get a few moments of fresh air—yet somehow, five hours later, when the kids come home from school, I'm still there. Apparently, I can become as lost as my husband. Bebe comes out to ask me what to make for dinner, and I mumble something about cold cereal and macaroni and cheese. I think she makes a little snort with her teeth, but she leaves me alone. Later, she calls the kids to dinner and I finally step inside. There are three bowls of macaroni and cheese on the kitchen table and also some hot dogs, which she must have found in the freezer. The kids are eating and chatting with Bebe, but they get quiet when I come in. I see the bowl that's been left for me but I ignore it, take a yogurt out of the fridge, and leave the room. I have no energy. I don't know what we're going to do.

That night I fall asleep with the TV on and have strained dreams about bank robbers and prison guards. I wake up in the middle of the night with a stiff neck and a cough. By morning, I feel awful. I think I'm getting the flu. I find my way out onto the deck again with a magazine, and that's where I stay for most of the day. Bebe comes out every hour or so with random questions.

"Miss Barbara, where the cleaning brush for windows?"

"I don't know, Bebe. Use whatever is there." There is that teeth snort again.

"Want me to make list for shopping? Plenty of things we need."

"I'm not going shopping today, Bebe." Half a teeth snort.

"What you making for dinner tonight?"

"Bebe, this is a bad time for me. Alan is in the hospital. I cannot think about food." Long, loud snort, with teeth and tongue involved. But at least she leaves me alone.

THE NEXT MORNING I know I must go and see Alan. One day is understandable, two would be inexcusable. I am in for quite a surprise. When I enter Alan's room, he is sitting up in bed, drinking what appears to be orange juice from a straw. It's like he is a completely different person. There is color in his cheeks, his hair is combed, and he looks almost like his old self. Certainly, there are signs that his body's been ravaged—bruising on his arms, blotches on his face from various electrodes, plus the bones are really sticking out around his neck and his lips are dry and blistered—but all in all, he looks less like he's been semiconscious for a week and more like he's had a rough day skiing in Vermont.

A nurse is leaning in and arranging a pillow behind his head. She has red hair and is about five feet two inches and must weigh about two hundred pounds. Her white uniform is so tight that there are at least three rolls that I can see, three tires from her bra to the bottom of her underwear. She looks just like a plump pig in a blanket, one that is about to burst out of its pastry. But the weirdest thing is that this overstuffed woman is leaning right over Alan, in his face, really, and he does not look even the slightest bit repulsed; in fact, he has a small smile. I walk into the room.

"Alan? Is it really you?"

"Apparently so."

I go to him. I reach out and touch his hand. I guess I should lean in and kiss him but something stops me; something in me or in him, I'm not sure. He doesn't seem to notice. In fact, it's almost like he pulls back, too.

"Mrs. Lerner?" The nurse stops what she's doing and comes over to me. I see her name is Louisa. There is something not quite right; I can sense it. She seems a bit panicked to see me.

"I . . . wait. Oh! The doctor has asked to be paged when you come in." I look at her and back to Alan. He still has this kind of dopey smile.

"What's going on?" I ask. She turns to Alan.

"We'll be right back, hon," she says, adjusting the fold in his top sheet. "You just keep drinking your juice." Then she puts her hand on my right shoulder blade and turns me toward the door and walks me out of the room.

"Dr. Morris will want to speak with you."

"Just a minute," I start to protest, but Louisa is remarkably strong. She is urging me out the door with both hands.

"Excuse me!" I go to take her hands off me, but she doesn't budge. "I don't understand what you're doing. My husband looks better than he's looked in a week and you drag me out of his room before I can even—" She puts up a hand to stop me and turns toward the front desk.

"Janisha, page Dr. Morris." Then she says to me, "Mrs. Lerner, your husband is doing better. His vitals are all stronger, and he's going to be fine. But there's something else. Really, the doctor will want to speak with you himself." She pauses, as if she has a dilemma. "It has to do with his memory. He . . . he's not quite back to himself. In the memory department. You know what I'm saying?"

"What? Like he doesn't remember why he's here?"

"I really must ask you to wait for the doctor."

"Well, can't I wait with Alan? I promise I won't say anything about what happened."

"It would be best if you'd just wait out here." I consider this. Alan is going to be fine, which is wonderful news. But apparently he is blocking out what he did. The whole Vicodin thing? Well, that's convenient for him. I mean, I've already realized that he is going to need to see a psychiatrist and things will never be exactly the same, and obviously I have to be careful because he is so stressed and fragile, but I did think at least he'd have to face things. I did think that maybe *we'd* even face some things together, and maybe in a very awful way we could look back on this one day and be grateful that we finally had to be honest with each other and with ourselves. So if Alan doesn't know what he did? How exactly are we to proceed?

"Dr. Morris is on his way." Janisha delivers this news from the desk.

"Why don't you have a seat in the family waiting room?" Because I don't want to go sit in the family waiting room, Louisa, whoever you are. Because I *sat* in the family waiting room enough last week when I was avoiding my mother-in-law. Because I *hate* the family waiting room with its shabby attempt to be homey and comfy. What's homey and comfy about commercial carpet and year-old copies of *Redbook* and a television nailed to the wall?

"I'll just stand here and wait," I offer, stubbornly. And though clearly Louisa would prefer me down the hall, she nods and moves away. I think she is afraid that I will dash into Alan's room and start yelling, "Don't you remember? The ambulance? The pills? Don't you?"

She would not be that far off. I am angry. A little part of me wants to hurt Alan for everything he's done. I pace up and down the hall outside his room, never quite reaching the opening or the window where I can see him or he can see me, but I am listening. Listening for any sounds, perhaps Alan calling out, calling my name. And that is the strangest thing of all. Alan knows that I am here, we spoke for just a minute, and then I left the room and he did not protest. *That* is not like

Alan at all. The one thing I know is that when he's feeling help-less, Alan needs attention. Usually mine. And he will go to any lengths to get it.

I desperately want to ask him about so many things. I will not press him, but I know I will be looking for some sort of sig-nal from him, a sign that he feels something, maybe an apology or at least an expression of regret. I wonder if he will be one of those people who, because he was near death, vows to live every minute to the fullest from here on in. That would be kind of wonderful.

I hear the doctor's footsteps before I see him. He comes around the corner at a brisk pace and heads straight for me.

"Mrs. Lerner, sorry to keep you waiting. Can we take a walk?" I nod. He goes on. "Have you had a chance to speak with Alan this morning?"

"Yes, just for a moment."

"And what did you talk about?" I stop walking.

"What? What kind of a question is that? What is going on here?"

"Please, Mrs. Lerner, indulge me. What did the two of you talk about?" Dr. Morris looks serious. I am getting very frus-trated, but also concerned. I debate turning my back on Dr. Morris and marching into Alan's room, but instead I find myself answering.

"We only had a chance to say hello. Why is everyone so concerned with what I say to Alan?" Dr. Morris stops and takes a breath.

"It's not what you say to Alan; it's what *he* might say to *you*. I want to prepare you. I've called for a neurological and psych consult. You see, Alan is displaying whole gaps in his memory. He isn't 'oriented times three,' as we say, which means he doesn't know person, place, and time. He knows his own name and what state he lives in and where he grew up, but he doesn't know anything about his current life. He doesn't know what he does for a living or that he"—the doctor pauses, looking pained—"or that he's married. To you. Or anyone, for that matter."

"What are you talking about? I just saw him."

"Yes, but all you said was hello, right? Did he recognize you?"

"Of course he recognized me. Why wouldn't he recognize me?"

"Mrs. Lerner, I can imagine how unfathomable this might be, that your own husband doesn't know who you are. Yesterday afternoon when I made my rounds I mentioned to Alan that he'd pulled a bit of a Rip Van Winkle, and he looked at me very seriously and asked if I was sure that was his name." Dr. Morris lets this sink in. I look at him like he is crazy, but I don't say a word. He goes on.

"I thought he was kidding, of course, but it soon became clear that he was actually quite confused. I began to ask him about his life and a few things seemed to come back to him as we were speaking, which is an excellent sign. He suddenly knew his name. Then he told me he was living in a house in Virginia and attending George Washington University. He spoke of his roommates, his dog, and said his mother was a schoolteacher. No mention of being a husband or a father. I noticed some pictures of you and the children on the windowsill, and when I showed them to Alan, he claimed to have absolutely no idea who any of you were. That's when I called for the consults. If you hadn't come in by nine, I would have phoned you and called you in because I sincerely hope that seeing you will bring much, if not everything, back, and perhaps it already has. I'd like to go back into Alan's room with you so we can judge whether or not that's true."

"This is . . . crazy." I manage these three little words.

"Please don't be nervous. The good news is that there's no evidence of brain damage, and in these cases most memory issues resolve. Also, Alan's physical condition has improved a hundred percent. Let's just take this a step at a time."

I know the nurses are watching me as we enter Alan's room. They pretend to be busy with paperwork, but I know. I am now the star of a new reality show entitled *Life's Weirdest and Wackiest Events: Medical.* We go in and there is Alan, sitting up in the bed just as he was twenty minutes ago. He is still sipping his juice and he is watching TV. It's *The Today Show,* and there is a dog trainer doing obedience training with several dogs. Alan looks at us as we walk in but then turns back to the TV. I march right up to the bed and take his free hand. He looks at me, questioning.

"Alan," I say, squeezing his hand and staring deep into his eyes, "you know who I am, right?"

Alan stares back at me, looks over at the doctor, and then back to me before he answers. "You're the lady in the pictures."

DR. TOBIAS, the chief of psychiatry at Bergen General, is beefy, hairy, and sweaty. He's a man who looks like he would be more at home competing in the all-you-can-eat hot dog contest at Coney Island than running a department at a major teaching hospital in New Jersey. Unlike his appearance, his credentials are impeccable. Princeton, Colombia, coveted fellowships and appointments. This, plus a regular-guy aura that eventually wins me over and allows me to overlook his un-kempt appearance.

"Dissociative disorders," he reads, from a big red book called the DSM-IV. We are seated in his office, on the couch, two days after my morning meeting with Dr. Morris. Alan has been seen by a whole squadron of medical personnel since then and he has had more scans and lab work than most people do in a lifetime. They have ruled out stroke, a seizure disorder, a brain tumor, and traumatic brain injury. They have done biopsies, spinal taps, and MRIs, and they have tested for growths, parasites, viral infections, and damage to the vagus nerve, which is just one among several body parts that prior to now I never knew existed. Other than calling in a psychic or a bucket of leeches, I believe they've exhausted all procedures. As Dr. Tobias reads, he shows me the paragraph, so, like a small child, I am reading along.

" 'The essential feature of the dissociative disorders is a disruption in the usually integrated functions of consciousness, memory, identity, or perception of the environment. The disturbance may be sudden or gradual, transient or chronic.' "

I sit back on the couch. I will just listen. The book is too confusing and the writing is too small. Dr. Tobias goes on to list several features of this disorder and what is needed to make the diagnosis. Then he slaps the book closed and turns to me.

"Look, this is not an exact science. And despite all the tests, no one knows for sure just how long Alan was unconscious. But the fact is, he can compute complicated equations and solve multiple-step puzzles, he demonstrates superior problem-solving and high-order-thinking skills. This suggests that he's lost no cognitive function. Is it possible that his brain has been damaged in an area of emotion or personality and we can't detect it? Of course. But right now I'd say we need to proceed with a diagnosis that is a hybrid of disassociative amnesia and disassociate disorder not otherwise specified." As an afterthought, he adds, "Although you could make a case for dissociative fugue. Based on his prior accident, and because one could argue that since he could not wander away with two broken legs, the only wandering he could manage was through a bottle of pills, it fits. But I'm leaning toward the amnesia."

I am now totally lost.

"Could you go over that list again?"

"Sure. Basically, disassociative amnesia commonly presents in adults, and almost always follows a stressful or traumatic event. Often, the amnesia follows a violent act, like a car crash, murder, or suicide. Also, there is a subset of the amnesia in which an individual doesn't remember a specific time period, which in Alan's case seems to be about the last twenty years. This is called continuous amnesia. It can present with depressive symptoms, even trancelike symptoms, which would explain Alan's slow rebound."

"Okay. Fine. So let's say he has this disorder. This amnesia. What happens now?"

"Well, it's unusual enough that we're going to want to observe him for a few more days, monitor his brain function and such. There's been some success with hypnotherapy, which we will also provide, assuming you agree. But the best hope for Alan's recovery will be the ongoing stimulation and attention of his family. Often in these cases, one breakthrough can open the floodgates, so we're going to have to pick away at him with reminders and memories."

"So you think I should bring the kids, too?"

"How old are they?"

"Twelve and nine."

Dr. Tobias leans back and looks thoughtful.

"I'm not certain that having their father *not know* who they are is in their best interests just yet. Why don't we begin with pictures, videos, but physically leave them out. You can tell them he has some memory problems and then ease them into the extent of it. Either way, he should be going home by the end of next week, so you'll have to prepare them."

HOME. AT THE end of next week. Alan coming home. To a home he doesn't remember and a family he doesn't know. Today is Wednesday, so that could mean about eight or nine days from now. Let's see what I might tell the kids to "ease" them into this. How about that their father remembers his damn unhousebroken dog, Paco, and not any of us, and also thinks he might be Rip Van Winkle. That should go over well. Then we can all go to the mental hospital on the family plan.

EIGHTEEN

t he next two days go by in a blur, each one a repeat of the day before. In the morning, like a zombie, I get dressed and lumber through the motions. Make coffee, pack lunches, feed Casey, and sign permission slips. The kids quietly step out of my way, and seeing this forces me to rebound a bit. I take a few minutes before they go to school to chat about what their days will be like. Anything special today? Ev, don't you have to run the mile in gym this week? Laur, how's that science project coming? I'm grateful when I see that Bebe is nodding approvingly as she loads the dishwasher, and it strikes me as strange that her opinion should mean anything to me at all. When the children leave, I go to the hospital. The first thing I show Alan is our wedding album. He makes one comment.

"My mom looks nice."

I try not to hate him. I try not to think about the seven visits to Milady Bridals with Eve of Milady, the actual gown designer, during which I had to nervously pretend to be a good customer's niece just so Eve would personally supervise the design of my wedding gown, and how both mothers were supposed to wear long evening gowns but Marian insisted on wearing a short burgundy cotton dress, which was barely dressy enough for an afternoon lunch, let alone a Saturday night affair.

—————

N E X T ,   I   P R O D U C E the albums filled with baby pictures; Lauren in the preschool play, then dressed up as a surfer girl; Evan as a baby in the stroller; all of us on horses on the beach two Christmases ago in Mexico. He thumbs through them as if they are travel brochures of lovely places he might one day visit, making comments now and then that have no meaning and float to the ground like dust in a ray of light.

"She looks good in pink," he says of Lauren, and "How old did you say the boy is?" This makes me nauseous. I take the pictures back. I pass him photos of his precious cars, and he is much more excited. "Sweet!" he says, about the Porsche. "I really know how to pick 'em! Do I own all of these?" How to answer that one? We've given back the Porsche and the BMW has gone to the little scrapyard in the sky. I mumble something noncommittal. He stares at the cars much longer than the kids, goes through the pile twice, but he doesn't remember anything. I try to forgive him, reminding myself that in his last conscious thought he was twenty-two years old. Sometimes he says things that don't make sense.

"Are you going to Fort Lauderdale?" he asks. I stare back at him, rack my brain. Nothing.

"Why would I do that, Alan?" He thinks, and then he shakes his head. He doesn't know. Another time he asks for Angela.

"Angela who?" I ask.

"You know," he says. "The one from the meeting."

"I'm so sorry, Alan. I don't know who that is." He stays silent. Thinking. As if there is a file; a file he knows he saved, but can't find. As if it's lost in the computer and he can't pull it up. Occasionally, I become suspicious. It's all too weird. I try not to doubt him, but sometimes a little angry thought intrudes, and I wonder if he could possibly be pulling off the greatest acting job of all time. And then I have an even nastier thought. If Alan had succeeded, if he had never woken up, might it have actually been a lot easier than this? We do have life insurance, don't we?

Quickly, I push those thoughts away and chastise myself for even thinking such a thing. I feel guilty then, horrible, so I bring him chocolates, the dark Dove bars he likes, and when he tells me they taste bitter and he doesn't like them, I almost cry. "You love them!" I shout. He shrinks back then, and I'm ashamed. I start to cry and have to leave the room. Suddenly, I *love* the family waiting room. Anywhere but that chair next to that bed with that stranger. I pull myself together, and when I go back in, I gently ask him what kind of candy I can bring him tomorrow. He asks for Chunkys. I tell him I haven't seen a Chunky in years but I will look. Then he asks if I can bring him some Junket, and I tell him I don't know what that is.

"My mother makes it. It's like Jell-O."

"Okay," I say, "I'll look for that, too."

WHEN I LEAVE the hospital, I am so drained that from the time I walk back into the house until dinner I just sit out on the deck. I am not even thinking, just deprogramming. When the kids come home, it's like I'm paralyzed. I am torn between wanting to attach myself to them and fearing that if I do, I will infect them with my despair. Somewhere inside I know that, like Alan, I am not making progress.

Absentmindedly, I twist my wedding band around and around on my finger. Usually, it fits snugly on the loose skin of my fourth finger, but today it comes right off in my hand. I tell myself I must be losing weight, but a little voice whispers back that it's more than that; it's a sign. "A sign of what?" I ask silently. "You figure it out" is the reply. I play with the ring for a few more minutes, and when I try to put it back on my finger, it simply will not stay on. Afraid to lose it, and for no other reason, I set it gently down in a little dish on the end table and close my eyes. Occasionally, I glance over at it, half expecting it to speak or fly away or do something supernatural. I should try to put it back on again, I think, maybe now it will stay, but I don't do it. As Friday afternoon slips away, Bebe is beside herself.

"I go leave today for weekend."

"Okay, bye."

"You be all right with no one here?"

"Yes, of course."

"Why you no talk with children?"

"Bebe, please. That's my business."

There is silence for a while. Then she says, "Famous saying: Give what you have. It may be better than you think."

"Thank you, Bebe." She doesn't move.

I get up not only to get away from Bebe, but also because there are great clouds of smoke coming from over on the Rabinowitzes' lawn, and I am curious.

"I leaving soon." Her voice follows me.

"Okay, fine." I continue walking away.

She calls after me. "See me Monday."

WHEN I PULL back the evergreen branches and step into the Rabinowitzes' yard, it's like entering an alternative universe. We are no longer on pricey, groomed, Autumn Court in upscale Glen Vale, but somewhere between the Catskills and Mars; somewhere the Unabomber might feel right at home. The yard is disheveled and overgrown; wild brambles merge with struggling fruit trees and sickly evergreens. Remnants of lawn alternate with flat bald spots and dry tracks of mud.

The dominant structure is the tall tower of metal and wires we fear is giving us extra Y chromosomes while we sleep. Beneath this structure, on a picnic table, are a number of appliance parts that may have once been radios or toasters but are currently unrecognizable. Near the house is a campfire, a circle of flat stones and tree trunks that surround a burning tepee of wood. Above the tepee is some sort of metal stand, from which a bucket hangs just above the flames. It is smoking. My first thought is toxic waste, but then I remember that Susan is an active environmentalist. The occasional Greenpeace volunteer who shows up at my door after visiting Susan is openly disappointed; my enthusiasm pales next to hers, as do my contributions. Also, she gives out oranges on Halloween, a reason, duly noted by the children of the neighborhood, to bypass her ranch.

To the left of the campfire are two easels, another picnic table, a sandbox, and a baby pool. The picnic table is covered in books and what looks like a chemistry set. On the ground are various projects in different stages of completion. Finger paintings and tie-dyed shirts hang on a laundry line between two trees. The overall theme is junkyard meets nature camp meets techno retreat; it's a hodgepodge of school and science and art colony. It is an unqualified mess—and I can't help but smile.

Susan and her son, Ross, are sitting in the campfire circle, deep in discussion. At the picnic table, Zory, who will be off to college in the fall, leans over her little sister and points to something in a textbook. They are all deeply involved with what they are doing, and I am struck by the simple synergy of the moment and this family: interconnected and efficient. A mother calmly explains to a fourteen-year-old son, a ten-year-old listens receptively to an older sister. If not for the strange backyard decor, it would be a classic American family portrait à la Norman Rockwell. I hesitate to break the harmony, but Zory sees me coming and waves, and then Susan looks up.

"Bitsy!" Her voice is so friendly as she calls to me. "How nice!" She is wearing a caftan and sandals; her frizzy light-brown hair is loose and flowing. She leaves the campfire and makes her way toward me. Ross, I notice, takes a stick from the ground and tends to the bucket. The girls go back to their reading.

"Hello, dear," Susan continues as she approaches, and before I can say a word she wraps one arm around my back and urges me further into the yard.

"It's so good to see you. We never see you enough, do we? Terrible for neighbors to go so long between visits. Can I get you some tea?"

"Oh, I don't want to bother you. I saw the smoke and, well, I just wondered what you were working on back here." As we step further inside the strange yard, I find myself relaxing. My own yard is manicured to the max, orchestrated for peace, with its flowering plums and bluestone patio bordered in designer impatiens. The hedges alone could be photographed for *Architectural Digest*. But when I sit there beside my granite-topped built-in gas grill on my Brown Jordan lounge chairs, I don't feel relaxed at all. I feel tense. Why is that?

"Oh, don't be silly, it's no bother. I need a break myself. Let's go onto the sun porch. I have chamomile, peppermint, or green; do you have a preference?" I don't protest. Suddenly, tea sounds just right. "Oh, anything is fine."

"Ross," Susan warns, "you're getting very close, see how the steam is changing color?" Ross peers into the bucket, stirring, and little Magenta joins him.

When Susan returns with the tea, I ask her about the substance in the bucket.

"Oh, well, that's Magenta's year-end goal. To make a gas that has glitter in it. She seems to have a knack for chemistry, so I let her choose it, but so far she hasn't had much success. You have to get the compound to a certain heat and . . . oh, I don't want to bore you with this!"

"Oh no, you're not boring me at all. But what do you mean by her year-end goal?"

"Well, they all have them, even Zory, it's a big part of our homeschooling. We have projects at the end of the year, instead of tests. I think they measure just as much, plus they require some creativity. Ross is working on a listening device, a sort of turbocharged hearing aid. Of course, we think it's because he likes to eavesdrop on everyone, but I have to admit he's making excellent progress. Poor Magenta only wants to see long streams of glitter traveling through the air"—she smiles—"like if you had a big bubble wand. She's even picked out a name: Sparkle-works!"

"I think that's incredible. Your kids are really incredible." As Susan pours the tea into my cup, she looks surprised.

"Well, you're kids are pretty incredible, too. I don't know Lauren that well, but Evan is just a sweetheart."

"You know my Evan?"

"Oh, sure, he wanders over here quite a bit. Likes to hang around the kids—Ross, mostly."

Well. I had no idea. Maybe Evan feels what I'm feeling when he's over here, some sort of tranquillity transfusion. Can you absorb serenity, like through osmosis? I wonder what else Susan knows. It seems impossible that she wouldn't know about Alan, but I've always thought her so out of the loop, I can't be sure. She quickly clears things up.

"Bitsy, I don't want to intrude, but with Alan in the hospital, is there anything we can do to help?" Maybe it's the tea, or the idea that Evan finds comfort here, or maybe it's just the sheer spirit of a young girl wanting to create Sparkleworks, but before I know it, I am pouring out everything to Susan Rabinowitz. She doesn't say much, but I see her mouth form a tight line when I tell her about Andrew Sloan, and she seems genuinely heartbroken when I mention that my father said I'll probably have to sell the house. I end by throwing up my hands and exclaiming that my immigrant housekeeper, who I am not paying, by the way, is probably a member of Mensa. When I finish, she hands me a tissue to wipe my eyes and blow my nose and smiles sympathetically.

"Aren't you sorry you asked me to have tea?" I whimper.

"Well, I'm just glad to see the truth serum is working."

"What?"

"Kidding. Just kidding." I look back at Susan, and when the shock fades, I start to laugh. This is possibly the worst moment of my life and she has decided that I can take a joke. It is the most validating, respectful thing anyone has ever done for me.

"Oh God, Susan, I thought you were serious. I thought maybe it was Zory's goal or something."

"Are you kidding? Ezora has actually changed her goal three times this year and I have no confidence that she'll actually complete it, but as she reminds me daily, Brown University could care less about a goal, so I'm thinking about giving up this fight. More important, let's figure out what we're going to do about your situation."

Just like that, Susan uses the word "we," and it's unbelievable how much I like the sound of it. We haven't had more than ten conversations in the past three years and we've never gone out socially, and yet suddenly we are a team.

"Thank you, but you've been a big help already, just for listening. There's really nothing anyone can do."

"Nonsense. I'm sending Mort over as soon as possible. I'm sure he can make sense out of your finances."

"Why? Is Mort knowledgeable about bookkeeping?" Mort Rabinowitz is the palest person I have ever met. He is about five feet nine inches tall, with thin red hair, round wire-rimmed glasses, and a skinny body. He wears jeans that are too big and have to be cinched with a brown leather belt, and he literally has no ass. Whenever he is outside, he covers himself completely. He is always in long sleeves, even in the middle of August, even in the shade. If he has to be in the sun, he wears a towel on his head, which he holds in place with a baseball cap. Whenever I see him standing next to Susan, who is on the hefty side, I have the sense that she could pick him up, turn him on his side, and carry him into the house like a ramrod.

"Oh, honey! Mort is just about the best CPA in Bergen County. I know what you're thinking, he doesn't look the part, and you're right, of course. But it doesn't seem to matter to PricewaterhouseCoopers, since he's been their Northeast vice president for fifteen years! Between you and me, all these companies are alike; they push for a certain look, but they're willing to overlook the image if the brain happens to make them millions every year."

"I . . . I never knew. I thought Mort had a . . . a business or something. I thought maybe he was an inventor." Susan starts to laugh.

"The only thing that man invents is new ways to drive me crazy." But she says it with warmth and affection, and I know instantly that they are soul mates. I start to tear up again and Susan thinks it's because of my situation, and that's part of it; the other part is that I covet that feeling she has, that affection for her husband. I haven't had that in a very, very long . . . maybe never. But I feel no jealousy toward Susan, maybe envy, maybe just a little; but even so, it's not the toxic kind, not at all. In fact, I'm reluctant to leave, and when I finally do, I feel more hopeful than I have in months. This, of course, is always a big mistake.

LATER THAT NIGHT, Evan and I are watching a movie and Lauren is at the library when the phone rings. I hit pause on the remote and answer.

"Hello?"

"Mrs. Lerner?"

"Yes?"

"This is Sergeant Kestner of the Glen Vale police, and I have your daughter here with me. She's fine, but you need to come down and pick her up." I feel the air go completely out of me. Once, when I was about ten, my brothers let me play a game of fungo with them. In fungo, you have to catch a Wiffle ball on a fly before the other outfielders. I was about to do just that when suddenly my brother Eddie charged into me from behind and lifted me right up into the air, and I came down flat on the hard ground and thought I was dead. No air to breathe at all. And that is what I feel like right now.

"Wha . . . what did she do?" I say in a small voice.

"You need to come down, ma'am. We'll talk when you get here."

NINETEEN

"Evan, we have to go in the car." Bebe is gone for the weekend, and I don't know what's more upsetting: going to the police station or having to drag Evan along to see his sister there. I am wearing sweats that don't match and I have absolutely no makeup on, but I don't care. I simply run my fingers through my hair, slip on sneakers and a coat, and off we go. At the police station, where I've been exactly two times in the eight years we've lived here (once when we moved in, to register our alarm and receive a Glen Vale sticker and alarm code, and again when I was a Brownie group leader and we needed some literature to create a DARE badge), I tell Evan to wait in the car. It's only about nine o'clock, but it's pitch black in the parking lot, so I leave Evan the keys and make sure he locks himself in.

I approach the desk and identify myself and the officer comes out from behind the counter and I hear him call out "Lauren," and suddenly there she is, my baby, looking nothing like she did when she left home. Her sweet face is covered with makeup: pink blush and lipstick, blue shadow on her eyes, and I think I see something glittering on her cheekbones. She is wearing her red jacket, but underneath she has on a shirt I've never seen. It is black, tight and cropped; *very* cropped. There must be at least eight inches of stomach skin showing between her pants and top.

"What? How? Where is your other shirt?"

"At Natasha's."

"But how did it get to Natasha's? I dropped you at the library."

"We walked."

"You walked all the way to Natasha's?" I do the mental math—at least two miles.

"By yourselves? At night?" I look at the officer. "I don't understand."

"Your daughter and her friend met up with some other kids tonight. Some boys." I stare back at Lauren. She turns away.

"Apparently, at some point they decided to play a few pranks."

"I didn't do anything." She says this quickly. I look at Lauren. She seems afraid.

"What did they do?"

"One of them had a baseball bat. They smashed some mailboxes along the east road. And a couple of lampposts."

"Oh my God. Are you serious?"

"Mom, I didn't do it, I swear. We saw them after they'd done that stuff."

"Some of the kids are known to us," the sergeant continues. "They're not what I'd call the best influence for a young girl. I don't know Lauren, but we've had a little talk, and I have the impression that these are some new friends. I've suggested that she reevaluate her choices." He smiles. This is not such a big deal. *To him.* "I don't think she set out to vandalize tonight, but where this group goes, trouble follows. So we're going to release her to you, and hopefully"—he turns to Lauren—"the next time we see each other it's at the PBA family fun day, right, Lauren?"

She gives him a little smile. "Right."

"Okay, just sign over here, Mrs. Lerner." In a daze, I sign the papers, thank Sergeant Kestner, walk my daughter out, and get into the car. On the drive home, she doesn't say a word. Nobody does.

"I have just one question," I say, after we are back inside the house and Evan has headed to the kitchen. "All the times you went to the library this year, all the times that I thought you were studying, were you someplace else?"

She looks at me as if debating what to say. A whole minute passes. Then she offers, "Not *all* the times."

ON SATURDAY MORNING at nine, Evan has been picked up for baseball and Lauren, who has been grounded for life, is still in her room when the doorbell rings and there is Mort, pad and pencil in hand, asking shyly if this would be a good time for him to take a look at my finances. Asking. I show him into Alan's office, and I don't hear from him for two hours. I interrupt him once to bring him a glass of water, which he accepts without breaking his concentration.

Around this time I hear Lauren on the stairs, and she enters the kitchen like quite the remorseful angel. She's wearing pink fuzzy slippers, her Hello Kitty pajamas, and a pink robe from The Gap. I laugh to myself. This is a not-so-subtle tactic on her part, trying suddenly to look the opposite of the way she did last night, trying suddenly to look like she's nine. I decide to say nothing, and watch as she grabs a bowl, fills it with corn-flakes and milk, and out of the corner of my eye I see her watching *me*. At some point we have to talk about last night. Or maybe not. Maybe this is one of those events that make a big enough impression just by the fact that they happened; talk might be redundant. It would be nice if I had someone to run this by—another *parent,* for instance—but since I seem to be in this alone, I guess I'll just have to go with my gut.

Another hour passes and Mort emerges. He suggests we sit down at the kitchen table. I see that he has filled several legal pages with notes and figures. My head hurts, I'm scared of what he'll say, and I'm embarrassed at what he may have found. Lauren is in the family room, thankfully engrossed in the movie *Clueless,* which she must be watching for the eleventh or twelfth time. I hear the female leads exclaiming "As if," and I wish more than anything I could be Lauren's age again and curl up on the couch with a snack while the adults handled all the worries and solved all the problems.

Mort's voice is level and soft as he explains to me what Alan has done. Overleveraged, undercapitalized, we are in financial crisis. Alan has refinanced our house so many times that there is not nearly as much liquid as I imagined, when I imagined at all. Not all the deals Alan entered into were bad, Mort says; some were just unlucky and others have not developed as quickly as Alan may have thought. I'm not sure whether Mort is just being kind when he says that; after all, what's the difference? There are some unresolved investments, Mort says, and some holdings that aren't clear. For instance, do we own any real estate in Hackensack? Not that I know of, I reply, and Mort stares at me for what I think is an awfully long moment. Then he looks down and quickly assures me that some assets may not be what they seem. Often, he says, financial statements are legally but creatively inflated or padded to bolster an applicant's credit, and he promises to continue to sort things out. Chapter 7 is a possibility, and yes, it looks like I may have to sell the house.

The good news is that Mort has found two accounts with several thousand dollars in each, so we are not totally broke. Also, he has managed to set up a payment schedule with the credit-card companies and the utilities and even salvaged our medical, life, and auto insurance policies. They will all accept minimum payments until the house is sold or some other money becomes available.

Then Mort looks at me seriously and says, "Bitsy, there is one thing you must do, and that is to get a job. There is no way around it. You need income, or you will lose everything." I just stare back at him, thinking, A job? Doing what?

"And something else you have to address, and this I really can't say strongly enough. There are papers here from the school about your son. Perhaps you didn't understand what they meant, I don't know, but he is having trouble, and you have to find out what is wrong. Look here."

Mort slides several papers over to me, letters I've seen and ignored. Honestly, I didn't pay much attention to them because I thought they were asking for money or donations and I just couldn't be bothered. They have the school's letterhead and one has the words "Child Study Team" underneath. I read them, really read them, for the first time. Apparently, they suspect that Evan has some sort of learning disability. I am so ashamed in front of Mort. His children are so brilliant. One letter is from Evan's teacher; she wants me to call her, and it's dated a month ago. Another is from the principal and school psychologist. The last letter states that if they do not hear from me, they have the right by law to test Evan for special education without my consent. I look at the date, and see that I must respond by this Monday! Mort is gathering himself up and I thank him profusely, but he just smiles and nods and wishes me good luck.

"You should talk to Susan about Evan. She's a certified special education teacher, you know." He smiles gently. "Has to be, to deal with all of us." When Mort leaves, I take a look at the school papers again. I hear Evan come in around 1:00 p.m. He doesn't even come in to the kitchen, just anticipates my questions and calls out that the team won and they all went for pizza and he's not hungry and heads up to his room. I am not far behind.

TWENTY

I knock softly on Evan's door and go in. He is on his bed, drawing in a sketchbook. He closes it when I come in.

"Hey, buddy."

"Hi, Mom."

"How ya doing?"

"Okay."

"Ev, I need to ask you something. How's school going?"

"Good."

"Really?"

"Uh-huh."

"Well, I don't know if that's exactly right. I have a letter from your teacher. It's been so crazy around here, I kind of let it slide, but she says you might be having a little trouble." No answer.

"Are you finding third grade tough, sweetie?"

"NO!" Evan sits up, gets off the bed, and slams his sketchbook on his desk. "Leave me alone, okay?" This is so out of character, it throws me. When I speak, I hear my own voice sounding a little frantic, and I try to level it.

"Evan, if you're having trouble, it's okay. We need to figure out what it is that you're not getting, that's all." Silence. His back is to me.

"Evan?" From behind me, there's a voice.

"He can't read." It is Lauren. He whirls around.

"Shut up."

"It's okay, it's not your fault."

"What? What is going on here?" I am at a total loss.

"He can't read, okay? Zero. Nada. Can't do it."

"That's impossible! We've been reading together for years."

"Really? Think about it, Mother. Who reads, you or him?"

I am mortified. I look from Evan to Lauren. Evan turns away, clearly miserable, and my daughter just stares, arms crossed, defiant. She is calling me out, challenging me to be accountable. I start to get a sinking feeling. I've spent many nights lying with Ev on his bed reading; he always likes when I read to him. But that's okay, that's what they tell you to do, no matter how old the child is—it's supposed to strengthen their desire to read, not sabotage it. God. All the problems with Alan. Can it be I've overlooked something as clear and important as this? I start to search for reasons why it can't be true.

"But he . . . he reads the cereal box. And comics." My mind is racing, searching. "He reads how to microwave the pizza bagels." I look from Lauren back to Evan. He doesn't say a word.

"He's faking it. He figures it out from the pictures. Tell her, Ev."

Silence.

"I told him it's okay. Donny Becker can't read, and he's like the genius of sixth grade. It's not like you're stupid, Ev. Donny says it's like being color-blind. You get what everything is, you just don't see it the same way."

"Evan?" I go to him. He is standing at his desk. I put my arms around him. At first, he pushes me away, but I hold tight and he relaxes, eventually turning to face me and burying his face in my stomach.

"Oh, Ev." I am just hugging him, holding him, feeling an energy I haven't felt for years and a love so strong it hurts. I would do anything for this kid, for both of them. I look over at Lauren, who has become seemingly schizophrenic in the way she can quickly change personas. I totally ignore the fact that she is now wearing a belly shirt and flannel sweat pants that are rolled so low she is practically naked, and I mouth "Thank you." She lights up for a moment, then the indifferent mask comes back, and the shrug, and she turns and leaves.

"Baby, it's okay. We're going to figure this out and beat it. You're going to read, I promise you that. I'm sorry I didn't know. I'm really sorry. But it's going to be fine. Mommy's here."

BEBE ARRIVES AT 8:00 a.m. on Monday, and this time she's the one who's surprised. I am dressed, sitting at the kitchen table, reading the classifieds. Coffee is on, breakfast dishes are in the sink, and the kids are on their way to school. The curtains are open, sunlight streams in, and the small television is on. This kitchen has a heartbeat and a pulse. It lives once again.

"Miss Barbara, you feeling better?"

"Well, Bebe, you know how the saying goes, the early bird catches the worm."

Bebe raises her eyebrows and snorts. But this time it is a satisfied snort, not a disgusted one.

"Are you going to supermarket today?" Damn. This woman has a way of continually making me feel guilty.

"Yes Bebe, I am going to see Alan and then I have to go to Evan's school and then I will go to the market."

"Good. Buy regular dinner. Not from box."

O N M Y W A Y to the hospital, I call Susan on my cell. Mort has pretty much told her everything.

"I'm sorry about the house," she sympathizes. "Are you going to put it on the market?"

"I'll be speaking with the Realtor later today."

"What about Evan?"

"Well, I'm going over to the school this morning. I don't have an appointment, but someone will just have to see me."

"That's the spirit. And don't let them bully you. But you know, it might not be such a bad idea if Evan did get tested. He might just need some extra help or different strategies."

"I guess. I want to hear what they have to say. I just don't want them to put him in a special class or make it like he's a weirdo or anything."

"Evan's no weirdo. I told you, he's a little doll. If it would help, I could work with him in the afternoons, you know, just sort of give him some support."

"Oh Susan, I couldn't ask you to do that."

"No, I wouldn't mind. Zory's gone in a few months and Magenta really likes having people around, she works better that way. You'd be doing me a favor."

"I highly doubt that. But it sounds so great. I can't thank you enough." Through the phone I hear great popping sounds and Susan says, "Whoops, gotta go! Send Evan over whenever you can. Bye!"

T H E H O S P I T A L L O O K S the same, and even though Alan is no longer in ICU, everything feels frozen, as if the world is on normal speed but time has stopped inside Bergen General. Everything is just as it was, from the pale-yellow color of the tile walls to the faint smell of canned soup and peppermint in the hall. I know that Alan's mother has been coming every evening. I know this because the evidence of her is everywhere in his new room. There are fresh flowers, lilies (my least favorite), in a vase by the door. The smell is nauseating. I go over to them and employ a little trick I've learned, pulling out the inner most stamen to eliminate the smell. Then I spy her signature blue tin of butter cookies on the table near his feet. Last week, on the one day we overlapped, I saw her coming down the hall with two tins. "Two tins?" I asked, wondering who was going to eat that many cookies. She looked at me as if I was the lowest form of life, "One is for the *nurses, of course.*" Obviously, this was information I should have known. It may not have occurred to my mother-in-law that not everyone is up to date on hospital brownnosing. It made me pity the poor mothers of children in her class at holiday time.

Despite the lilies and the cookies, Alan, too, looks the same in his new bed. Occasionally, a nurse comes by, checks his vitals, inserts something into the bag above his head, gives me a small smile, and urges Alan to get up and walk around to prevent bedsores. I get the sense that the hospital staff has subtly dismissed him. Since he's in no physical danger, their job is done. In a way, though far from recovered, he is overstaying his welcome. I sit in the chair by his bed and look into his face. The truth is, even looking at him, I have no thoughts of him; it's like I've entered another zone, as if I'm the one not still in the world, his world. Instead of feeling connected to Alan, I'm antsy, distracted, and anxious to get to Evan's school. We make small talk. Finally, though my heart isn't in it, I pull three videos from my purse. Dr. Tobias has arranged for a VCR, and

Alan looks at me strangely as I push the cartridge in and press Play.

"You know how to work a Betamax?" I turn. A what? And then I remember. It's 1982. "No more Betamax," I respond. "It's a new kind. Easier." He looks puzzled, but that's all I'm prepared to offer right now. As our little family starts to come to life on the screen, I think, just wait till he hears about DVDs.

On the screen, Lauren, age four, is running back and forth from the sand to the edge of the ocean, based on the comings and goings of the waves. Each time the water pounds the beach and the surf creeps up toward her feet, she squeals and runs away, laughing, then tentatively takes a few more brave steps back to wait for the next wave. The camera follows this game. From off camera there is a voice, "Go closer, Lauren, the water's not going to hurt you." She shakes her head at the voice, her father's voice.

"Oh, for Christ's sake." The camera leaves Lauren then and tilts upward to me, tanned and squinting in my postpregnancy utility tankini with a six-month-old Evan in my arms. "Can't you get her to at least get her feet wet?" says the voice. I pull the baby's hat farther down over his head and make a visor with my hand to shield my eyes. "She's happy doing what she's doing," I shout. "Just let her be." The camera flips back to Lauren, but her smile has faded and she's backed up even farther, no longer flirting with the water or even the wet, hard sand. She stands, twisting a little, digging her big toe into the soft, hot, dry sand. The camera stays on this awhile, then wanders toward the ocean, where two parents are swinging a little boy up and out of the waves. They are foreign, Spanish I think, based on snippets of their shouts of *"Alay!"* I turn to Alan. He points to the TV. "Who's that?" I look back at the screen, at the strangers; strangers who are occupying more of our home video than our kids. "I have no idea." I wait to see if Alan says, "Well, that's weird," or even "Why was I filming them?" but he doesn't. I stare at my husband. Anything? Eventually, the camera pans back to Lauren, who is hunched down, her little butt resting on her heels, playing in the sand. Her red two-piece with the yellow quilted fish is all scrunched up in the middle. I see my feet come into the picture and hear my voice. "Honey, you look hot. Let's go put on some more sunscreen and get a drink." Lauren stands up. "Shut it off, Al, we're going back to the blanket." The camera pans up and then zooms in to a close-up of me holding Evan. In the bed, Alan lets out a whistle. "What?" I say, with a little flicker of hope. Does he remember something? Anything?

"Your chest," he says, "is enormous." I gasp.

"What?" I ask. Alan smiles.

"Sorry. It's just that . . . well, I mean, you do have . . . and there, you just had a baby, right? So, you know, they're . . . well . . . um . . . they're really big."

I stand up. I walk to the television and pop the video out. I don't say a word.

"Hey, I'm sorry. Really. I just mean, who wouldn't, I thought that . . ." I don't help Alan as he fumbles to make it right. The truth is, I don't know what to say. He is my husband, after all, and I do have a big chest, and this shouldn't be such a big deal.

I walk around the room, inventing things to do: put away the video, wipe the ledge that doesn't need wiping, and straighten the tissue box and the plastic water bottle and the flower vase. Finally, I look toward the door, out the window, up at the clock, and wonder how much longer I need to stay. Outside, it is an almost cruelly perfect spring day, complete with blue skies, budding trees, and the first faint notes of returning wildlife. On my way into the hospital, a blue jay swooped down, a robin flew by with a twig in its mouth, and two baby rabbits hopped into the flower bed as I stepped out of my car. It was like a Disney movie, an animated rainbow of movements; surely, just around the corner was a babbling brook and a family of deer. I felt as if at any moment two furry chipmunks with oversized eyes would pop out, sit back on their haunches, and start to sing, "Welcome! Oh welcome! Welcome to this beautiful day."

And now here I am in this closed, air-conditioned, climate-controlled room. I flip the TV back to regular programming and up the volume and force myself to sit for another half hour. Alan and I pretend to watch a morning talk show; or maybe he is really watching, I don't know. Then I escape as if for my life, with a "Take care" and a pat to his hand, down the corridors and into the day, bursting through the hospital's main doors. Now their really is a song in my head: I'm Dorothy waking up from the poppies, spying the Emerald City in the distance. "You're out o' the woods, you're out o' the woods, you're out o' the way!"

I am so giddy with release that inside my heart I can feel the hope physically return, carried by arteries and veins, and then just as suddenly there is something else along for the ride; there is anger and regret and guilt. With a new day in front of me and a broken husband to my back, the juxtaposition is so wrong as to be obscene. It's as if I must make a choice. And the choice is becoming so simple. I think of Alan, his disdain, his denigrating grin. I think of Lauren and the shadow over her four-year-old face. I think of my baby, Evan, the sweetest little boy on the planet, trying not to let anyone know he can't read, and I think of foreigners who are starring in my vacation video and there *is* no choice. I do not slow down, not even for a second, and there it is: a defining moment, a cleansing breath. I know in which direction to go.

I gulp the fresh air and lift my face toward the sun, throw my hands out wide dramatically, symbolically, to affirm that I am becoming healthy by breathing in the clean air. In doing so, I notice the tan line on my fourth finger, where I haven't replaced my wedding ring. I will continue to do the right thing, for sure; I will try to be a good wife to Alan, to help him through this, not just for him but for my children and myself. But inside, I will make a change. Inside, I will begin to search for me, for the me I want to be. The moment is as powerful as it is pivotal. As I reclaim the day, I begin to reclaim my life.

TWENTY-ONE

"I'm sorry, but Miss Ashton is in class until eleven, and then she has lunch."

"I'll be happy to wait until eleven."

"Teachers don't usually see parents during their lunch."

"I know, but it's important."

"Even so, I'm afraid you're going to have to make an appointment." I sigh. This is uncomfortable. My new confidence and strength begin to fade almost as quickly as I sucked them in. But perhaps not entirely. There is about to be a confrontation. The old me would have shied away, accepted the rules, the structure, the firmness. The old me may have attempted to see Principal Cummings, who I've known for years. But Jay Cummings retired last year, and I have absolutely no pull with his replacement. In fact, I've never even met him. Bitsy would settle for an appointment for a week from Thursday. But Barbara is much less compliant. Barbara doesn't care as much about not making waves. Barbara thinks maybe the world will not fall apart if she raises her voice.

"I don't have time to make an appointment. I . . . I have these letters, they have dates. I really need to see Miss Ashton today."

"As I've already explained—"

"Look"—my voice is raised, but I am fighting tears—"this is about my son, okay? It can't wait."

"Excuse me! But you—" Her tone is haughty, insulted. Luckily, she's interrupted.

"Eleanor? Can I help?"

The man who comes out of his office and puts his hand on Eleanor's back is tall, tan, and vaguely familiar. He exudes warmth and strength, and his eyes are smiling. He's also kind of cute, in a Clark Kent kind of way; scholarly but muscular. Eleanor visibly tries to look softer and more composed. I do the same.

"This is Mrs. Lerner; her son, Evan, is in Carolyn's class." I notice just a hint of disdain. "She doesn't have an appointment and she's very upset." This is a good tactic from Eleanor. She sounds like the reasonable, rational, adult and I feel like the nine-year-old who's been sent to the principal's office, which, in fact, is just where I am.

"Mrs. Lerner?"

"I'm sorry. I just need to talk to Evan's teacher. I *am* upset, she's right."

"I'm Ken Davidson, the new principal." He offers his hand. I take it, relieved to find it big and warm and comforting, just like him. Instantly, I know that all of the kids must look up to him and like him even though this is his first year. His size alone is worthy of respect. Coupled with that smile, well, he's a sure thing. "I specialize in upset parents." His eyes are twinkling. "Why don't you come into my office and we'll see what we can do."

As I follow Mr. Davidson into his office, I'm tempted to turn around and stick my tongue out at Eleanor, but I restrain myself.

TWENTY MINUTES LATER, I feel much better. Principal Davidson knows quite a bit about Evan from Miss Ashton. Apparently, the staff at school is even aware that Alan is in the hospital and nobody was going to act on any of the testing without my consent. But Evan's reading skills are a source of concern, and I do agree to have him tested. Then, to my surprise, the principal praises Evan's artwork. There is more than a moment of embarrassment, since I know that he sketches, but I have no idea that he is so acclaimed at school. It seems that Evan is one of the best artists in all of Cherry Lane, and his drawings are all over the walls. We take a walk down the hall, and I have to say I am overcome with pride. My kid is amazing. This leads to a discussion of art, and the principal is asking about my background and the next thing you know he is telling me that they are looking for an aide to work with Mrs. Cultierri, the art teacher, three days a week. Back in the office, I fill out an application and try like crazy to make nice with Eleanor. When I leave, I not only have a bunch of materials to read about Evan, but also about Cherry Lane School and the New Jersey state requirements for reactivating a teaching license.

ON THE WAY home, I stop at the supermarket for the first time in about two weeks. In addition to the standard cereals, pasta, and cookies the kids like, I load up on fresh fruits and vegetables, chicken breasts, and yogurt. I'm just about to turn out of the last aisle, lost in thoughts of children's art, memories of Escher and Sendak, when I come face to face with my neighbor Peggy Winston. I have to admit that she looks amazing.

Not only is she flawlessly dressed and achingly thin, but she looks like she just came from a professional stylist; her hair is salon shiny, her makeup smooth, her eyes strategically smudged. Her outfit is right out of the Neiman Marcus catalog, all butter-colored leather and taupe pumps, a linen scarf wrapped around her head and neck à la Grace Kelly, and atop it all the most perfectly tinted brown sunglasses I've ever seen. I look down at my own black trousers and lime knit sweater, run my hands through my hair, and try not to feel like a Glamour Don't.

Peg is standing in front of the vitamins, holding a jar of Silver Palate Dijon mustard in one hand and studying either the coenzyme Q-10 or the garlic capsules. Why is it that you never see women like Peg doing a real food shop like the rest of us? Where is her full cart of overflowing groceries with a twenty-four-pack of toilet paper sticking awkwardly out at the top and a package of chicken cutlets leaking all over the bottom? Where is the embarrassing store-brand laundry detergent because she's too cheap to pay for Tide? Don't her children have to eat? Has she hired someone to do it? Who is able to run into the market looking like they've just chaired the annual March of Dimes charity luncheon and then get out with just a bottle of designer mustard?

All of these thoughts plague me as I look at Perfect Peg, but mainly I want to kick myself for not seeing her in time to avoid her. There is an art to avoiding someone in the supermarket, a formula. You factor in the moment of awareness times the distance between the two of you divided by the contents on the shelves of that aisle. I'm serious. You can avoid your own mother in the market if you do it right, and certainly a catty neighbor, but the key is to spy her in time. Then you employ a subtle shift of the cart, facing it slightly in and well out of the way so that you can be easily passed (if she has to maneuver, forget it; you will almost certainly have to say hello when you turn to move the cart), and a turning of the head so that there's only the shadiest of side views and thereby the possibility that it is not actually you. Assuming she has just as little interest in seeing you as you do in her, this uncertainty will be plausible enough for both of you to pretend that you are each too absorbed in shopping to start investigating. Plus, your face will be pressed up against the boxes of Jell-O, presumably engaged in the life-altering decision of whether to buy strawberry banana or raspberry or sugar free. Since I do not see Peg in time, this does not happen.

"Oh. Peggy. Hi."

She lowers her sunglasses, peers through them at me as if I am a species of tropical fruit she can't quite identify, something bumpy and dark green. A guava?

"Oh. Helloo, Bitsy." She really does say "helloo," like she's a duchess or a duchy or, as Alan used to say, a douche-y. Then she says nothing at all. Cue the awkward silence. Neither one of us says "How are you"; not me, because I suddenly remember how angry I am at her sleazy son, and not her, because, of course, she doesn't care how I am. I begin to check out the eggs and turn my cart toward them. She turns toward the jelly and I think we will not even say good-bye when suddenly I hear her voice. "Ooo, Bitsy, I almost forgot. How is Alan?" It comes out "Aahlan." I am forced to turn back. I look at Peg. We both know she couldn't care less how Alan is. "Doing great!" I force out. Too cheery. But I can't stop. "Very well. *Very* well!" She looks suspicious, and why not? I suck at this. I suck at in-person bullshit. I am not too terrible with phone bullshit and somewhat better with Alan-is-beside-me bullshit, but not great on my own. "Mm-hmm? Is that so?" she croons. "Well, please send my best. Tell him it will be nice to see him . . ." She hesitates for a moment and then says, are you ready for this, "It will be nice to see him . . . erect." And she smiles right at me.

I just about die. I don't even pretend to look at the eggs. I just stand there with my mouth open and watch her go. It will be nice to see him erect? But, of course, she meant without casts on his legs, when he is able to walk. What else could it be?

As I finally unfreeze and turn up the aisle I think to myself, Ahh, another soul-affirming encounter in the suburbs: land of open space, greenery, and goodwill toward man.

THOUGH UNSETTLED, I refuse to let Peggy ruin my mood. At home, Bebe is delighted that I have gone shopping and asks me what I am going to cook for dinner.

"Bebe, please. You cook the chicken and whatever else you want. I'm sure the kids will love it." She makes a little sound again, a sucking noise, then speaks.

"Famous saying: Best thing to spend on children is your time."

I smile and shake my head. I am getting used to Bebe's sayings. It's her way of trying to make me feel guilty, sort of like a Hindi Jewish mother. By summer I'll probably be an expert in Far Eastern philosophy. Before the kids come home, I force myself to make the call I've been dreading.

"Phyllis Katz Realty. How may I direct your call?"

"Phyllis, please."

"Who may I say is calling?"

"Bitsy Lerner."

"Hold, please." There is a short pause. Then Phyllis's smooth tones. She can say about twelve sentences in the time it takes other people to say two.

"Bitsy? Hello, honey, how are you and how is that sexy husband and those adorable kids they must be practically in college by now it's so good to hear from you after all this time I hope you're not looking for a job in this crazy business, that's not why you're calling, hopefully, but anyway this is great so tell me everything."

"Phyllis, I don't need a job in real estate and the kids are fine, they're twelve and nine, and Alan is, well, he's actually kind of sick." I wait. Silence. "Phyl, I need to sell the house."

"Oh dear. Okay. I see. I'm sorry. Really. Well, then." Phyllis was a great broker, very decisive, not too gushy, didn't try to talk us into anything, but touchy-feely was not her strong point; she is a businesswoman first, and clearly she doesn't know what to do with my news. If I want the best broker in northern New Jersey, I have to let her off the hook.

"Look Phyl, Alan's probably going to be fine, but he's not up to running his business right now, so we need to cut our expenses and that's all."

"I see. Right. Well, it's no problem. Where are you going to go?"

Where, indeed.

"Oh, somewhere here in Glen Vale, I think. Smaller, I guess." Then I add, "I mean, if that's possible." Phyllis recovers and perks up, probably calculating the commission she might earn on both ends.

"Okay, Bitsy, tell you what. I'm looking at my schedule, and I think I can come by tomorrow and take a look. I'll make some suggestions and run the numbers and we'll have it on by the weekend. You'll need to do an open house for the brokers first—"

"No," I interrupt.

"Bitsy, you have to at least—"

"No, Phyllis. No open house. None." I am thinking of my kids, my neighbors, myself. I am thinking of all those nosy women stopping by, slinking through my bedroom, eating deli sandwiches and Danish from my kitchen island, making catty comments about my choice of window treatments and sharing rumors about my husband. I want to throw up. No open house. I tell Phyllis that I'm firm.

"Fine. Have it your way. But it's against my advice."

WHEN THE KIDS come home from school, I know I made the right decision about not having an open house. They've had everything turned upside down enough. I decide to say nothing about the house just yet. Lauren is especially cranky, a little snooty. I notice her jeans are so low in the back that I can see her underwear, which isn't really underwear at all but a thong. I know all the girls Lauren's age are wearing thongs, but I'm not sure they are letting them show. We need to talk, my little Britney-wannabe and me. She needs an attitude adjustment big time. Last year, I attended a seminar at the high school about parenting teenagers. I figured it was good to get a jump-start on what to expect. One technique the social worker described stuck with me: Sometimes you have to compliment teenagers on a behavior you want them to have, as if they already do. The idea is that they will want to embody the wonderful quality you tell them they have and actually acquire it. I thought I might be able to try that here.

"Hey, honey," I called to my daughter. "Can I talk to you for a minute?" Wary and distrustful, Lauren sashays over. I go to her and give her a big hug.

"I just wanted to say that I'm so proud of you." She looks at me, stunned. I go on as if it's the most natural thing in the world. "A lot of kids would be acting out even more after an incident like the one you had. A lot of kids would try to push the envelope by being even more rebellious. But your attitude has been excellent despite the fact that you're grounded. I really appreciate it, and I'm just really proud of you." I look her dead in the eyes and smile warmly, and she even smiles back a little. So that we don't enter into an awkward moment, I release her, call to Evan to come down, and prepare myself for round two.

I GUESS I had expected a fight, so when Evan is actually delighted to spend time at the Rabinowitzes', I have an unreasonable jolt of jealousy. I push it away, call Susan, and agree that he can start tomorrow afternoon. I want to pay her, but she reminds me that it's her pleasure and that an extra kid actually fuels her own kids. Evan and I also make a date to read together every night.

"I hear you're quite the artist." He blushes.

"Nah, I'm okay."

"Oh, I don't think so, Mr. Modest. I saw your stuff at school today. That one with the lady who has all the rainbow hair is unbelievable." My baby is smiling; he can't help it.

"You saw that? It's an angel. Like from heaven."

"Wow. I loved it. I'm hoping you'll make me something for the house that we can frame. What do you think?"

"All right." He is beaming. I bend down and hug him close.

"I love you, Evan."

"I know."

"Okay, just so you know."

"Okay."

"Okay." Then I tickle him to break the mushiness. "Okay, okay, okay, okay!" We both end up on the floor, laughing. In the doorway, I see Bebe. She is drying a plate. She is nodding her head and forming her version of a smile, which is to say she is not frowning. "Famous saying," she begins. But before she can finish, Evan and I look at each other, then at Bebe, and start to laugh. She knows that we are not laughing at her and continues to smile, enjoying, I think, the fact that we feel close enough to her to tease.

"Famous saying," she continues. "Laughter is sun that drive winter from human face." Score one for Bebe.

TWENTY-TWO

When Evan goes upstairs to do his homework, I sit down at the kitchen table, intending to look at the papers from Cherry Lane, but I find myself daydreaming instead. I'm remembering how art was such a big part of my life before Alan and how much of it I shut out after we were married. The paintings on the wall, except for the earliest ones, are more or less "decorator art," without character, without soul; bought to blend or match, not to stir up feelings. I've exposed the kids to a few of my favorites: Monet, Kandinsky, Boulanger. They know I'm the best at making costumes and holiday decorations, and the dioramas that come out of this house are legendary (no ordinary clay or LEGOs for us; we've used baked goods and once live goldfish to tell a shoe box story), but I wish I'd imparted a little more of the spirit of art, the joy of sliding your hands along the wheel, the pride of carving your initials into something that has the stamp of your spirit. We've been to some museums, a smattering of galleries, and, of course, I've been the parent on the class trips to MoMA and the Met. But I should have told them about the passion, about the first time I fell in love with painting. It was in first grade, when the teacher gave us each small Dixie cups containing blue paint, then went around pouring swirls of yellow into the blue. We all stirred the cups with Popsicle sticks to make the color green. I was trans-fixed, mesmerized, *changed.* Somewhere in the swirls, or in the metamorphosis, I fell in love with color and texture and design. I was hooked.

The thought of school reminds me of Principal Davidson: his warm eyes and easy manner and the way he looks just a little too big for his suit, as if he's all hard muscles underneath and no thin, tailored fabric could ever quite contain him. I feel a quick ripple of shame, thinking about him this way, but I can't help wondering how old he is—fifty, I'd guess—and if he's married. He wasn't wearing a ring, but some men don't. I'm actually blushing, even though I am sitting by myself. The thing is, he has this way about him, strong and soft, so different from Alan, who is all hyperenergy and fire, and not only am I wondering if he's married, I'm hoping he's not. Enough! This is completely unproductive. I need to shake these thoughts off; then, suddenly, I know exactly what I want to do.

THE BASEMENT OF our house is unfinished and cold; it's not a warm, fuzzy place. Our suitcases are there, along with out-grown toys, extra ceramic tiles, stained patio chairs, boxes of record albums, and old photographs from all of our child-hoods. Only in the far right corner is there anything of interest: my potter's wheel and kiln; three metal-and-wood racks for drying; a long, wooden, bench for displaying vessels; and above the bench, built-in wooden cabinets for storing everything from glaze to brushes to tools.

I recognize a few old projects still sitting on the racks. Each year, the clutter of our basement has inched farther and spread deeper, eventually infringing upon the pottery corner. Cans of kiln wash and enamel are covered by canvas sport bags and Hello Kitty backpacks. A work sink holds Rollerblades and a variety of deflated balls. I circle the space, at once mourning but also wondering. Above the kiln are the necessary windows, the separate electric line we had to install, and the vent. I check the kiln; its pilot light is still on. The wheel is hardened because the last time it was used, I forgot to clean it. Who knew it would be the last time? Suddenly, I am longing to get my hands moving, kneading, pounding, to wedge the clay in slow downward pushes, removing the air and my tension simultaneously. It isn't lost on me that there is symbolism here; that I am the lump of clay, begging to be molded and stretched, to be prepped, the process that prevents cracking or exploding later on. The task of cleaning up this mess is awesome, but for some reason I'm smiling as I plunge in.

HOURS LATER, I ascend to the living part of the house. There is quiet, but somehow it's already a different quiet, free of tension and shame. I climb the stairs and stand outside Evan's room. His door is open, he's studying at his desk, transferring numbers from a math textbook into a workbook. I lean my head in.

"Almost ready for our date?"

"Just two more problems."

"Did you pick something out for us to read?" Without breaking his concentration, or looking up, he reaches over and holds up a paperback, *Challenge at Second Base,* by Matt Christopher.

One of our favorite family movies is *Don't Tell Mom the Babysitter's Dead,* and we've all watched it about thirty times.

Whenever I ask the kids if they've done something I've asked, they quote the main character, Sue Ellen, who says to her boss, "I'm on top of that, Rose." This is exactly what Evan says to me as he holds up the Christopher book. I smile and turn down the hall. Lauren's door is closed. I knock.

"Come."

"Hey." I enter the sanctuary, a combination of little-girl pink (her bedspread and furniture) and early teenage prostitute (her bulletin board, rap posters, and growing makeup and jewelry supply). She is on her stomach, reading a book for English, something about a young girl in the French Resistance, but she is also doing her nails, using the open book as her table. She is doing her nails blue. Without looking up, she asks, "What's up?"

"Nothing. I just wanted to see how you're doing."

"You mean in my cell?" This doesn't make me panic. The high school social worker warned that the behaviors often got worse before they really improved.

"Well, I think it's a little more comfortable than what Sergeant Kestner may have provided, but yes, for now it is your cell, but that doesn't mean that the warden doesn't care how you feel."

"Oh." There is silence, then she says, "I'm fine." I move closer to the bed, wait till she finishes a nail, and sit down.

"Laur, there's something I've wanted to say to you for a while."

"Uh-huh." She doesn't look at me, but instead continues to apply what I now see is *metallic* blue to her nails.

"Well, I think we went over this, but I just wanted to say it one more time . . ." I am faltering, because I want to get this just right. "What happened on Halloween"—I see her whole body go tense—"well, I never, ever, ever thought that it was your fault. Not at all. You know that, right?"

For a moment, I think she's going to smile. Then it looks like she might cry. I think we are having a moment, that she will stop polishing and throw her arms around me, and even though she will get blue nail polish all over my shirt I won't care because she will be Lauren again and not this tortured creature who has moved into her body. I think this will happen, and then immediately I know that it won't. The almost-smile and the possible tears fade away and the wall returns. So hardened for twelve. And without even looking at me, she says evenly, "I'm fine. I forgot all about Halloween already. It's no big deal."

"Okay," I say, unconvinced. "But I'm only a room away, and I'm here if you want to talk." I get up to leave. She isn't ready, she's still locked away, and I know that much of that is my fault. But I won't give up; I saw the smile and I saw the tears; she's in there somewhere. One thing I know, I'm not going to find myself and leave her behind.

TWENTY-THREE

Surprisingly, my credentials from ten years ago are still good. I need only to submit to a background check and to accrue enough continuing ed credits to be reactivated, but I am cleared to teach provisionally till it all comes through. Now I just need a job. Any job. An art aide position at Cherry Lane would be a godsend. I wait for news.

On Tuesday morning, hopeful but impatient with waiting and needing a distraction, I grab Bebe and take her down to the kiln. We spend the morning trying to continue what I started, cleaning most of the dust and organizing my art supplies. We are only about half done, but it's a beginning. Then I release Bebe to the friendlier world upstairs. I check the bricks of clay. They are dry, as expected, but a little water fixes that, and with a bit of ceremony, I drop the clay onto my plaster bat and work my first piece of clay in over seven years, and when the tears mix in I'm reminded of my grandmother, who died when I was just fifteen. She used to grate potatoes for potato pancakes and sometimes her knuckles would get caught and bleed.

"Tsk, that's nothing," she'd laugh and say to me with a wink, "a little blood . . . makes them taste better." And that's how I feel as I push down and out, kneading and crying, punishing the thick, wet lump. I throw it on the wheel and it takes me three tries, but eventually it's like riding a bike. I get it perfectly centered, and my foot finds the cadence, and in a half hour or so I have a shape that satisfies: half platter, half bowl, something in between, something not necessarily with a defined purpose, and, irony aside, something just like me. I set it to dry and go to work on another, then another, working feverishly—obsessively, I guess—for hours. When the doorbell rings, I know who it is, and even though I've been dreading Phyllis's arrival, the clay and the kiln have had a calming effect on my soul. I still want to scream at the thought of moving, but for now it feels less like the shower scene in *Psycho* and more like taking a soccer ball in the gut.

Phyllis is no-nonsense and professional and does nothing to turn me into a crying mess, which I appreciate. She approves of my decorating, maintenance, and color scheme and feels the house will be an easy sell. I am tempted to point out every leaky faucet and quirky drawer, just to inhibit a quick sale, but content myself with a high-end, negotiable number as an asking price. "We'll see," she says, with a quick air kiss and stiff hug. "I'll be in touch." On only one point do I remain resolute: no showings after 2:30 p.m. I'm still too chicken to tell the kids.

On Wednesday, it's back to the hospital with Alan. I've still heard nothing from the school and try to push down my anxiety and focus on him. After the last video fiasco, I decide to bring Alan the VHS tape from his thirtieth-birthday celebration at the club we would eventually join. I've a growing suspicion that this may have more of an impact on his memory than our family vacation did. We'd invited all the couples from the neighborhood and a lot of Alan's business associates and pretty much everyone we ever socialized with. It was cocktails and a DJ and a buffet dinner, and we'd hired a professional to film it, so the opening shot is of the room laid out with black tablecloths and gold napkins and white flowers with gold and black balloons that all say ALAN on them. The camera pans to Alan and me standing at the bar waiting for the guests to arrive. I haven't seen this particular video in years, so my first thought is that I look so young and also much thinner. Alan is impeccable in a black sports jacket, white shirt, and gray slacks. He is holding up a drink.

"Here's to me! My birthday! C'mon, Bits, drink up for the camera." In the video, I smile and take a sip. Alan has obviously started the party early.

"Alan, you're not supposed to look at the camera; you're supposed to act natural."

"I am natural," he says to me. Then he turns back to the camera. "Aren't I natural? She thinks I'm not being natural. Hey, how about we take a walk?" This to the camera and not to me. "C'mon, follow me. Look how great this room looks. This club never looked so great. See these centerpieces? Bitsy arranged for all of this and it cost a fortune, but you only turn thirty once, right. Don't I look young? C'mon, you can't believe I'm thirty, right?" The videographer answers him. "You're wife looks great, too." "You bet she does. I know how to pick 'em. Oh, there's Jeffo and Wolf." Instead of following Alan the camera turns back to me. I see myself smile. But now, fifteen years later, there is something else. I realize that behind the smile is a feeling I've experienced for years and never acknowledged. It is a cross between discomfort and the urge to apologize. I remember that I pushed that feeling down.

My memory is suddenly interrupted by Alan, who is sitting up and shouting, "Wolf! I know him! That's . . . that's Jerry Wolfson!" On the tape, the camera has panned to the entrance and is filming the guests as they begin to file in.

"Calm down, Alan. Wolf was one of your college room-mates at GW. That's why you know him."

But he is all excited. "And the other guy! Jeff somebody. Wait, I know—Jeff Ostrowsky, right?"

"Well, sort of right. He dropped the 'sky' right after school. Now he's just Jeff Ostrow. *Dr.* Jeff Ostrow, by the way." And he doesn't speak to you anymore, I want to add, since he lost a ton of money in one of your deals, but I don't.

"No way! He's a doctor? Ostrowsky? Jeffo? That guy was the bong champion of Thurston and maybe of all McLean, too. What kind of doctor?"

"The rich kind," I say. "He specializes in weight loss."

"No shit." Now Alan is more animated than I've seen him in weeks—make that years. He is scouring the video for people he knows, and I can understand that. He keeps asking me who certain people are. "Who's the stiff guy?"

"That's our neighbor, Peter Winston."

"Do I like him?"

I look over at Alan. What a question. This is so bizarre. I can't help myself.

"You hate his guts."

He doesn't even flinch. "Thought so," he says.

A little later, the videographer tries to get various people to speak for the camera. Most of our friends just wave him away, but occasionally one of the guys takes the microphone. "Yo, Lerner"—it's Alan's attorney, Hal, speaking—"you better have enough left after this shindig to pay my bill." And then another friend grabs the mike and chimes in. "Hey, get in line, age before beauty and taxes before legal, right, bud?" They all break into great guffaws of laughter. I want to cringe a little now, knowing what I know about our finances, but I look at Alan and he's smiling. Then there is a shot of us dancing. Alan is being dramatic, whirling me around, but watching it this way, it's like I'm seeing this video for the first time. Alan is dancing with me but he's looking everywhere else, at all the other couples, his eyes darting back and forth. Suddenly, he notices the camera is on us and smiles widely and falsely and gives me an extra spin. I wonder if he'll have any sense of this, see the transparency, the phoniness. Not a chance.

"I'm a good dancer, right?" he asks, and I tell him yes, he is, though I say it with some sadness, which really isn't fair. What do I expect? That this new, fragmented Alan will see what the old one didn't and what I suddenly see for the first time? Which is just how disconnected we were, even back then. And then, a little surprise.

"Can I ask you something?" He says it politely, like he knows the next question might be an intrusion. I am a little afraid but excited, too. I nod.

"Are we . . . happy?"

I look down. At my lap. Then up at the video and back to Alan. He is very still and quiet. My hesitation is, of course, a partial answer. There is no going back.

"I guess I thought you were."

"But not you?"

"I never really thought about it before."

"How is that possible?"

"You get good at it."

"At being happy?"

"No. At not thinking about whether you are."

THE VIDEO ENDS, and Alan and I sit quietly for a while. Dr. Morris comes in to talk about Alan coming home, and I notice that Alan gets physically agitated; his palms start to sweat and his breathing quickens. It turns out that there is a problem with Alan's white count and Dr. Morris thinks he will have to stay in the hospital a bit longer than expected. Alan actually seems relieved to hear this news. When I ask for a specific date, the doctor reiterates that Alan's memory could return any day and that home is an excellent place to spark such a return, and, if all goes well, he could go home at the end of next week. When the doctor leaves, Alan asks questions about our bed at home and the food that he will be eating and whether the children will be there, too.

"Of course the children will be there. Where else would they be?"

"I . . . I don't know. I thought maybe they had, um, camp or something."

"It's barely May, Alan. They're still in *school.*" A little part of my heart turns cold. For a moment back there, I thought perhaps we'd had, well, a moment. Now I wasn't so sure. Was I really going to be able to do this? I'd heard stories of people caring for Alzheimer's patients, the frustration as their loved ones became suspicious and disoriented. Could it get any more bizarre than a man not knowing his wife and children? I'd finally told the kids that their dad had some memory problems and they were familiar with the term "amnesia" (from some Adam Sandler movie) and they were probably less skeptical than me about its existence. But I hadn't come right out and told them that Alan had absolutely no idea who we were or that he thought it was still 1982. Dr. Tobias gave me a booklet on dissociative disorders and also a DVD about memory issues that he said would be age appropriate for the kids if I watched it with them. We would do that tomorrow night.

FROM THE HOSPITAL, I go right home and head down to the basement, the organizing of which seems to calm me. On Thursday, I still haven't heard from the school, and by now I've cleaned up all my tools, unstuck the brushes, and categorized the glaze. I think this weekend I might be able to fire the kiln. It will take several hours to heat up, first on low, then medium, and finally high, and by then the platter, bowl, and plate I cast on Tuesday should be dry. It will be a shame to fire the kiln for so few pieces, but I need to see this through.

I am looking through my stock of enamels, trying to decide if I want to dip or pour, create a dribble effect or use a brush for lines. I am cleaning up and putting away my tools when the phone rings, and then I hear Bebe calling from upstairs.

"Miss Barbara, you come! School for you!"

TWENTY-FOUR

t he secretary from the Board of Ed says that I am to come in on Monday and fill out some forms. "Okay," I say. She details what I need to bring. Never once does she say anything about my being hired, and finally I can't contain myself.

"Does this mean I've got the job?"

"I assume so, dear. Why else would you need to come in?"

My other line is blinking. Ecstatic, I thank the secretary and switch lines.

"Hello?"

"Mrs. Lerner?" I know exactly who it is.

"Mr. Davidson?"

"Actually, it's Doctor."

"Doctor?"

"Davidson."

"Oh!" I'm an idiot. So he's a *doctor*. "I'm so sorry."

"Not at all. If it were just me, I wouldn't even mention it, but after four years of college and six years postgraduate, my mother would kill me if I dropped it." He is smiling, I can tell. But what really strikes me is that he doesn't say his wife would kill him, only his mom.

"I can understand that." Brilliant comeback, Bitsy. Scintillating.

"I have some good news for you."

"Actually, I just heard from the secretary at the Board of Ed."

"No kidding? That Janis is quick. I should steal her over here."

"And replace the charming Eleanor?" He laughs, and I relax a bit. I think I remember how to do this, how to casually chat, how to kid.

"Now, now"—he drops his voice—"you two just got off to a bad start. She can be, well, almost civil, when she wants to be." My turn to laugh.

"Oh, I'm sure. I bet at the Christmas party she really goes out on a limb and cracks a smile."

"Yep. That's about the size of it. So, can you stop in Monday either before or after the Board of Ed? Maybe early afternoon? There's a lot of paperwork, orientation materials, things about school policy, plus you need to watch a video about germs and one on violence, lots you probably never did years ago but are now required to by law. Also, I want you to meet Ann Cultierri. You'll be working with her—"

"Isn't she the one they call Mrs. C.?" I interrupt.

"They do."

"Bright colors, kooky jewelry, and red hair?"

"Yep. That's her."

"She seems like a lot of fun."

"An understatement. She's wacky and talented, and the kids love her." I am suddenly nervous.

"And you will, too," he adds. I'm sure he's right. I'm sure I will love Mrs. C., but will anyone like me?

THE NEXT DAY I arrive at the hospital at 2:00 p.m., much later than usual, but I calculate that if I only stay an hour, I can miss my mother-in-law. I make my way down the hall to Alan's room, thinking that despite my doubts about his return home, I will not miss this place with its sterile steel and medicinal smells. I am not exactly humming as I enter Alan's room, and I'm not exactly thinking about Alan, but rather my new job and my renewed spirit and all the possibilities that both have sparked. Alan is on his side, facing out, his eyes half closed. I move toward him, and he holds up his hand as if to say stop.

"Alan? Are you okay?"

"Mm-hmm." He is sort of mumbling. "I'm tired," he sighs. "I don't . . . I don't really feel like a visit today if . . ."—he looks at me hopefully—"if that's okay with you?"

If that's okay with me? I hate to admit it, but that's fine with me. I move a little closer, smooth the side of his hair with my hand, and wonder if he actually flinches when I do so or if I'm just imagining it.

"I'll just let you rest," I say. He closes his eyes. I wait a minute or two, but he doesn't open them again. With a little guilt, some nagging discomfort, but much more relief, I turn and leave.

WHEN BEBE LEAVES on Friday, the kids accompany her to the bus stop, which is on Lake Street, just a few blocks farther than their school bus stop. When they come in, they are "talking Bebe," as Evan puts it. "You must need jacket, Evan boy," he imitates, laughing. "Kids must be good for Mommy, please!" warns Lauren. "See me Monday!" They shout together, hysterical, but with love. I shake my head and smile. They are getting attached to Bebe. They're not the only ones. Even Casey listens to her and follows her around the house. She has an earthy calm to her and a quiet confidence that literally infuses the air. Her presence in the house has had a very positive effect.

I GO BACK to visit Alan on Saturday, not my regular day, since it's when Marian goes, and, sure enough, I narrowly miss bumping into her and another woman (can she actually have a friend?). Luckily, I spy their backs, walking away, just as I turn into the corridor toward his room. Once again, I sit, fidgeting, in a hard orange chair, watching Alan beep and pump and survive. He is awake this time, but just as reticent and a bit morose. I make small talk, focusing on snippets of our current life. I had attended Evan's baseball game, so I'm able to give a complete play-by-play, inning by inning, accentuating his personal highlight, an amazing catch in the outfield to end the fourth. Alan doesn't pretend that he's interested or excited. He asks me to bring him some "records." He asks if I know where his cassette player is. I try to explain about CDs and finally give up and just ask him what "albums" he wants.

"Jethro Tull, Sly, Hall and Oates, Springsteen." I stare back at him for a moment. Thank God for Springsteen, I think. Everyone else may be dead. By the time I leave, I feel sprung from prison, and even a traffic jam on Route 17 feels like paradise. My mother calls and asks if I'd like them to come for dinner on Sunday, and she seems relieved when I lie and say that we have plans with the people next door.

"Oh, the Sloans?" She asks. "Were they able to help straighten things out?"

No, Ma, I want to say, but the husband did try to rape me . . .

"Not the Sloans, the, um, Rabinowitzes."

"The who? Oh! Not those people to the side?"

"Yes, Mom, them." And then, to end the frustration, I let the lie grow. "They've invited the whole neighborhood. To a barbecue." I should shut up now.

"Oh dear. You'd better eat before you go." And suddenly, I'm just incensed. I've had enough.

"You know, Mom, the Rabinowitzes are very nice people. *Very* nice people. You shouldn't be such a snob. Now I've got to go." Whoa. Is this me!

By Sunday afternoon, I am able to fire the kiln. It heats up slowly, over many hours. The heat cones will tell me when the first stage, the bisque firing, is done. Then, after the kiln cools down, the pieces will be ready for glazing, and then they'll be fired again. If everything goes well, and I can get to the glazing by Tuesday, I could have my finished pieces by the end of the week.

I STILL HAVEN'T said anything to the kids about moving or my new job because the mood in the house is surprisingly cozy, and I don't want to risk disturbing that peace. On Sunday night, we bring in Chinese food and plan to watch a movie together. Between dinner and the movie, Lauren asks about her dad, and I begin to educate them both about dissociative disorders. I tell them much more than I have before. I tell them I have a DVD. They are somber. Lauren wants to know if we have to watch the DVD tonight, because she really wants to watch *Romy & Michelle's High School Reunion,* and Evan protests that he wants to watch *Ace Ventura,* and before I know it they are fighting about a real movie. Somehow, I don't have the heart to force the documentary on them.

I wait for the inevitable: One of them will ask to go to visit him. But the request never comes. When the movie is decided upon with a coin toss, I notice Lauren positions herself on the couch so that her feet are scrunched up next to my thighs, and Evan puts a pillow in my lap and just lays his head down right there. Within fifteen minutes, my right thigh and left butt cheek are totally numb, but I wouldn't move for the world.

PRINCIPAL DAVIDSON (*Dr.* Davidson) is out at a meeting when I arrive for my orientation, and although I'm reluctant to admit it, I'm disappointed. I'd dressed with extra special care, going for classic but clingy, not knowing why I was doing so much thinking about him, but doing it anyway. However, two minutes with Ann Cultierri and I'm transported to another time, before Alan, before college, when oils, enamels, and even origami were my natural habitat, and I suddenly realize how much it used to define me, comfort me, shelter me.

Back in junior high, when art was about the process, instead of the result, you were never wrong, and as a shepherd of young souls, Ann shares that mind-set. Her art periods are over for the day and we have the art room to ourselves. She imparts her philosophy from atop a small stepstool as she hangs mobiles and enlists me to do the same. Eyeing a peculiar-looking creation (the others all look like stiff but colorful birds, and this one is a round black blob), she holds it up, turns it around, then shrugs and smiles.

"Oh well. You never know what's going to come out of the little ones, tra-la! Whatever they come up with is what they should." She stops. With a mobile hanging by a piece of yarn in her teeth, she passes me a thumbtack, points to a pile of other mobiles on the floor, shoves a stool at me with her foot, and presses a bird into the porous ceiling tile so it will stay. Satisfied, she steps down. "Ah, tra-la! Such a pretty one." For the next half hour or so we hang these creations while Ann tells me about some of the upcoming projects. She mentions that Evan will be a big help to her with the end-of-the-year mural, a block-length Cherry Lane tradition that depicts the highlights of the past school year and hangs in the main hallway until the following spring. Her conversation is punctuated by her animated exclamations of "tra-la," her signature expression, and her bubbly giggle, which discharges like a string of mini hiccups and is strangely musical. I am being rather meticulous about my pile of mobiles, trying to press them into the ceiling in some sort of spatial complement, and more than once I notice Ann studying me. When I look up, she smiles and nods approvingly. "So he gets his talent from you, yes?" I blush.

On her desk is a boom box, and inside there is a tape that might easily be entitled *School Favorites from 1966:* an odd assortment that includes "Val-de-ri, Val-de-ra," "She'll Be Coming 'Round the Mountain," and "Kumbaya." When we are done, she takes me on a tour of the building, most of which I know. We finish up in the teacher's lounge, and I am beginning to feel right at home, until we run smack into Eleanor. I remember my first job in the city and my first teacher's lounge. Despite my college degree, I'd felt guilty, like I didn't belong. It had taken a full year to get over that feeling, and Eleanor's look takes me right back to the guilty place. But I'm not twenty-two anymore, so I suck in my breath and raise my head high and nod to Eleanor in my most adult, postured way.

"Eleanor," I say.

"Mrs. Lerner," she replies, dripping reluctance.

"Actually," I begin, making a quick decision and wondering where the hell I get the courage to do so, "please call me . . . Barbara."

On Tuesday morning, the kiln is cool enough to open. I start by opening it a crack and peek inside. Not bad, I think. I've still got it. An hour later, I open it all the way. I spend the day glazing, and by evening I'm ready to refire. As the pottery begins to take shape, so do I. I haven't been able to visit Alan since Saturday, and I resolve to go first thing in the morning. I will have to try harder at this. I just need to remind myself that this is my husband and he is sick and he needs my help and he is coming home on Friday to get better. Wednesday morning, I drive to the hospital with a sense of strength; I even wear his favorite shirt, a clingy orange tank top from Theory that I think is too tight. I am completely unprepared for the tribunal that awaits me in Alan's room.

"Morning," I begin, in my fake, cheery, voice, the one I use when I don't know what the hell is going on. I notice that Alan is sitting up and his mother is standing at his side. Dr. Tobias perches on the foot of the bed. "Marian," I question, "no school today?" There is silence, a decidedly loud silence. I walk toward the chair at the foot of the bed, drop my bag on it, and my insides begin to quake. *What now?* Something is terribly wrong. Have they found some unusually rare tumor or incurable cancer, or maybe now he thinks it is 1970? Oh God, I'm going to have to buy him bell bottoms and a Nehru jacket.

"Alan?" I look from Alan to Dr. Tobias to Marian and back to my husband. He looks at me for a second then quickly hangs his head. Dr. Tobias appears sympathetic. Finally, my mother-in-law speaks. "We've been discussing Alan's release," she says, straightening herself, "and he prefers to come home with me." There it sits, her proclamation, like a boulder, crushing me. I have never felt like such a complete failure in my entire life. My husband of fifteen years is rejecting me, not for another woman or even another *man,* for God's sake, but for his mommy!

"You can't be serious." I squeak this out with hardly any breath at all. Dr. Tobias stands up. "You know, this is not that uncommon. While I think it would be better if Alan were to be around his family, his current family, I'm not sure it will make a difference in the long run, and given the anxiety Alan has about returning to a place he doesn't know, I can hardly advise it." I take this in. As much as I can. Apparently, this has all been discussed; apparently, it is a done deal. By the smug look on Marian's face, it appears that she doesn't care whether this is in Alan's best interests or not, only that she seems to have won. And what a prize. I look over at Alan, who is unable to look at me. He feels my stare, I know it. Finally, he peeks up at me and with a pained expression says, "I . . . I just . . ."

Marion grabs his hand. "It's all right, Alan," she says. "You don't have to explain. I'm sure Bitsy understands." I don't. Not really. And I don't say that I do.

Alan does not let go of his mother's hand, but he does continue. "What it is," he says, struggling, "is that . . . I just don't know you."

And that, as my mother would say, is that. I can't help but feel sorry for Alan. He looks so pathetic. But there is something else I feel. Alan, I think to myself, it goes both ways. You don't know me, but I also don't know you. And that may be the understatement of the decade—not just the one you're in right now, but all of them.

"You do what you need to do," I say, chopping my words. I am speaking pretty much to everyone. "Of course, I won't be able to visit that much, Livingston is pretty far, and I'll be working now." And then I can't help it. "I'll be working because we are in financial hell, by the way." I look at Marian. "We'll probably have to sell the house." I turn to Alan. "You know, the house you don't know, but the rest of us call home." There is no response. I am near tears, and still I feel guilty. It feels like I am attacking a sick person. "Well. If you . . . if you want to see the children, we'll work it out."

"I'm still advocating immersion in the familiar," Dr. Tobias offers, "and Alan will be able to drive, so perhaps he can come for visits." I don't say anything. I retrieve my purse from the chair. No one, I note, has responded to my assault or asked me about the financial problems or where I'm working or anything else.

"Well," I say. "Good luck."

It sounds stupid. I'm not leaving the country, nor is he. But I don't know what I'm supposed to say. "Okay, good-bye then, everyone." I start to leave the room and I hear Alan call weakly "Bitsy . . . ," but he doesn't follow it up. As I reach the door, I have a thought.

"By the way," I say, turning and surveying the room. I end up looking squarely at Marian. "I'm going by my real name now. It's Barbara."

No one says a thing. Later, it will become clear to me that the last little bit of Bitsy was joyously and ceremoniously left in that room, left right back in 1982, which is where I probably should have left it in the first place.

OVER THE NEXT few days, I try to prepare the kids for the changes in our lives. We watch the video, and they are remarkably sympathetic to their father's fears about living in a strange place. They don't take it personally at all. And I am thankful that they are still children. Unlike me, they are not prone to doubt. They don't dismiss what I call the convenient disorders like amnesia or multiple personality or temporary insanity due to PMS. They also don't seem to mind one bit that their father isn't coming home. So, which is it, empathy or self-preservation? Of course, I could ask myself the same thing. But not today.

I tell the kids that my job starts Monday, and Evan is delighted that I will be working at school. He is already blossoming after just a week with Susan. It turns out he has the most minor of learning deficiencies, a perceptual impairment not unlike dyslexia, but much milder. In fact, he didn't even have to be classified for special education because there is a kind of loophole for kids who don't test out as extremely deficient; it's called 504, and thanks to Susan I know all about it. Evan and I have been reading together every night and using some strategies that Susan taught us, and my little boy is like a confidence sponge, soaking up more and more each time. If I had any worries that he would resent my presence at Cherry Lane, they were unfounded. Even Lauren seems fine, if a little suspicious. I am not treated to any especially sarcastic barbs, but she does stare at my face a lot, and tonight at dinner she asked some pointed questions.

"So it's just part-time?"

"Just part-time."

"But like every day?"

"Yep. Every day from eight-thirty to twelve-twenty."

"And just in the art room, right?"

"*Right.* What's the matter, honey?"

"You're sure you're not like serving lunch or anything?"

"Lauren, I'm not serving lunch."

"Good. Because I would just die if you were going to be a cafeteria lady." She says the words "cafeteria lady" as if she means "bag lady."

"Lauren, relax. I'm an art aide. I have a background in art, remember? I'm trained and qualified to teach art." She looks somewhat relieved, but there's something else.

"What?" I ask her. "What is it?"

"How come you suddenly feel like you want to teach again? Is it 'cause of Daddy?"

I need to level with her a bit. I take a deep breath.

"It's partly because of Daddy. When daddy had the accident, I realized that sometimes things happen that we don't expect. I love you guys so much that I want to begin to take steps to make sure we have everything we need." Lauren seems content with my explanation.

"*And,*" I go on, "I'd forgotten how much I love to be around art of any kind." Now she smiles. That part she understands. It's the same for her with makeup.

"Too bad you don't love science," she tosses out. "I have to write a paper on global warming."

"What's global warming?" Evan asks.

From the doorway, there is a voice.

"Everybody make big damage . . . change earth in a bad way . . . too much exhaust, cutting down forest, these things . . ." We all turn around and look at Bebe. "Modern things . . . let in too much sun—make world too warm."

I don't know what to say. In her chopped way, Bebe has explained global warming. I feel a little guilty. Since she came back this morning and I told her about my job, Bebe has been ecstatic. She's been smiling from ear to ear, and tonight for dinner she made chicken the way *I* prepare it, baked, and not fried in oil with curry or hot peppers. This is Bebe's way of letting me know she approves of me, at least for today. Now I have to say I am awfully approving of her—and much more curious as to her background.

"Exactly right," I say, in response to her explanation. And then I add, "Hey, kids, why don't you get started on your homework. You're excused from clearing tonight." They don't stay to argue.

As Bebe and I clear and wash the dishes, I ask her about what she's doing here in the United States. With very little emotion, she explains that she has left her two children with her mother in Guyana, because she was unable to earn enough money to care for them. Her husband, the children's father, is an alcoholic who began to abuse her shortly after her second child was born. She kicked him out from her hospital bed at the clinic, a hospital bed she ended up in with a broken arm and bruised spleen after he beat her with a broom. Fortunately, she made friends with the clinic staff, and because she had finished high school, they offered her a job. For the past several years, she worked as a nurse, and had even begun to go back to school for medical training, but then the government closed the clinic due to lack of funds.

Without a degree in nursing, she couldn't get work in another hospital, and the family was struggling, barely getting by. Realizing that her country held no promise for a future and adamant that she must create a better life for her children, one in which they can go to college, she came here.

Bebe's children, ten-year-old Raj and seven-year-old Jenny, are living with her mother and two sisters and one brother-in-law and *their* children in a house she describes with a small smile as "different from this." All of them depend on Bebe to send money each week. So except for a small amount for food and the rent for her room on the weekend, she sends practically her entire paycheck to them. I gently probe her a bit about her plans for the future. She won't meet my eye, and in a matter-of-fact voice says that some things simply cannot be helped. "Like famous saying goes, One generation plants the trees, other gets the shade."

I turn away, with a new sympathy and certainly a new respect for Bebe, and I can't help noticing that despite her stoic proclamation, she has to use the back of her hand to wipe her eyes. I can't imagine leaving my kids. Of course, I can't imagine a life in which a mother would have to. I resolve to help Bebe as much as I can. In fact, tomorrow the kids and I will go through all of their clothes and toys and put aside everything they've outgrown or underused and make a package for Bebe's family.

That night, I don't sleep well at all. I keep dreaming of island women with pots on their heads calling for my children to follow them. I am watching helplessly, stuck in a boat on a river, yelling for them to come back. In the morning, I creep down to the kiln, not just tired but strung out. I am more nervous and expectant than I imagined I'd be. For some reason, the pieces have become symbolic of my new life; they must be beautiful and meaningful. I work myself up into a bit of an irrational theory. The pieces are a litmus test; if they are well done, then I will be successful in my new job. The kiln is cool enough to open just a bit. Gingerly, I throw back the locks and peek inside. First, I start to smile, then cry, then laugh. Soon, I am actually doing all three. It's just a peek, but they don't look half bad. An hour later, I open the lid all the way. The pieces are still hot, the glaze soft, but I can tell that they look great for a first pass.

With a sense of purpose, I leave the pottery to cool and decide to start on my closet, not just because I'm sure Bebe's mother and other relatives can use clothes, but also because this is my version of shopping for new clothes for a new job based on my budget, which is minus zero. When the phone rings, Phyllis's voice on the other end is an unwelcome jolt. She has someone who wants to see the house. Tomorrow, 11:00 a.m. There is nothing I can do. I say yes. Reluctantly, I tell Bebe that we need to get the house in perfect shape, and I tell her why. She makes that little mouth snort but there's a twist, this time it's not *at* me, it's *with* me. And then, without thinking, I make it right back at her. We are both surprised. I start to laugh and Bebe smiles. For a moment, she and I are sisters, or at least teammates. I guess soon I will be quoting Buddha.

BACK IN MY CLOSET, I guiltily uncover more clothes than I ever realized I had, some with the tags still on. It is easy to imagine that without buying anything new, I have enough of a wardrobe to go for at least sixty consecutive workdays without repeating an outfit. I am folding and hanging when I hear Bebe scream.

don't know who is more upset. Bebe's screams have become little squeaky grunts, and I am hyperventilating, my breath coming in short spurts of "It's okay, it's okay, it's okay." No one is hurt. No one is sick. No one is dead. Well, no one human. The pottery that is sitting in the kiln, still warm and pliable, is ruined. Bebe has managed to explain that she was trying to clean the top of the cabinet when she slipped, and in trying to get her balance knocked some things off the top. Well, it was really only one thing. My old mah-jongg set. And, of course, it opened right up. I stare down into the kiln at the pieces that just an hour ago had given me so much joy; they are now a distorted mess. Little mah-jongg tiles are scattered randomly on top of them, some flat, some sideways, some actually standing upright, and they are held fast by glaze and clay, which is still warm and acting like superglue. Bebe started to pull some of them out and stopped; she saw that they were leaving little depressions, little holes, and that's when she began to scream. "Bam," I think to myself, looking at the Chinese pieces. It is an apt name for this mess. "Bam and crack." I look up at Bebe. There is total devastation in her eyes, almost fear. Suddenly, instead of being concerned for myself and these pieces of clay, which really do not symbolize anything, I know that it just doesn't matter. Not enough to put such a look on Bebe's face. And not just because I am capable of making more, but because there are two children named Raj and Jenny who don't have their mother and there are two more named Lauren and Evan who don't have their father, and I am suddenly so clear that life is about so much more.

"Oh, Bebe," I say, putting my arms around her, "it's just some clay. Who cares?" Bebe doesn't say a word, but she does stop shaking, and together we clean up the pieces from the floor.

LATER THAT MORNING I purposely go on an errand. I don't want to be home when Phyllis brings the people to look at our house. I make Bebe promise not to worry about the pottery, and I also make her promise to be nice. I've seen her when she takes a position, and while the image of her being rude to the prospective buyers makes me smile, I really do not need her sabotaging a sale. I decide to go over to Cherry Lane and offer my help to Ann, even though I don't officially start until Monday. I might as well start familiarizing myself with the art room and the routine.

Ann is thrilled to see me and quickly puts me to use. The children are adorable. They are all so happy to be in art, and they love Mrs. C., One little boy even asks me if I am as nice as Mrs. C. and I tell him that she is teaching me and I will try very hard to be. He hugs my leg and tells me I am learning "really good." I want to kiss him. I am in heaven. I even forget to check my watch to see if it is safe to go home. At 12:30, Ann has her free period, and I collect my things to leave. Just as we are about to head out, a familiar face pops in.

"Mrs. Lerner, what a surprise," he says. "Hey, Ann, I told you we're not supposed to torture her till Monday."

Ann laughs and heads out the door. "Bye, Barbara," she calls over her shoulder. "You were such a help today. Come by anytime." Then she says to Principal Davidson, "Whatever you do, make sure they don't cut my budget. She's a keeper." And with a wink to me, she leaves. I, of course, am totally flustered. Luckily, Dr. Davidson doesn't seem to notice.

"Wow, high praise. You must have really hit it off with the kids."

"Oh, they're wonderful. Especially the little ones. I'd forgotten how honest and open they are when they're that young."

"Stick around. Wait till they start asking you all kinds of personal questions. The other day a little girl in the first grade asked me how come I don't have a wife anymore. Can you imagine? I don't even know how she knew that, but there I was, trying to explain it without scarring her for life."

My heart skips a beat. Stop it! But I can't help myself.

"So, how *did* you?"

"What?"

"How did you explain it?"

"Hmmm." He looks back at me, pauses, then smiles.

"Who wants to know?"

I giggle. "Excuse me?"

"Well, it's kind of a personal question, don't you think?" He's really smiling.

"You brought it up!" I say, mock accusingly.

"Well, okay, if you absolutely must know." He is teasing me, I know, and it helps me recover my cool.

"Well, it's really not that important." I begin to turn away. "In fact, I have to go, so have a lovely day, *Doctor.*"

"Ken," he says, still smiling that damned irresistible smile.

"Ken. Fine. I'm Barbara."

"Fine."

"Okay, so bye. See me Monday. I mean, I'll see you on Monday."

"Barbara." His tone, both pointed and soft, stops me.

"Yes?"

"I'm divorced."

"I see. That's nice."

"It is?"

"Well, no. I mean, I guess so. I mean . . . well, *is* it? For *you?*" God! I don't even know what I'm saying. Ken's voice gets soft.

"Yes, it is. I had a lousy marriage. It's been two years now. So I'm definitely over it. There were no kids, which is good, since I have about 356 of them anyway." He spreads his arms out to indicate that the school is his family. He is still smiling, but it's a quieter smile. I can tell that he is reflecting on a time of pain, and his face radiates sincerity. I am trying to quiet the voice that is in my head, the one that is singing and shouting, "Single, single, single!"

"I see what you mean. Well, okay, sorry . . . I mean, well, I didn't mean to pry."

"I don't think you were prying per se."

"You don't think—*per se?*"

"You want to know what I think?"

"Um, I'm not exactly sure."

"I think you were flirting with me." I am flabbergasted. He is so smug, and he is smiling again, and, damn it, he is so cute, and I don't know what to say. So, of course, I use a trick I learned from Alan: I go on the offense.

"You're crazy."

"Am I?"

"I'm married."

"Uh-huh." He acts like he doesn't believe me. I remember the empty space on my finger.

"Did you hear what I said? I'm married."

"Are you?"

"Principal Davidson, what are you—"

He interrupts. "Ken."

"Excuse me, I have to go." I must be about the color of the primary red paint in the oversized can on the shelf. I turn to get my things, practically hyperventilating. I thought I could keep up, but my bantering skills are rusty.

"Wait, I'm sorry, I didn't mean to insult you, or . . . or marriage, but I just thought, well, I guess what I meant was . . ." I don't wait for him to finish. Clutching my purse to my middle like armor I push past him toward the door. He calls after me.

"What I meant was . . . I liked it."

Now I stop. I look back. My coat is on and I am halfway out in the hall and I am a married woman and I need to keep walking right out of that classroom and right out of the school. So, naturally, I cover my face with my hands and burst into tears.

KEN AND I sit in the art room for a half hour, at the end of which I've told him everything about Alan and me and my family and Alan's mom and possibly all of my childhood. Mostly he listens, asks sensitive questions occasionally, and laughs at all the right moments at the jokes I make through my tears. He, in turn, tells me about his failed marriage, and

I notice that a lot of the words he uses to describe it closely mirror my own; words like "ignored," "denied," and "pretended." Before we know it, the door opens and Ann Cultierri walks back in to her class. She looks at the two of us and shakes her head.

"Oh, for God's sake. Have you two been here this whole time? No, don't tell me, I don't even want to know." She turns and walks toward the supply cabinet, shaking her head and muttering. But just like the two of us, she is smiling.

TWENTY-SEVEN

When I come home, I am moving around the house like Annette Funicello in one of those boy-meets-girl beach movies: humming, gliding on air, the whole thing. Occasionally, I smile for no reason at all. All I need is a beehive hairdo, a linen dress, and Bobby Darin to walk in with a surfboard. Bebe eyes me suspiciously but says nothing. When I decide to bake, she snorts, but I can't tell if she is pleased or disturbed. The kids come home to the smell of oatmeal and cinnamon, and even Lauren loses her attitude long enough to attack the batch of cookies. Their faces say it all; things are getting back to the way they used to be.

After the kids gorge themselves, I tell them I'm going to take the leftovers to the Rabinowitzes. Evan grabs his book bag and says he's "coming with" and—will miracles never cease—Princess Lauren casually remarks that "if it's okay," she'll come, too. Well. I suppose being grounded does not preclude a family walk to the next-door neighbors, and I am thrilled that she doesn't make her usual remarks about the Rabinowitzes.

When we push through the blue firs and enter their yard, everything is the same as when I last visited, except that this time when Ross looks up and notices Lauren is with us, he begins to act weird, brushing his hair back with his hand, shifting from foot to foot, and backing awkwardly away from his little sister. Magenta waves to Evan, who runs over to the picnic table, as comfortable as he can be. I don't know what the relationship is between Lauren and Ross, since Ross is a year older and home-schooled, but clearly she makes him nervous. Susan notices, I'm sure, especially when Magenta pokes her brother in the leg and says, "Hey. What's wrong with you?" Zory, who is eighteen, seems to be struggling not to laugh. To Susan's credit, she stares at Ross for a long moment and then smoothly ignores his behavior.

"Oh, hey, neighbors! Do I see baked goodies?" Susan comes right up to my daughter and stuns Lauren by giving her a big bear hug, as if she is her long-lost niece. Then she takes the plate of cookies and does the same with me. We make our way over to the porch and there is a moment when Lauren is unsure where to put herself, but then Zory calls her over, and by the time Susan and I sit down, the Rabinowitz girls have her surrounded. Magenta is touching Lauren's hair and looking at her nails, which today are purple, and Zory is telling her sister to calm down. Lauren is actually smiling at them both. Poor Ross doesn't seem quite as happy, but then Evan decides to jump on his back and they start wrestling, and it appears that the kids will find their rhythm with each other.

Susan and I start chatting, and before I know it an hour has gone by. I look up and notice that Evan is working with Magenta and Zory. Lauren and Ross are sitting (together) on a large boulder near the swings. They are talking. Together. I need to blink to make sure it's not an apparition. And they make quite a picture. Ross, with his red hair, clean-cut khakis, and yellow Izod shirt, and Lauren in her low-cut pink Juicy sweats and cropped white T-shirt that has an imprint of a pair of red lips. Not to mention the plastic bracelets, the earrings, and the lip gloss. When I announce that I'm heading home, *both* kids call out that they'll see me later. I look at Susan, and we both smile and shrug at the same time.

Back at home, I ask Bebe about Phyllis and the people who came to the house, and she says that "they no like house," which makes me wonder if this is Bebe's opinion or whether Phyllis actually said as much. Phyllis is not big on fluffy conversation. She would not bother to call me and make me feel good, saying something like the people loved my taste but felt the house was too small for their needs. That's just not her style. But neither is sharing information with the housekeeper.

"What do you mean they didn't like the house? How do you know?"

"They say this."

"They told you they didn't like it?"

"No, they say it in front of me."

"You mean in back of you, behind your back?"

"No, no, front. Say in front."

"Like, they didn't know you were there?" Bebe turns to me with a sour smile.

"They don't care if Bebe is there. Bebe is just the maid." Ouch.

"Oh, Bebe. That's terrible. You mean they acted like you didn't exist?"

She doesn't answer.

"Bebe," I say, "you're very important. Especially for us. I don't know how I would have gotten through the past three weeks without you. You know that, right?"

"Not ruined pots if Bebe isn't here."

"What? Oh, Bebe, I told you I don't care about the pots."

The only answer is a snort.

WHEN THE KIDS come home, I remember to talk to them about Bebe and her family, and both of them are thrilled to go through their closets and rooms to find things they can give away. By the end of the night, we have three piles, one of clothes and one of toys and one of books. I go down to the basement to find some boxes we can use to pack them up. As promised, Bebe hasn't touched the ruined pottery. Without much care, I lift them out of the kiln, set them on the counter, and clean up the remaining mah-jongg tiles at the bottom. Then I close the kiln, wondering when I might have the energy to attempt another round.

With work starting on Monday, I guess my life is going to get pretty busy. So much is happening so fast. I think of Ken, and get a little shiver of excitement, and then the guilt begins to seep in. I haven't even called Alan since the showdown in his room. I will have to figure out a plan for visiting him and vice versa.

The weekend is quiet. The kids help me pick out an outfit for my first day of school, and Sunday afternoon Ross knocks on the back door and hands me an apple from Susan. There is a toothpick stuck in it that has a little flag at the end which says *For The Teacher,* and I am so touched that I start to cry. Ross continues to stand at the door, and then in a croaky voice manages to ask if "Lauren is around." When I call up to her, she comes down in a flash, and the two of them walk out onto the patio and into the backyard. "Go figure," I say to myself as I hug the apple to my chest.

SINCE I DON'T have to be at school until 8:30, I can go at the same time as the kids. They are ecstatic not to have to take the bus. We drop Lauren at Glen Vale, and then Ev and I go to Cherry Lane. Evan thinks it is hysterical when he says, "Have a good day in school, dear, and play nice with the other teachers." I go to the office to sign in and check my box as instructed. Actually, I *try* to check my box, but notice that it hasn't been set up yet. The box is there, at the bottom, but not my name. I look up to see that Eleanor is watching me from her power position behind the front desk. I quickly surmise that it is her job to assign my name to the box, so I purposely pay no attention to the slight. Thankfully, there are other teachers and a few kids milling about, so I can get past the awkward moment of a greeting with a cheery, general "Good morning" to everyone in the room as I make what I hope is a cool and composed exit from the office.

My nerves disappear as I step into the art room, which is like stepping into your favorite children's book, all soft colors, friendly shapes, comforting music, and waves of generous warmth emanating like sonar impulses from Ann Cultierri, aka Mrs. C. This is the room you might design if you were asked to create a utopia for your inner child. In stark contrast to my welcome from Eleanor, behind Ann's desk a set of containers and a cubby is set up for me, my name announced in multicolored bubble letters on each. I am touched. Ann comes up behind me and pats me on the back. "The kindergartners did it on Friday. They can't wait to meet you."

BY MIDMORNING on my first day I am covered in glue, paint, and glitter. As each class came in, no matter if they were five or nine years old, they all greeted me warmly, and accepted me immediately. It seemed that if Mrs. C. said I was okay, then I was okay. Ultimately, someone in each class would realize that my name was Mrs. Lerner, and they would find that really funny, to have a *teacher* who was a "learner." They all made jokes by asking me if I "learned anything today," and when they left they made me promise to "make sure you learn something 'cause you're a learner, okay?" Oh well, grade-school humor. I thought they were adorable.

EVAN'S CLASS WASN'T scheduled on Monday, but some other fourth-grade classes were, and I knew many of his friends. I was a little worried about how that might play out, but I needn't have been. The kids all wanted to know if I was the one who "taught him how to draw so great." I couldn't help but be proud. Especially when one little girl named Lindsey came up to me and said that Evan was the best artist in the whole school. She showed me her binder and said that Evan had made this picture for her. It was an amazing bird, which was kind of like a dragon but with weird stars and lightning bolts shooting out of it. My little Dalí.

When it was time to leave at 12:30, I was almost sorry to go, although I have to admit I was exhausted. Elementary school kids are mentally and physically draining. The younger ones need you to help them hold and cut and fasten; the older kids ask questions incessantly. They also tend to be perfectionists and don't always trust themselves, so they want *you* to draw or cut or paint *for* them—not because they can't, but because they already think they're not good enough. One part psychologist, one part handyman, and one part nurse, a school art teacher wears many hats. By the end of the day, I realize that I have one agenda, which I share with Ann, and that is to communicate to these children that expressing yourself is about the feeling you get, not the end result. Technique will come later, but only if you have the passion, and the passion starts early, right here, right now. I, too, want them to love the creation of art, the process of it.

Leaving the school, I feel a little twinge of disappointment that I haven't seen Ken. I have to be cool about this, I know, but I've felt so bottled up and intense for so long, it's nice to look forward to something light and breezy. I've been thinking about him a lot, and I thought for sure he'd find at least one second to stick his head in and say hello. In the parking lot, I toss my purse onto the passenger seat and am about to get in when someone calls my name. I turn and see Ken jogging over from his car. When he approaches, I can see he's out of breath.

"Hey, I'm glad I caught you. I was at a meeting all morning in Bergenfield and didn't think I'd get back. How'd it go?" I get a nice, warm feeling thinking that he must have raced back to school, knowing I leave midday.

"How does it look like it went?" I open my arms and look down at the various stains and soils that snake up and down and around my smock.

"Looks like an A-plus day, especially the touches of blue and green right here." Ken leans in and with his two fingers gently rubs at a piece of my hair just above my ear. He is so close that I can smell his skin. It is my new favorite smell.

"Oh, I must look like a mess." I fidget a bit, not sure if I can take another minute of this without getting dizzy.

"Hold still, it's almost out. Okay, there you go." Unfortunately and thankfully, he steps back.

"Well, thanks. I guess I'd better get home and wash up."

"Wait, Barb, I just want to ask . . . um . . . how's Alan?" He looks so sincere, so solid. I had been wondering whether it would be awkward seeing each other after our heart-to-heart last week, but it isn't; it is just as genuine as the first time. We've made a connection, of that I'm now sure.

"The same."

"Okay. Well, look. I don't want to do anything unorthodox, but do you think we could have dinner sometime, you know, and pick up where we left off?"

This is the part where I tell him that it's impossible, that I am still married, that I wouldn't know what to tell my kids, that somebody might see us, blah, blah, blah.

"I'd like that," I say. And then, of course, I have second thoughts. "We'd just need to make sure it's all aboveboard."

"Of course. We're just two friends, two coworkers, having a meal."

"Except I'm not going to tell my kids who I'm dining with."

"And we should probably go someplace about ten towns away."

"Yeah, since we have nothing to hide."

"And it's all aboveboard." We both crack up.

"Okay," he says, "we'll work it out. Saturday night okay?"

TWENTY-EIGHT

t he rest of the week goes by in a wonderful blur of construction paper, cotton balls, and chalk. The fourth graders are hard at work on the end-of-the-year mural, and the rest of the school is concentrating on various projects for the spring art show, which takes place on Earth Day, the Friday before Memorial Day weekend. With only three weeks to go, Ann is unusually hyper, though still cheery; her tra-las are coming more frequently and at an even higher pitch. We are working with many natural ingredients, from pinecones to blades of grass, and even using forsythia blossoms as yellow dye to demonstrate the correlation between nature and art. On Saturday, both kids are preparing to sleep out. I am shameless, having ungrounded Lauren for my own, selfish purposes. Of course, I didn't put it that way. Instead, I did what any brilliant, manipulative parent would do: I complimented her on her improved attitude and rewarded her with a Saturday night, although I did give her a list of appropriate friends to choose from, and I spoke with the mother of the one she picked. Evan was no problem at all, because his All-Star baseball team has a three o'clock game, and he was invited to sleep over at Zach's, one of his friends on the team, so we will pack him up before the game and he will leave with Zach right from the field. Ken and I are going to a restaurant in Wayne, some three towns away, which is not really being sneaky, since it is a well-lit, popular place and therefore, I tell myself, I have nothing to be ashamed of and nothing to feel guilty about. That works for about a second. The guilt comes in frequent waves, but they are gentle, lapping. They do not knock me down or pull me out to sea; they are easy to fight.

AFTER EVAN'S GAME, Lauren and I come home, and she begins to get ready for her sleepover at her friend Lindsey Diamond's house. They will be going to a movie in Ridgewood and then out for ice cream. The Diamonds are older and conservative, so I know that the girls will be on a tight leash, home by eleven. Lauren has turned her room upside down looking for a belt that she's sure was "right here," and she insists that her whole outfit is ruined without the belt. Once it becomes clear that she is stuck on wearing only this outfit, I suggest that Bebe might know where it is and why not just call her and ask.

"Oh, Mommy, please, will you?" She smiles, uses the puppy dog eyes, and I start to laugh.

"*I* should call?"

"Please, please, I need to finish getting ready."

"Okay, let me go find her number."

"Thank you, Mommy. You're the best!" She gives me a hundred air kisses.

"Mm, mm, mm, mm, mm!"

I go down to the kitchen and search out the phone number I have for Bebe, then dial and wait. The phone rings about seven times, but no answering machine kicks in. Finally, someone picks up, but no one says hello.

"Hello?" I say. "Hello?" I hear what is maybe a little kid's voice, then a screeching noise and then nothing. Next thing I know there is a dial tone. Okay. I will try again. Again I dial, again it rings, and rings, and rings. Nothing. I'm about to hang up when once again someone picks up.

"What the fuck you want?" The voice is male, young, and angry.

"Hello? I . . . I don't know if I have the right number, I'm looking for Bebe. Bebe Jaikaran?"

"Fuck you, aw-right? Don't be callin' here no more." And then there is a click. Even through the phone, I find myself afraid and quickly drop the phone back in its cradle. This can't be right. Maybe I didn't dial right. I check the number in my book and then gingerly press redial, just enough to see the number, which, horrifyingly, is correct, and then quickly hang up. Feeling disturbed, I head back upstairs and tell Lauren that I couldn't reach Bebe. It turns out that it doesn't matter, because *naturally* by now she's decided to change. A few minutes later, the Diamonds beep for her and she is out the door.

It's finally time for *me* to get ready, I've only picked out my outfit about a hundred times, but instead of feeling excited I am troubled by the call to Bebe. By the time Ken picks me up, I have a plan. I have no idea how he'll feel about it, but before he even steps into the house I spill it.

"Of course, we can check it out. Fair Lawn's on the way to Wayne anyway, so it's no problem." I smile. Good guy. And I begin to feel better. I'm sure there's an easy explanation for the guy on the phone. I take a breath, and as I start to relax I realize that this is the first time I haven't seen Ken in a suit, and those muscles I suspected are in clear view tonight. He's wearing a black, long-sleeved knit shirt, and even though it's not that tight, the fabric seems to cling to his shoulders. Whenever he moves, you can see the upper area of his sculpted arms. And when he leans in to give me a friendly kiss hello, and for just a moment I grasp his upper arm, I almost faint: solid as steel. Jesus. After we leave and he opens my car door and then walks around to his side, it's all I can do not to stare at his butt.

WE DRIVE ABOUT twenty minutes and don't say much, but I find myself thinking that these might be the most pleasant twenty minutes of my entire life. There is just something so warm and comfortable about being in Ken's car.

"You know, Barbara," he says, as we pass a sign that reads ENTERING FAIR LAWN, "I'm not one to dance around the elephant in the room." He glances over at me. I wait, then can't resist answering, "Yes, but which one?" We both laugh.

"Seriously," he begins again, "I've really put you in an unfair position, asking you out this way, friends or not."

"I'm a big girl, Ken. I could have always said no."

"True, but technically I'm in a position of authority. If something were to happen, you could always say you felt pressured or coerced, that you were afraid for your job."

"Are you serious?" He looks dead so. "What do you mean by happen?"

"Nothing specific. I just . . . well . . . I may not have been thinking straight. This is very unlike me. People are sure to talk, and you could get hurt and I—"

"Whoa, whoa, whoa," I cut him off. "Just hold on. First of all, thank you. I appreciate your thinking of my reputation. *And* my career, fledgling that it is. Second of all, we haven't even made it to one dinner, let alone to the 'What's Happening' page of the PTA newsletter. I *am* a married woman, we are just going out to eat, and who knows if we will even do that again." I say this all in a rush. "Besides, I don't know if I want to go out to dinner with you again! I've never seen your table manners. Maybe you chew with your mouth open or pick your teeth with your fork." I smile at him. There is a slight pause.

"So the teeth picking thing is really out, eh?"

WHEN WE FIND Bebe's street, Ken slows down as I begin to read off the numbers. When we reach the matching number, I check the address three times. My stomach starts to sink. It is impossible that Bebe would live in this place for even one night, let alone every weekend. The street is depressing enough, but the house at 3217-40 Fairmount Parkway is the biggest eyesore on an already run-down block. It's unbelievable to me that a structure could look so dilapidated, so dirty, and so close to collapsing and not be condemned.

"Whew," Ken mutters. "Not exactly the Ritz."

"Oh God." I am at a loss. The house is almost sideways. It may have once been white, but so much of the paint has peeled off it's hard to tell. A front porch is barely attached to the house, its broken railing sporting slats of wood that hang and swing at various angles. Only two windows have glass; the rest are covered in plywood or flowered sheets. Beneath the porch, some sort of latticework has given way and it's possible to see under the house. There are some remnants of a foundation—cinder block and a wooden platform—but mostly there is junk: a broken bicycle, a wheelbarrow, hubcaps, great tangles of wire and piping. The front walk is cracked, broken concrete overrun with weeds, and the front door is gouged, stained, and noticeably warped. The house in which Bebe lives looks like the neighborhood crack den. The house has given up.

"I can't believe Bebe's in there." I turn to Ken. "You can't really understand what I mean. She's so elegant. And neat. She makes faces at me if I put a dish in the sink without rinsing it." I look over at Ken. "Of course, I would *never* do that." I smile, and so does he, but really, I'm upset. How can I eat dinner and think of Bebe in this house at the same time?

"Well, what do you want to do?" I'm struck by the fact that Ken is not annoyed. That is a new response. Alan, I know, would not think twice about rolling his eyes and imposing his opinion. Alan would already be driving away, explaining why we shouldn't get involved. But Ken seems open to my feelings. Suddenly, I know what I want to do, and that's to get Bebe out of that house. I am a little scared, especially since the guy on the phone sounded like he'd have no problem shooting me, but looking over at Ken, who is waiting patiently for my decision, I have confidence. Of course, it doesn't hurt that Ken looks like a pro wrestler.

"I'm really sorry about this. You're going to think I'm nuts."

"You're not going to throw all my clothes out the window onto the front lawn are you?"

"What?"

"Because you mistakenly think I have a girlfriend?"

"Ken, what are you talking about?"

"I was reminiscing about someone who was . . . never mind. Anyway, sorry, too much information. What I mean is, no, I could never think you're nuts."

There is nothing to say. He's put a little piece of himself out there, and the one thing I'm certain of at that moment is that

I want more. I touch his arm, acknowledging that I understand he's got some war wounds.

"I'm sorry."

"It's fine." Time to move on.

"You know what I want to do, right?"

"Let's go."

WE HEAR THE RAP music before we even get to the front steps. After a full minute of pounding, a child of about six answers the door. She is tan-skinned, dirty, half naked, and carrying a ratty yellowed blanket. When I ask for Bebe, she screams out something unintelligible and disappears. A few minutes later, a woman approaches. Like her daughter, she appears to be of mixed descent, possibly Indian or Polynesian. And like her daughter, she looks like she hasn't had a shower in days. Her face is wrinkled and grimy, and she is annoyed. Before I can say a word, Ken leans his imposing six-foot-two-inch frame forward and announces that we are looking for Bebe. The woman considers, and then opens the door a little wider and turns away, mumbling something that seems to mean that we should come in. She shuffles through a decrepit living room and we follow, but not before I notice the source of the rap music: a boom box on the floor next to an old filthy sofa on which is sprawled a young Indian man, either asleep or dead, it's hard to tell. As we get to a staircase, the woman points and motions toward the top and says what sounds like "Up there." Ken and I exchange looks, and then we go up. Me first, him close behind. At the top, there are three doors. I feel like I am on a game show. Monty Hall, where are you? Like he's reading my mind, Ken whispers, "Please pick the one with the car, not the goat."

"Ssh," I say back, and start to giggle. I think the giggling is a reaction to the fact that I am truly uneasy. In a really small voice, I call, "Bebe." Now Ken starts to crack up.

"Oh, that'll work."

"Okay, okay. I'll just knock on this one," I say, pointing to the first door.

"Fine. Go ahead."

"Stop pushing me." I poke him.

"Okay." He pokes me back, struggling to cover a laugh, but I can tell that he's not so comfortable, either.

"Ken!" We are now poking each other and generally acting like we're five. I knock on the door. Only it's more like a little tap, tap, tap. I am not too good at this. Ken sizes this up pretty quickly. The next thing I know, he is banging on the door. I jump back and grab his arm, horrified. He shrugs, and since there is no response we start to move to the next door. But then a voice calls, "Come in." I look at Ken. That's Bebe!

I swing the door open and take in the room. It is about eight by ten and there are bunk beds on three walls. Not just double bunk beds, but triple ones. It looks like one of those pods they have in Japan for businessmen to take naps, like a room full of open coffins. There are several men and women sleeping, many without any linen or covers. In fact, some of the beds don't even have mattresses, just some balled-up blankets. In a corner to the right, scrunched up on a grayish sheet on the lower bunk, half sitting, half lying down, is Bebe. I don't know who is more surprised, she or me. Neither one of us moves; we just stare at each other, not saying a word. I feel Ken looking down at me and I recover.

"Bebe," I say, though it's more of a croak, "let's go." She doesn't say a word, just unfolds herself from the bed, smoothes out her skirt and her hair, and grabs her satchel from behind her head. Before she leaves, she looks around the room and then slips her hand under the bottom bed and pulls out a paper bag and tucks that under her arm as she follows us down the stairs, out of the house, and into the car.

"Bebe," I say, just before we get to the car, "please don't ever come back here, okay?" She looks at me doubtfully. "You will stay with us on the weekends, too, okay?" She nods slowly. "Not to work, just to live, okay?" She nods again, then gets in the backseat. I can't see her face, but I hear her take a tissue out of her bag, and I hear her blow her nose, and I need to do the same. Luckily, Ken breaks the silence.

"Well, ladies, I'm starving. Anyone for Wendy's?"

the kids are ecstatic that Bebe is living with us full-time. In some ways, they are shockingly untraumatized by their father's absence. I'd like to think this is because they've transferred an attachment to Bebe, but I can't help wondering if it's really because they have always had such a small attachment to Alan. Whatever filial bond they share seems all too easily severed. Point in fact: They have not asked about their father in over a week. I haven't broached the subject, either. Truth is, it's all I can do to concentrate on my new job, the kids' mental health, and the financial plan that Mort laid out. I had no idea that the credit-card companies would be so willing to work things out; it won't be easy and I must sell the house but at least for now we have phone, lights, and air-conditioning.

True to her word, Phyllis has been showing the house quite a bit, but only during school hours. No offers yet, and I walk around feeling a strange combination of relief that it isn't selling and fear that it won't. I'm starting to feel anxious about the school year coming to an end. Not just because of the money, since I've already been inquiring and have found out that the day camps in the area are starved for art counselors, but I've become so comfortable with these children and this school that it feels like I've been here forever. It's Monday, and in just a week it will be Memorial Day, and then there are only three weeks to go. Right now, we are busy preparing for Earth Day, so I have little time to contemplate the end of the year. Suddenly, Ann comes rushing in with her arms full.

"Thank God you're here! Five days will never be enough to get this all done! Have you seen the poor mural?" She unloads her booty, an assortment of potted plants, trowels, and bags of moss. From my perch on the stepstool, my mouth full of tacks, I try to answer.

"Merrll?" I answer, between closed lips. "Is smthng rong?" Ann takes a breath and wipes the dirt from the plants off her chest.

"Well, no, not exactly, nothing that can't be fixed." She marches over to the paint cabinet and frantically searches above and below, unable to locate whatever it is she needs. I climb down, spit out the tacks, and walk over.

"What do you need? Can I help?"

Out of breath, she explains in a rush.

"Yesterday at recess the fourth graders glued grass to the bottom of the mural, on the parts where the athletic fields are depicted. They thought it would be more realistic, and I missed it. But they don't realize that grass dies, so by Earth Day it will look as if Glen Vale's children play all their sports on dirt, and I can tell you that the PTA, who paid for some beautiful landscaping last year, and the board, who approved five acres of new sod, are not going to like the looks of that!" She is laughing but clearly a little frantic. "I need to find some green paint. We were ready to start hanging it up, but now we have to go back and paint over the bottom of the whole mural!" With that, Ann turns around, hands on hips, frustrated. For just a second she doesn't move and then her entire face breaks into a smile.

"I know! Mrs. Kendall in music needed to paint circles on the blacktop and she used the green paint!" Like a woman possessed, she dashes for the door. By now, I've learned to stay out of Ann's way as she flies through the art room like a happy fairy, albeit a fairy on speed.

"Tra-la!" she cries. "I shall return!" I smile and have a moment of relief that it will all work out, but the smile vanishes suddenly as Ann nears the classroom door. There, on the floor, is a small trail of wet dirt that must have spilled from the plants. As she reaches for the doorknob, her front foot slips right out. In almost comical form, she tries to right herself but her arms simply flail while the other foot slides sideways and she lands hard on her side.

"Awwgh." There is a moan of pain as she hits the floor. I'm there in a flash.

"Ann! Ann! Oh my God, are you all right?"

"Oohhh."

This doesn't look good. I grab the phone on the wall and ring the office. "Send the nurse to the art room! And while you're at it, call 911."

As the EMTs, some of whom I unfortunately recognize, load Ann into the ambulance, she grabs my hand. By now, the paramedics have determined that she most likely has a broken hip.

"Barbara, dear, you'll have to do it all, and I know you can."

"Oh, Ann, I don't think—"

She cuts me off. They have given her a shot for the pain and she is oddly calm.

"Now, now, don't worry, you can do it. Start by repainting the mural so it has time to dry. And make sure the second graders are gentle with the pussy willows. And remember to defrost the . . ." And that's the last thing I hear before they shut the doors. Suddenly, I am the art teacher. In charge of the most important event of the school year. I would laugh if I wasn't completely paralyzed with fear. And then I have two thoughts: First, there is something I must defrost, but I have no idea what it is. Second, there's no way I can pull this off. A crowd of us back up as the ambulance pulls away and some of the teachers pat my back and shake their heads and smile. "You'll be fine," they murmur, or "Piece of cake." I am not consoled. Ambulances have a way of turning my life upside down. Then Ken is there and we're the only two left outside, and he's wearing that grin.

"Well, the good news is that we'll move for a quick approval from the board to hire you full-time for the duration of the school year."

"And the bad?"

"The bad news is that we'll move for a quick approval from the board to . . ." I give him a little smack on the arm.

"The bad news is the same as the good news?"

"Well, it's just that Earth Day is our most anticipated event and I know it's a lot for you to take on." I look over at him. Is it possible Mr. Easygoing is just a tad anxious?

"And you don't think I'm up to it?"

"Hey, I never said that."

"But you were thinking it."

"I was *not* thinking it. I thought *you* were thinking it."

"Right." We both turn and start to walk back toward the school in silence. Ken calls out, "Hey!"

I turn around.

"Are you trying to start a fight or something?" I look back, ready to defend myself, and then I stop and smile.

"Maybe." He seems surprised, and then he relaxes and smiles back. I wag my finger at him.

"Don't say it." I keep walking. I'm afraid he's going to say something cute like "our first fight," thereby acknowledging that we are an "our" or something like that, and I'm just not ready for that. Thankfully, he doesn't say a word. He does start to hum rather loudly, which makes me want to give him a big playful shove, but I restrain myself. Despite this, as we enter the school I look to the right and see Eleanor standing at the office window looking out. She stares right at me, raises an eyebrow, and then turns away. It actually gives me chills. One thing's for sure, if I happen to run into a jam, and I'm sure I will, Eleanor will not be the go-to girl.

THE WEEK GOES by in an adrenaline blur. On the last afternoon before the big day, I am still in school well after the kids have gone home. I am dabbing at the mural with a solution of water and turpentine, cleaning up the stray splatters and drips. The mural is about twenty-five yards long and runs the length of the main hallway.

"Do you know it's almost seven o'clock?"

"Morning or evening?"

"Cute. Have you even eaten anything?"

"You mean besides paint chips?"

"Wait here. I'll be right back."

"No, really, I'm not hungry, I'm fine." But he is gone. A few minutes later, there is this incredible aroma coming down the hall. The waiter's not bad, either. Ken pulls over a child's table and two chairs and commands me to sit. I have to admit, the smell of whatever he has is suddenly making me realize that I'm ravenous. And he looks so cute squished into the little seat. There are two paper plates, and on each is a portion of some kind of fish and a side of something orange.

"What is this?" I take my plastic fork and start to taste.

"Cod with pecan crust and roasted butternut squash. It was my lunch, left over from last night's dinner, but I didn't get a chance to eat today, either."

"So I'm taking half of your lunch?"

"Don't feel bad for me. I raided the baked goods, the ones for tomorrow, about ten times today. Each time I told myself it was the last time, but I'm a sucker for homemade brownies." I try to respond, but my mouth is full of the most delicious bite of food. Even microwaved, this dinner is spectacular.

"Where did you eat last night? This fish is amazing."

"I made it at home."

"Get out."

He looks at me, tilts his head. Even with his mouth full he manages to grin.

"I swear."

"Oh God. You cook like this? What else do you do in your spare time, rescue animals? Rush into burning buildings? Save the world?"

"Well, I used to, but I wasn't crazy about the suit. So *blue,* you know."

My turn to grin evilly.

"I think I might have liked to see you in that suit."

"Oh yeah?" There is a moment, me grinning, him staring, when everything freezes. Maybe it's because we are totally alone in the school without even a janitor in sight. Or maybe it's because we are both folded into these tiny, dwarfed chairs, our knees unnaturally bent up near our necks, and it feels like

I am twelve again, sharing secrets with a boy in the park. But just like that, in this cramped, awkward position, Ken leans in and kisses me on the lips, and I let him. It's kind of a long kiss, not a child's kiss; our mouths are open and we find each other with our tongues, but it's kind of sweet, too. No hands, the position won't allow for it, so it's all lips, serious and slow, kind of chaste, and because of that, kind of tantalizing, too. All in all, it really is like being twelve. Then we sit back, satisfied little smiles on our faces, and finish our food without saying a word.

We clean up the makeshift dinner and I tell Ken I'd better get home, that the kids will think I fell into the foam pit that's been set up outside. Ken grabs my hand before I can go and pulls me to him, and I stop him stiffly. I am suddenly afraid.

"Why are you pulling away?"

"I don't know what I'm doing."

"I do. I want to kiss you again."

"I don't think that's such a good idea."

"You didn't like it?"

"Ken."

"Okay, okay. But I want to cook you dinner."

"Now?"

"Not now! I mean—" Then he sees that I'm kidding him and laughs. "Barb, seriously, we have to talk about . . . everything."

"I know. We do. But just let me get through tomorrow, okay?"

"You got it. By the way, is everything set?"

"Oh, suddenly you're the responsible principal."

"That's right, and you better watch your step or I'll have to take disciplinary action."

"So much for the guy who thought his position gave him an inappropriate edge! Do I need to get a written reference now, before I start my harassment suit?"

"Oh!" He fakes getting punched in the gut. "You definitely know how to kill a mood." Then he adds, softly, "But you're right, too, of course. Sorry."

"Stop. I was kidding. Come on, we're both tired." I start to walk away. "But I'll see you tomorrow, very early."

"Barb, I . . ."

I turn back and stop. It's hard enough walking away from him. I feel like if he says one more flirtatious thing and smiles, I'll be totally lost.

"I want to say that I . . . I always have fun with you." Oh God. He's not being flirty or sexual, he's being nice. There's an underestimated adjective. I know that I need to just turn around and keep walking or I might never make it home, so I do, but just before I turn, I murmur, "Me too." I don't see him smiling, but I know he is.

THIRTY

e arth Day is a huge success. The weather is perfect, seventy-two degrees and partly sunny with big puffy clouds moving slowly about. It's a day for children to frolic and grandparents to stroll, and young mothers to push baby carriages while they throw crumbs to the ducks; a day from a Rousseau painting. I have two mishaps: the first, when Lucy Steckler's little brother, two-year-old Abe, tries to eat the macaroni necklaces and actually does ingest at least two hard rigatoni; and the second, when Shannon Feldman is stung by a bee at the World in Flowers display. After being stung, Shannon flailed so hysterically and frantically that she managed to tear down half of what was once Asia. Naturally, for Asia we used orchids, which were the most delicate and expensive, and they are now trampled and shredded and lying in piles on the grass. Oh yes, there is one more thing. I was supposed to defrost an ice cream cake in the shape of the earth. Of course, I didn't know about the cake until it was time to serve it and the lovely Eleanor came to tell me so. I'm sure she enjoyed the look of panic on my face and was equally disappointed when Jill Toller's mother announced that there was no need to worry since she'd brought a chocolate sheet cake because her kids couldn't eat dairy. Later, I got to see both of my kids, since Glen Vale Middle comes over to Cherry

Lane by class throughout the day. Lauren, running over to me with two other girls, was suddenly proud, beaming even, that she has a mother who is a teacher.

"Everything looks so cool!" she exclaimed, before she ran off to other booths.

By the end of the day I am exhausted, more mentally than physically. I must have been conceptually holding my breath since Ann broke her hip and left me in charge. Thankfully, a committee of parent volunteers stays to help clean up, and by four o'clock I am walking into the house. Bebe is waiting for me with this news:

"Miss Phyllis say you must call her."

We share a look. I plop my bag down on the kitchen table and whisper to Bebe, "Ssh, where are the kids?"

"Not here. Over there." She points outside toward the Rabinowitzes.

"Oh well, then, might as well get it over with." I know how this conversation will go. Phyllis will say she has a couple who just love the house. She will say they've made an offer. It will be a great offer. Phyllis will encourage me to take it and ask if I can be out in two or three months. I will think, well, at least it will be summer, which is actually the best time to move, so how can I not take it. Then I will throw up.

"Hi, Phyl, it's Bitsy." I haven't told Phyllis that I've changed my name to Barbara.

"Hi, hon, I have to ask you something."

Here it comes. I will not move in two months. I need three. "Uh-huh."

"That piece in the basement, what do you call it?"

"What?"

"That . . . you know . . . plate. In the basement. What's it called?"

"Phyllis, I don't know what you're talking about. This is *Bitsy.*"

She gives an exasperated sigh. "Hold on, Bitsy, I'm doing three things at once. Okay, there. Now, Bitsy, in your basement, there is a plate near the kiln, with little tiles all over it, yes?"

"*That* plate? Yes, why?"

"And you made it, right?"

"Yes."

"Well, okay, today I showed the house to a couple from Fort Lee. The husband is an art dealer. He didn't like the house, but he loved the plate."

"You have got to be kidding."

"Why would I do that? He was practically transfixed. I had to haul him upstairs. He kept saying something about it being the most original representation of suburbia he's seen since somebody or other. Anyway, I promised him I'd ask you about it and give you his number and persuade you to call him."

I am dumbfounded. Too dumbfounded to be smart.

"Phyllis, the plate was . . . is . . . a mistake." There is a small pause.

"Yeah? Well, so what? Isn't that how great art happens or some such thing? Anyway, you know I love you, but I don't really have time for this, so let me just give you his number." As Phyllis rattles off the man's name and number I mechanically write them down. Before she says good-bye, Phyllis adds, "If I were you, I wouldn't say it was a mistake, I'd just call it something. Something suburban."

A half hour later, I am at the Rabinowitzes, sitting with Susan and all of our kids, and relaying the conversation between me and Julian Soltes of the Julian Soltes Gallery in Soho.

" . . . so then he asks for 'the title of the work,' and it was either burst out laughing or come up with something. I didn't think *Bebe Slipped* would go over, so I just said I call it *Tuesday Afternoon,* you know, like because Tuesday is Mah-jongg Day. And he loves it! He says it's perfect, and then he asks me what other pieces I have, and I say I have several but they are not done yet, and he says he is really excited about my work; it's so fresh and original! Can you imagine? My work! Bebe knocks over a mah-jongg set and suddenly I'm Andy Warhol!"

"Oh, Bitsy, this is so wonderful!" Susan is beaming for me.

"Forget wonderful. You all have to help me come up with other ideas about suburbia and I have to get to work. He wants pictures as soon as possible. Pictures! He told me to send them digitally and I almost died. I would have an easier time sending them by ESP!"

"I can take the photos and send them." It is Ross. He is so sweet.

"Of course you can. I should have known. Ross, I swear you could probably build the camera to do it." He turns red, embarrassed but pleased.

"How about one called *Soccer Carpool*?" Lauren sits up, excited. "You could stick a torn piece of the team roster and the black-and-white ball and some net . . ."—she stops to think— "ooh, and a long shoelace and one of Evan's trophy heads!" Then Zory pipes in. "And two tickets to the World Cup."

I smile at them. "That's fantastic!"

"How about *College Bound*?" Ezora offers. "You could do dorm keys and sorority letters and SAT stuff and like a suitcase tag, and some university stickers, things like that?" Everybody loves it.

Then Evan says, "*Movie Night!* No, wait . . . *Family Night.* I don't know, I was thinking TV clicker and take-out menus."

"That would work," Ross says, "but you need pieces of a pizza box and ice cream containers, too."

"Wait a minute," Evan continues, "what about something with housekeepers, you know like Bebe's roti and rice."

Lauren stands up. "Yes! We can call it *See Me Monday!*"

Everybody is laughing and testing ideas. Suddenly, Magenta clears her throat.

"I have an idea," she says quietly. We all turn to her. "You could do one called *Girl Geek.* You could have glasses and book-marks and a library card. You could even put in some saxophone flints—I could give you mine—and you could put some Band-Aids 'cause when you're a geek you get beat up . . ." She trails off pitifully. There is a moment of silence as we all stare at this rare moment of vulnerability. No one knows what to say. Except, as usual, Susan.

"Oh, knock it off, Mags! Too many Lifetime specials for you! If you're going to imagine a role for yourself, you should definitely go for Drama Queen, you've got that down pat!"

I just watch to see what will happen. Suddenly, Magenta smiles and says, "Oh well, just an idea," and we all crack up and the tension is gone.

We are having a great time when Evan suddenly asks, "How come the man was in our basement anyway?"

Shit. Think fast. I do. "Oh! The kiln. He was looking around for one of his own, and got a list of people who had them in their homes. He wanted to see how it fit." It works. I think. I don't know for sure because I turn away, suddenly very busy scratching a fictitious mosquito bite on my right ankle. After a minute, the chatter resumes, and I excuse myself to start planning my new pieces. One piece of information I do not share with the kids or anyone is the dollar amount that Mr. Soltes mentioned when he referred to my pieces: four figures. Of course, that's quite a spread, anything from $1,000 to $9,999, right? Also, I guess there's some sort of commission involved. But right now, any version of four figures sounds like the lottery to me. I ask Susan if she wants to walk me home by tempting her with the leftover muffins I know are on the kitchen counter.

"Let me guess," she says, when we are out of earshot, "there's more."

"I want to tell you about something," I begin. "Actually, it's some*one.*" Susan's face is neutral. She lets me tell her about Ken, my beginning feelings, my misgivings as well. Just like Ken did, she questions the appropriateness. I tell her he was first to bring that up. "Score one for him, then," she says, and then adds, "Or two or ten or however many that lovesick expression of yours says the man's up to." I laugh. She takes my hand. But she also doesn't let me off the hook.

"I am concerned. It's not just your marital status," she adds, "although that counts. From what you've told me about Alan, the relationship is pretty toxic and it may never recover, but I don't want to see you or the kids get hurt. I don't want you to do something you're not proud of—if this is a good thing, then you ought to do it right, when the time is right, you know?" Of course I know. I give Susan a hug and thank her, tell her that she is such a good friend and I have a lot to think over. She doesn't push it. Only tells me it's her pleasure. But when I go up the steps to the house, I hear her ask, "Wait a minute, you mean the leftover muffins were just a ruse?"

I WORK ALL through Memorial Day weekend. Luckily, the kids are invited to all sorts of events and don't even complain. Ken calls and I feel a twinge of guilt, but before I can dwell on it he suggests that I sculpt a vase with a cooking motif. I love the idea. So I run around collecting food-related items all day, everything from a cooking thermometer to measuring spoons to chopsticks. Then I feel guilty that I haven't even been to visit Alan once, and I tell myself that as soon as school is over I will be more vigilant about that. In my defense, Alan hasn't called once, and he and his mom have my number.

Bebe is amazing. By Tuesday morning, I have her trained to understand most of the nuances of drying, cooling, and glazing, and she will be able to speed up the process by helping when I am at school. My goal is to have three new pieces to photograph by the end of the week. Things are going so smoothly, almost too smoothly, that I begin to worry. Everything is falling just a little too conveniently into place. By midweek my anxiety level matches the latest color on the terror threat scale, orange, and Bebe notices. As I leave for school, she tells me not to worry. Actually, she quotes one of her gurus. "Where there is great love there are always miracles." I want to believe Bebe, I really do. As it turns out, it's a good thing I don't, because she couldn't be more wrong.

THIRTY-ONE

at the end of the school day, my usual routine, if you can call it that after only two weeks as the sole art teacher, is to check all the projects just to make sure they are intact, rather than risk the tears of some poor first grader who *thought* he used enough glue. After that, I clean up, which takes about an hour, depending on the materials used. All in all, I've managed to head for home by four o'clock this week, and I'm right on schedule with my pieces for Mr. Soltes. Today is Wednesday, and for the first time I'm running late, because I've been gathering materials for the last of my themed pieces, the one I plan to call *School Project.* It will have all the things parents are familiar with by the time their kids finish middle school: feathers, Popsicle sticks, LEGOs, pipe cleaners, felt, glue sticks, markers, and so on. In fact, I might actually make it in the shape of a rectangle (cheeseboard?) and call it *Diorama.* By the time I grab my purse and head out, it's close to 4:30 and my cell phone, which is set to vibrate, hums and buzzes. I look down and see my home number flashing, and I also see that I have nine new messages.

"Hello? Bebe is that—" I am immediately cut off. It's my daughter. She is agitated.

"Mother! Where are you?"

"Why? What's wrong?"

"I've been trying you for an hour!"

"Lauren, what is it, baby? I'm at school. Why didn't you call the school?"

"I *did* call the school. They said they couldn't find you." Damn. Eleanor. She probably didn't even try. How could she do that?

"Lauren, tell me what's going on. What's the emergency? Is Evan okay?"

"Evan's fine. It's Daddy."

"Lauren, baby, hold on. I'm on my way home."

"No, Mommy. You have to go to the hospital. They said to come right away."

"Why? What is it?"

"Daddy knows. He knows who he is. He knows us."

FOR ONCE, I beat Alan's mom to Bergen General. In the emergency room, I tell them who I am and they say just a minute. I have so many questions, the first being, why is he here? Nobody said that when his memory returned there'd be any physical problems. A nurse tells me to follow her and leads me to a large room with curtained-off beds, each in its own bay, and suddenly there he is, and I know right away that he is himself again. I can't say how I know, I just do; it's in his mannerisms, his posture, the way he reclines on the bed. Even from a distance, it's clear that he's Alan. The doctors and nurses are pretty much hovering around him, going in and out of the bay with excitement. They are monitoring and checking, and I just sort of watch for a minute, thinking that it is monumental, this waking; this returning to the world. Alan sees me and raises a hand to wave. Dr. Morris turns and ushers me over to Alan's side. "Alan?" I squeak. It is déjà vu, and I am suddenly terrified. "Hey, Bits," he responds. Just that. So simple, a phrase he might have said a thousand times in the past fifteen years that meant absolutely nothing and now it's as if he's said, "I know the meaning of life." It is that powerful. I start to cry, the emotion just floods out of me. Dr. Morris hands me a tissue and puts his arm around me.

"Why is he here?" I manage to sniffle.

"Well, I think Alan may have had a sort of panic attack. Apparently, he was at home in his mother's house when his memory came back and the confusion caused him to think he was having a heart attack, so he called 911 and here he is." Alan's mother comes in then, calmly holding a cup of coffee, and it turns out she's been here for two hours, the time it took for the kids to finally track me down. Dr. Morris explains that Alan gave our number as his emergency contact, but when I couldn't be reached they called his mom. Marian and I exchange a glance, but for once we are just quiet with each other. Dr. Morris assures us that everything looks fine, but that he's going to admit Alan just to be on the safe side, and run some tests. He will stay tomorrow, and then he can come home on Friday morning.

I notice that Alan is no longer in his casts, and I ask about this. "We saw the orthopedist on Monday," Marian offers. "He goes to physical therapy three evenings a week."

Alan doesn't say a thing. Then after a minute, he turns to his mother. "Could I get some water?"

We sit in silence. After a few more minutes, I leave the room to call the kids and wait for them both to get on the phone so I don't have to repeat myself. I tell them it's true, that their father seems to have his memory back, and that he'll be coming home on Friday.

"Okay," Lauren says.

"Did he ask about us?" This from Evan.

"Of course he did," I lie, "first thing." That seems to satisfy them, and I tell them to tell Bebe I'll be home a little late. I go back into the room, but they are taking Alan for some sort of scan, so Marian and I go back to the waiting room. When he returns, they are ready to transfer him to a real room. Finally, we are told to follow them up to the third floor. It takes a long time before Alan is settled and checked in. He has the room to himself for now. By the time I walk up to his side of the room, his eyes are closed, and when I take his hand he opens them and says, "Wow, I'm beat. This bed really sucks. Think you could bring me my own pillow tomorrow?" I drop his hand, trying hard not to let my heart fill up with ice. *Yes I'm fine,* I want to say, *and your children are fine, too.* But I bite back the words. Alan just settles back, throws an arm over his eyes, and appears to sleep.

When I get home, it's late, past twelve, and the kids are asleep. Bebe hands me some tea and I take it upstairs, crawl into bed, and have a dream-riddled sleep. In the morning, I call in to school and explain my situation to the answering machine, then head back to Bergen General.

Alan looks extremely comfortable in his bed. He's got his cell phone and a mug with coffee and his hair is combed and he's reading the *New York Times.* I walk over to him and he lays the paper down.

"You look different," he says.

"I do?" I touch my hair, smooth it down. "A lot's happened."

Alan looks down, then, into his coffee. He looks like he wants to go back to reading. He doesn't ask me what's happened. He doesn't ask how I've been. He doesn't ask about the kids. He does ask if I've thought to bring his razor. And then he says, "So, through all of this, how's my mom been?"

I STAY WITH Alan for most of the day. It's amazing how exhausting it can be to do nothing all day. Three times I try to bring up the subject of our home situation and three times Alan changes the subject.

"I'm working now," I say, the first time, "at Evan's school." Alan just stares back and nods.

"I'm the art teacher," I continue, hoping for some response.

"That's nice for you," he says, nodding, and then asks if he can get some juice. I bring him the juice and try again.

"You know, Alan, I'm not just working for the joy of it. There are other reasons." Alan responds as if he hasn't heard me, complaining that the room is too hot even though he's got the thermostat set to the coolest setting. He asks if I can get them to raise the air. I get up to do it and look directly at him before I go. "We'll have to talk about it sometime," I say.

His mother comes later in the morning. We sidestep each other, taking turns going out for breaks or for coffee. We meet with the doctors. Alan's vital signs are good. He will continue to need physical therapy, but if all's well and he continues to improve, he can go home in the morning. Home. Our home. This time Alan does not protest. In fact, he asks if we have an adequate supply of cranberry juice, Dole fruit bars, and some of his other favorite foods. His real, 2006, favorite foods. There is no question as to where Alan will return. I tell everyone that

I will bring Alan home in the afternoon, that I have to work until 2:30, and that I will come right after school. Nobody protests. Not even Marian. I take a deep breath and try to process this. I want to talk to Alan about our lives, about our finances, about how we are going to proceed. I also want to know about the Vicodin. The insurance company has raised questions, and if they refuse to pay for Alan's medical care, then we might as well just go right from the rehab to the shelter. But I don't bring up any of this, because how can I? It is too soon and his mother is there and I don't want to look like a barbarian. Besides, we will have endless hours to discuss this at home. But a little part of me thinks that a real man would at least ask how his family is doing. I mean, if he can worry about his beard.

Finally, I confess to myself how I really feel. The idea of Alan coming home is like a huge boulder sitting on my chest. But there is nothing I can do. Alan is my husband and my children's father, and I can't just suggest he get a room at the Holiday Inn. For better or worse, that's what we said. On my way home, the melancholy sets in, and I do what needs to be done. I call Ken on his cell.

"Hello."

"Hey." I sound like I've just been given two weeks to live.

"How's he doing?"

"Good. He's doing well. They say he can come home tomorrow." There is silence. He doesn't know what to say. Neither do I.

"Barb, it'll be all right."

"No, no, it won't be all right. I don't know what it'll be, but not all right."

"Were you able to talk to him about . . . anything?"

"No. How could I? I can't. The truth is, he's my husband, and six weeks ago I couldn't even imagine another life—and now, even if that's all I think about, I'm still his wife, and he doesn't know that anything's changed. I'm his wife. That's it. That's what I have to be right now." More silence.

"So what are you saying?"

"God, Ken, don't make this so hard. You know what I'm saying. Maybe he's a real shit, maybe he doesn't deserve my loyalty, but I have to be there for him now. I can't just abandon him." I hear him sigh. A big one. The tears are running down my face. I hear him clear his throat. I have an ache in mine.

"Are you coming back to school?"

"Yes, of course. I wouldn't do that to you. In fact, I told Alan that I won't be able to come tomorrow until late afternoon. I explained about the job."

Now Ken's voice is all business. "Well, you can amend that. Tomorrow is parent conferences all day and specialties are excused, but we'd appreciate it if you were back on Monday."

"Oh, I forgot about the conferences. Okay, I'll see you Monday, then."

"Fine."

"Ken?"

"Yes?"

"I'm sorry."

"I know." There is a click. I lean my head down on the steering wheel and cry.

ON THE WAY HOME, as I turn down Autumn Court, I see poor little Aly outside her house again, and I feel so badly. She and Lauren used to have so much fun. I am not relishing the idea of another afternoon of the kids furtively asking questions about their dad and them trying to deal with their mixed emotions and me trying to normalize everything. Suddenly, I decide to take a risk, and two minutes later I am marching into the house with a stunned Allison in tow, calling to Lauren to come downstairs. When she enters the hall and sees Aly, her initial expression is shock, but then, thankfully, she smiles.

"Okay, look," I say, turning from one to the other. "*You* are sitting in your room alone and *you* are sitting on your lawn alone and there is no reason in the world why two almost-thirteen-year-old girls who have known each other as long as you two have can't have their differences and still be friends. Now, I want you both to go upstairs and hang out together, and don't come out till you figure it out." I am expecting a protest. A big one. Instead, Lauren crooks her finger and rolls her eyes but it's not really *at* Aly, more *with* her and *at me,* and she says, "C'mon Al," and Aly hops up the stairs and then the two of them disappear. Wow. Did I do that? That was too easy. I barely have time to congratulate myself when there is a knock at the back door. I had forgotten that Ross was coming to digitally photograph my pieces, which, thanks to Bebe, now number four. Ross is accompanied by Susan, who just puts her arms around me and hugs me like she knows I need it bad.

"Do you have a sixth sense for needy people or am I wearing a sign?" I ask her.

"No, nothing like that. I just know you or Bebe always have something baking." While Ross goes down to photograph the platters, Susan and I dig into Bebe's famous powdered sugar and almond cookies, and I catch her up. She doesn't say anything, just nods when I explain about Alan and what I had to tell Ken.

"You have to do what you have to do," she says. "I don't have any profound words, no quotes." She smiles and tilts her head toward Bebe in the next room. "I'll leave that to our resident philosopher."

I smile back and then suddenly from the family room we hear Bebe call, "Famous saying, Miss Susan." Susan gasps and smiles broadly. "Our character is what we do when we think no one is looking." Susan shakes her head. Bebe comes to the door, and she is smiling. We all laugh at the truth of Bebe's words. We're still laughing when Ross comes up and asks if I want him to send the photos, too, and I say, "You betcha," as I lead him to the computer.

Just then, a door opens upstairs and loud music fills the house, along with my daughter's voice as she bellows, "Attention, friends and family, now presenting the famous model, Mademoiselle Allison!" The song playing is quickly recognizable as the famous striptease song "Big Spender" (the one that begins, "The minute you walked in the joint . . ."). Susan and I walk into the hall and Ross follows. We look up. At the top of the stairs, now sashaying down, is sweet, innocent Allison, dressed up and made up to look like Miss Teen Slut of the Year. And she's working it. I gasp. I look quickly over at Susan, who is laughing. Then I look over at Ross, who is riveted. I want to cover his eyes with my hand.

Allison is strutting, she has a boa and she's twirling it, crouching down now and then and leaning against the railing. In the background, I hear Lauren laughing. All I can think of is that Aly's parents will kill us both. But then I look at Aly. She is so happy. She is laughing hysterically, too. In fact, in a minute, Lauren rushes down and they collapse together in a fit of hysterics. At some point, they call out, "We didn't know Ross was here!" Then they laugh some more. Ross, who is now blushing, starts backing up toward the kitchen. It's then that I notice that my daughter is also dressed rather strangely.

"Hey, giggleheads, stand up." They are still laughing, holding their stomachs.

"Lauren, let me see what you're wearing." Lauren drags herself up. I am shocked once again. She is wearing a gray knee-length skirt from my closet, a cute little Ralph Lauren three-button white shirt, a pink cardigan from two years ago, closed-toe shoes, and fake pearls. She looks like a preteen Young Republican. And she looks beautiful.

"We switched! Cool, right?" And with that, they head back upstairs. But not before Lauren calls out, "Bye, Ross. I'll come by later." Susan and I exchange a glance and look over at Ross, who grins for just a second then turns an even deeper shade of red and heads quickly toward the computer. Cool, indeed.

THIRTY-TWO

Since Friday is a parent conference day, I decide that the kids would be better served by coming with me to pick up their dad than by going to school. For all their indifference, once we get into the car, they are remarkably excited and upbeat.

"Does he look different?"

"Does he have tubes?"

"Does the place smell weird?"

"Can we go for sushi after?" This, from Lauren, who I notice has steadily toned down her whole appearance. Gone are the purple nails and fake tattoos. She still sports several play earrings running up and down her earlobe, but her outfit is remarkably boring: just a simple pink T-shirt and jeans.

Alan doesn't know we are coming this early, since I thought I had to work today, and I'm hoping the surprise of seeing his kids will snap him into a little husbandly, fatherly mode. Evan goes in first, then Lauren, and I bring up the rear. At first glance, I think I'm in the wrong room. Sitting on the bed next to Alan in a very intimate way is a woman. She is not a nurse. She is in street clothes. And she is a stranger. In a chair next to the bed is Mrs. Lerner.

As the kids come in, there is a moment of complete paralysis; nobody moves. Then, at the same moment that Evan says

"Daddy?" all hell breaks loose. The woman jumps up, as does Alan's mom. I look from Alan to Mrs. Lerner to this woman then back to Alan again. He doesn't move, doesn't say a word, doesn't shout his kids' names with delight, just looks helplessly at me. In fact, everyone is looking at me. And, suddenly, I know. It just all falls apart, like a series of dominoes, one toppling over onto the other, all the pieces coming to rest on a most unbelievable truth. In that moment, I am many things: wife, daughter-in-law, and also "the last to know." But first of all, I am a mother. So I march closer to the bed, get in between Alan and the kids, and turn to them.

"This is not a good time to see Daddy, okay? I want you to go down to the lobby and wait for me there." Something in my voice tells them to do as I say. I recognize this voice; it is my old Mommy voice. And yet it is a new voice, too. With a little shove, I turn the kids and usher them out the door. Lauren looks back at her dad, hesitates a minute, then gives him a look filled with pain. She puts her arm around her brother and they leave.

"Bitsy," Alan says, and the way he says it changes it from a name to a novel. It is at once an admission and a confession: full of sorrow and regret. But I hear one thing above anything else: weakness. I wait for more, but there is no more coming. Apparently, he will not even attempt to explain. "Bitsy" is all I will get. There is so much I want to say, to ask, but suddenly I have just one question. I turn to the woman I don't know.

"Let me guess," I say, "I bet you live in Hackensack. Am I right?" I remember Mort asking me about real estate in Hackensack, I remember the extra long pause and his urgency to move on, and I shake my head. A stranger was protecting me; a stranger was kinder to me than my own husband. The woman looks surprised and unsure. She looks from Alan to Marian. "Never mind," I tell her, laughing to myself. "I already know." There is silence now. I have a kind of smile on my face, a grimace-smile, a little twisted, a little strained.

"Her name is Yvonne. She's a lawyer." This from my mother-in-law. Amazingly, she is not even a bit embarrassed, which at least Yvonne has the courtesy to be. Marian Lerner is defiant, almost like *she* has had the affair. Suddenly, I start to laugh. It's a little crazy, but a good crazy, because I realize I don't really care about Yvonne at all. I've already dealt with Alan's betrayal; it started years ago when he pulled away from me with his secrets. He never fully committed to me; he couldn't. He was too confused, and I was so focused on the picture that I just refused to see him for what he was: an imposter. So I'm laughing because it doesn't hurt the way it should. Because I'm not devastated. But I'm also not a damn saint. I inch closer to Alan's bed and petite Yvonne backs up a bit further.

"Alan, I'm really glad Yvonne's a lawyer," I say softly, "because you're going to need one."

I turn around and head for the door and at the last minute I stop. I look back at Mrs. Lerner. I should go, really, she doesn't matter. And yet my feet do a little pivot and I find myself walking purposefully back toward my mother-in-law. She actually shrinks. Does she think I'm going to sock her? It gives me strength.

"Oh, Marian," I say. "Shame on you. Shame on you for not loving your son enough to teach him to be a proper man. Everything you said you despised in your husband you now sanction in your son? You're not only a hypocrite, you're a pathetic, bitter, sad little woman. The only positive thing I can say is that for the last fifteen years you've been such an awful grandmother that Evan and Lauren have been spared from getting to know you. You are mean-spirited and judgmental." I look at Alan. "And you should have told her so a long time ago. If not for me, then for your children." Back to Marian. "I pity your students. They must be celebrating like hell every day you're not there. But mostly I pity you." I stretch out my arm and point to Alan, but I don't take my eyes off his mother. "See this?" I say, pointing at him, "This is your doing, your handiwork. A plus. Well done." As I turn, I do not even dignify Yvonne with a look.

I AM SHAKING as I walk toward the door. It was a well-delivered speech, but even so the tears start to fall before I exit the room. By the time I'm in the elevator, I am crying out loud, and I continue to wipe away tears as I proceed toward the lobby, ignoring the curious looks and awkward stares, and then I remember the kids. I dash into the nearest ladies room and lock myself in a stall and there I sit, composing myself. I feel as if I'm crying away years of resentment, cleansing all the unhappiness from my system. Somewhere amid the betrayal and the anger and the humiliation, a wonderful notion is beginning to form; a small, syrupy liquid feeling that spreads from my stomach to my heart like anesthesia but with the opposite effect. Instead of numbing me, it awakens every sense, every nerve, and with each passing moment announces, I'm free. I'm free. I'm free. I'm free!

IN THE CAR on the way home, no one speaks. I want to wait for questions, not deliver answers. Mostly, I want to stay conscious of not trashing Alan, because what child needs to think their dad is a big shit? Better to frame it that just because Mom and Dad don't get along it doesn't mean that they don't have two parents who love them. I've seen enough *Dr. Phil*s to know that's the best gift I can give them. Nevertheless, I have a sweet daydream in which Samantha tells Tabitha that Darrin is a big fat cheat and together they wrinkle both their noses and turn him into a lovely puss-eating warthog. Only that would never happen because Darrin would never cheat. And Samantha defied the Witches Council over and over again to defend her position as his wife. I defy the great Beberman Council and what do I get? A bankrupt adulterer. Something's just a little wrong with this picture. Possibly it's time to let Samantha go altogether.

BEBE IS WAITING expectantly when we come home and is clearly dismayed when she does not see Alan and is greeted with stony silence. Lauren brushes past with obvious annoyance, banging into cabinets and doors in her path. Evan is more somber, but equally uncommunicative. We all ignore Casey, too. Bebe calls after me, "Famous saying . . . ," but I cut her off with a sharp "Not now, Bebe. No Buddha, no Gandhi, no sayings. Please." She shrinks back. I am a little sorry, but I am in no mood for platitudes. I follow the kids up to their rooms and declare a family meeting. No more of this solitary stuff, I say. No more moody silences and not talking and dealing with our emotions alone. We are a family, and right now that's me and you and you, I say, and we will get through this together. Evan joins me on Lauren's bed.

"Look, I know you're hurting," I say, "and so am I. But we're not the first family to have problems and we won't be the last. The most important thing for you to know is that I love you and Daddy loves you and you've done nothing wrong."

"I hate Daddy," Lauren says. "He was cheating, right?" I look at Evan. Does he even know what cheating means? I sigh. My poor kids. They shouldn't have to be dealing with this. They should be worrying about baseball and pimples and passing English.

"Daddy has had a very hard year. Sometimes when adults feel a lot of pressure they don't handle it well, they don't always do the right thing. Daddy has made a lot of mistakes this year. So have I. It doesn't matter if he was cheating or not, the main thing is"—I take a big breath—"you need to know that Daddy and I don't love each other like we should, like two people deserve to. Sometimes that happens to people. But it never happens between moms and dads and their children. We could never stop loving you, you know that right?"

"Are you gonna get a divorce?" This from Evan. I look at the two of them, think of a million ways to answer, and figure it's best to tell what I know to be the truth. In a very soft voice I whisper, "Yes." And there it is. Lauren reaches out and puts her arms around me and then Evan does the same, and I envelop them back and we just sit there, cross-legged and hugging, dripping tears on Lauren's pin-and-white bedspread. Then there is a knock on the door. The door is actually open and Bebe is standing there, knocking on the frame. She is carrying her knapsack, the one she took from under her bed at the horrible house, and I think she is so insulted that she means to leave.

"Oh, Bebe, I'm sorry I was so short with you." Bebe walks over to the bed and begins to dump out the contents of her bag.

"Oh, Bebe not mind. Want to show you something. Bebe tries to be so smart. Family is thinking quotes from Buddha, right? But Bebe is too much pride, not honest. Here is famous sayings." One by one, little books drop onto the bed from Bebe's sack. They are all pocket-sized, and they are all almost entirely the same: *Chicken Soup for the Soul.* Abridged *Chicken Soup for the Soul.* Pocket-sized *Chicken Soup for the Soul.* Then there is Chicken Soup for the College Soul and the Golfer Soul and the Middle-aged Soul. It goes on and on. She must have twenty books. The Best Friend Soul and Teacher Soul and even the Irish Soul. I start to laugh.

"Bebe, you've got to be kidding. All of your sayings come from these?" Bebe looks mournful. "All from this, from Chickie Soup." Now the kids are looking and laughing, too. Evan picks one up and begins to read. " 'The two most important things a parent can give a child . . .' " All of us stop and look. Evan is reading. I get tears in my eyes and Lauren smiles and we share a glance. He goes on. "I think this is wrong. It says 'roots and wings' but I was thinking the two most important things would be PlayStation and TiVo." We are all smiling, and I go over to give Evan a big hug. Then Bebe starts to leave, but I call her back.

"Oh, Bebe! Why are you telling us this now?"

Bebe looks back. "So many lies. Everyone so unhappy. Bebe make lies, too. Famous saying: 'Time is always right to do right thing.' "

van's Little League team is in the play-offs. The last place I want to be is at Veteran's Park, sitting in the bleachers, pretending to watch the game while fielding nosy questions from the other parents, but we need some normalcy and Lauren is sleeping later and later these days so there is really no excuse for me to just drop Ev off, especially since I have only made it to one game this season. Because the game is at ten, I am spared the usual crush; an earlier game is generally a quieter game—not because all of us type A, obsessive, enmeshed parents are still asleep, but because we're more likely carpooling to any number of games, recitals, or lessons with our other children. Each field in the large sports complex that makes up Veteran's Park is a sea of color. Evan's team is in bright primary green, with Walsh Plumbing (their sponsor) plastered in large white letters on their shirts and hats. They are playing DiBella Trucking, who is in purple. Watching Evan make his way out to left field, I get a shiver of pride. Despite everything that's gone on, despite the discord in our home, or maybe because of it, Evan is at home on this field, in his uniform, and with his peers. It is not that everyone cheers when he arrives; it is more subtle, this fitting in, this belonging. It is the way that Greg Babson, the pitcher, good-naturedly grabs him by the shoulders near the watercooler, and how Jason Grimes, the first baseman, tosses him the ball even before he hustles out to left field. It is in Evan's gait, his posture, his easy smile. And I think it's a miracle.

THE COACH IS batting flies and grounders out to the team. He is a big guy, the catcher's dad, I think, and his size reminds me of another big guy. I look down at my hands, massage them, and think about Ken. I've really screwed things up, first by encouraging him and then by abruptly cutting him off. Well, I've made the decision to contact a family therapist—I think we can all benefit from that—so maybe there will be a point when I can ask about relationships, about how they work, since I clearly don't have a clue.

The umpire shows up and the game is about to get under way. A woman slides into the bleachers next to me and reflexively I shy away. It's a gesture calculated to reduce conversation, but the woman, who I don't recognize, is just as uninterested in small talk as I am. She has a cup of coffee and a look that says it's her first and she hasn't yet had a sip, plus she has a tote full of what looks to be paperwork. I glance back at the game, grateful to be sitting next to a working mom, and not some chatty Miss Junior League. After a few moments, a cell phone rings, and in trying to answer, the woman upsets her coffee cup and her tote. Papers fall and begin to fly everywhere. "Oh God," she yells, dropping her cell phone as she tries to grab the pages. I hop down to help and end up running back and forth like a squirrel after nuts, grabbing and stepping on pages as the wind makes a game of it. Finally, we seem to corral the mess, and both of us stand there breathless, me afraid to lift either of my feet, since they are still acting as paperweights, and she, covered in coffee, and panting. We are quite a picture, and despite the early hour, we both begin to laugh. Then she thanks me as she leans down and helps me lift one foot, then the other, and gathers up a now mud-covered clump of official-looking documents.

"I'm so sorry," she says. "I shouldn't have brought my work to the game, but I've missed so many and Trevor had his heart set on my being here."

"No problem," I offer. "I'm in the same boat."

"Oh, are you also one of those rare creatures who work?" she asks. I'm about to say no, I don't work, when I suddenly remember that I actually *do* have a job.

"Yes," I say, proudly. "I teach art at the elementary school and I, um, sculpt."

"Wow," she says, "and here I thought being a divorce lawyer was impressive. I'm Janice. Janice Smart." I reach out and shake Janice's hand, already knowing that in some big, spiritual way this meeting was fate. "Barbara," I say, "Barbara Lerner." And then I start to giggle. "Lerner and Smart?" I add. "I think we were meant to meet."

EVAN GETS ON base every time he comes to bat, with the highlight being a line drive to center field for a stand-up double, followed by an overthrow, which ultimately allows him to score, and earns him an inside-the-park home-run. The green team wins easily, and when the coach asks to take the kids for pizza, I happily say yes. Evan dumps his bat bag and glove in my arms and with a quick "Thanks, Mom" he's off. I watch with tears in my eyes as he and the other boys high-five and smack and shove each other as they make their way to the coaches' cars. Janice and I have already made a date for lunch, and I have somewhat unashamedly informed her that I will need her professional services as well.

At home, there is a note from Lauren that says she is next door, at the Rabinowitzes', and again I find myself smiling and shaking my head. A few months ago, Lauren couldn't even say Ross's name without groaning. I am feeling so good that I decide to call my mom. My parents had very mixed reactions when I told them Alan had come out of his fugue. Of course, they said, "Thank God," and "Now you can begin to straighten things out," but they also became very curt and awkward. I don't think they really believe that we will be okay financially, and they are probably calculating how that might affect them. The older they get, the more nervous they get financially, and I could almost hear them stepping back, inch by inch, even over the phone.

What would I do if my mom stopped paying Bebe? That's one disaster I don't even want to contemplate. When I told them about the art dealer and my pottery, I could *hear* the color come back, feel them relaxing, once again, over the phone. I wonder if they realize how transparent they've become. Or maybe I just see them differently, through a different lens— through Barbara's eyes, instead of Bitsy's. Of course, there was no way I ever would have predicted my mother's reaction to my sculpting success; it completely stunned me.

"Well, that's wonderful, dear, I told you years ago to focus on your art."

I couldn't speak. "You did?" I finally asked, unsure whether to scream or laugh.

"Yes, yes, I did."

Now I was angry. "And when exactly was that, Mom? Was it before or after you told me to get a teaching degree? Or was it when you told me to stay home and be a full-time mother?"

Silence.

"Well, I feel sure I must have encouraged you. You were so talented. And a woman needs something for herself."

I am dumbfounded. There is no other way to feel. My mother comes into her own at the age of sixty, twenty years after I'm out of the house, and now she thinks she modeled self-actualization all along? I take deep breaths. I let it go. There is just too much to deal with in the present to try to go back and fix the past. And now I wonder how she will take the news that Alan has been cheating, that I plan to leave him.

Although my dad never liked Alan, and looking at his financial shortcomings only solidified that, I will not get any bonus points for announcing my intentions to divorce him. My parents may not be in favor of Alan, but neither do they favor divorce. So, basically, it's a lose-lose. But it has to be done. And who knows: Since my mother has become Mrs. Unpredictable—no, make that *Ms.* Unpredictable—I may be surprised. Although it is Saturday, I know she'll be at work. I don't have to worry about my dad answering the phone. He can give up his practice and depend entirely on my mother's flair for placing domestics to support them, but he will never reduce himself to answering the phones, which, in his opinion, is always done by a woman.

"Evelyn's Eminent Helpers, may I help you?"

"Mom."

"Bitsy? Is that you dear?"

"It's me."

"What's wrong?"

"Nothing. Well, that's not really true. I have something to tell you."

"Are you sick?"

"No, Mom. Just listen. Alan and I are getting a divorce."
Big silence. And then I hear a little whisper.

"What? Mom, I can hardly hear you." She speaks a little louder.

"I *said,* good for you."

"Really?"

"Yes, you're too good for him." And now the tears are just spilling out.

"Oh, Mom." I think I hear her sniffling, too.

"I want you to be happy Bitsy."

I wipe my eyes and my nose, clear my throat, and say, "Well, then, I need you to do something for me. I need you to stop calling me Bitsy. I want you to call me Barbara. I'm Barbara, okay?"

"Fine. Yes, I can do that. I have to go now Bit . . . I mean Barbara, your dad needs me."

"Okay, bye. And thanks, Mom."

I hang up the phone. Then I start to cry all over again. Sad tears, happy tears, cleansing tears—who knows? Probably all of the above. Bebe comes down into the kitchen and hands me a tissue and without asking goes to make a pot of coffee. She sits down at the kitchen table and for once she doesn't say a single word, just reaches across, covers my hand with hers, and squeezes.

ON MONDAY I go back to school. Ann is back, on crutches and in a brace. She is supposed to just be visiting for an hour but keeps trying to do too much, and I keep forcing her to stop. Although her hip surgery was just two weeks ago, she insists that the doctors want her to move as much as possible. By lunchtime, when she realizes I won't be bullied, she resigns her-self to directing while I follow her instructions. We are cleaning up and out for the end of the year. Ann, as always, is sweet and wonderful. I tell her a bit about Alan and Ken, and she knows just how to listen. It occurs to me that when my life was all "perfect" I basically had no friends, and now that everything is upside down I have two wonderful friendships, one with Susan Rabinowitz and another with Ann, not to mention the begin-ning of a third with my lawyer, Janice. How this happened is a complete mystery to me, but it occurs to me that needing other people might have something to do with it—and, of course, shedding the need to put out that perfect press release helps.

Ken is clearly avoiding me. He is never in the art wing or the parking lot or the teacher's room. I see him at a dress rehearsal for the end-of-the-year music show, but I am in the back and he is at the front, and sometimes I think I catch him looking at me. At those times he smiles briefly and then looks away. I want to go to him, to explain, and to tell him that I am free, but I don't know how. I feel like I've led him around on an emotional leash, first one way and then the other; how would he respond? Eleanor seems to sense something is up or, more accurately, that things between Ken and I have soured. I know this mainly because she is happy and humming all the time.

NEAR THE END of the week, Mr. Soltes calls with good news. They have a sponsor, a very generous sponsor, who has already asked to acquire two of my pieces, and my very own show will take place in ten weeks. I decide to go over to Susan's and tell her the news. Halfway there, I run into Susan, Ross, and Lau-ren, who are coming to find me.

I AM SITTING at the kitchen table, still unable to comprehend what I've just heard. Susan, Ross, and Lauren are looking at me, waiting.

"Do you want me to rewind it and play it again?" This from Ross. I look at him, somewhat in a daze, then at Susan, who shrugs, and, finally, at Lauren.

"Honey?" I ask.

"I'm fine, Mom, really." She smiles, then looks at Ross. They share another grin.

"Maybe you better play it one more time." Susan says this to her son. I just nod my head. Ross presses Rewind and the tape whirs and then there is a click.

"Wait, Ross," I say. "Tell me again how you managed to tape this?"

"Well, that's the part Mom says I have to be careful with," Ross says sheepishly as Susan rests her head in her hands, shaking it back and forth. "I didn't realize it would work so well, that I'd be able to listen in on conversations in someone else's house. I mean, I knew it was sensitive and all, but now that I've done it, Mom says I can't use it because it's illegal to eavesdrop." He trails off.

"Ya think?" his mother asks.

"But you knew it was my goal! I told you it was going to work. I told you I was going to call it Super Spy and I was going to need a patent!"

"Ross, for God's sake! I thought you were going to be able to hear conversations a few feet away, maybe ten or twelve feet across the yard, not tap into conversations clear across the street in someone else's house!" They are both yelling, both somewhat disgusted, but underneath I notice something else: They are both a little proud. Ross has managed to come up with a device that can hear through walls.

"Well, you're right about the walls part, but it doesn't exactly work at such a far distance." We all look back at him, Susan especially.

"What does that mean?"

Ross hangs his head. "I kind of got a little closer."

"Oy. *How* close, Ross?" Susan says this last part through gritted teeth.

"Sort of right outside their family room window. But it was a closed window, you know!"

"Oh, Ross, now you're not only an eavesdropper, you're a Peeping Tom." Ross turns bright red.

"I didn't *look* inside; I just put the microphone there. Besides, it's going to work from across the street some day, just as soon as I get the kinks out."

"Please! Just leave it the way it is, kinks and all, before you really get into trouble."

"Can I hear that tape again now, please?" I wasn't even sure I wanted to, but I thought it best to break up this little mother/son conflict.

Ross presses Play and the tape rolls. I instantly recognize Peter Winston's voice. He is calling, yelling to someone.

"You tell that little pussy to get his ass down here."

I hear Peggy respond. "Peter, please." She is crying, her voice is high-pitched. Then there are some sounds, unrecognizable, and then Keith Winston. He, too, is yelling, but his voice is higher, frantic, almost desperate.

"I don't care what you do to me. I'm not scared of you anymore. You wanna hit me? Go ahead. I can't pretend anymore.

I'm not you or Trev or Darren, I don't like sports and I don't like fighting. I'm just me."

"No son of mine is gonna be a sissy, do you hear? I told you to stop babying him, didn't I? Didn't I tell you that?" It's obvious that he has said this to his wife, because Keith jumps in, still shouting.

"Leave her alone, okay? I may not be as tough as you but you're just a ——." We can't hear this part. "You think you can scare everyone, but you can't."

Then Peter.

"What the hell happened to you? I thought you were okay when you messed around with that girl across the street. I thought, Thank God, my kid is finally normal. What was that?"

Keith Winston is screaming now.

"What was that? You think that was normal? That was assault, Dad! You don't just go around touching girls! She was a nice girl and she didn't deserve that—and you had no right to threaten her father, either. I was so scared that I wasn't like you or Trevor or Darren that I tried to be like you. But after, all I felt like was an animal. It made me sick. You make me sick."

"If we all make you so sick, you can just take yourself right out of this house and don't come back."

"Fine."

"Peter! Keith!" Peg Winston gives a desperate cry but nothing more. There is a door slamming and the tape goes dead.

ONCE AGAIN, we all sit around the table in silence. Finally, I look at Lauren. "You know, this probably wouldn't hold up in court, but if you want to press charges or something, I think we probably could."

"Oh my God," she says, "that's the last thing I'd want to do. I feel so bad for Keith. Ross taped this two days ago. Where do you think he might have gone?"

I look over at Susan and we share a smile. We have two great kids. One thing is for certain: If Lauren can be more concerned about Keith Winston than her own revenge, she has healed better than I ever thought she would. And Ross taping the Winstons and getting their dirty laundry on record was the tenderest of gifts. As everyone gets up from the table, Lauren comes up behind me and gives me a little hug.

"Thanks, Mommy."

I am thrilled, but it is unexpected. "For what, sweetie?" I ask.

"For not being Mrs. Winston." As good a compliment as any.

A LITTLE LATER, as I am about to go up to bed, Bebe passes me in the hall. "Famous saying," she says, smiling.

I smile back. "Okay," I say, "I'm ready."

"To love deeply in one direction makes us more loving in all others."

I look at Bebe, trying to decipher her meaning. Is she saying that I have done well with the children? That she is proud of me and my relationship with the kids? I don't say a word, but as I start to walk away she calls after me. "In all others. You see? In all others, but *first have to be in one deeply.*" I think I get the picture. Once again, Bebe is trying to prod me along a road I find most difficult to navigate.

"Good night, Bebe," I say, without turning, but she's done the damage. I lay awake for hours, finally falling asleep just before the sun comes up.

THIRTY-FOUR

Sunday afternoon is brutally hot and humid, and I'm feeling cranky because I got so little sleep. I need a break from working at the wheel and it's too hot to bake, so I wander outside, thinking that I will just clean things up in the garden, but the air is stifling and I have to go back inside. Sometime between yesterday and today someone planted a big For Sale sign on the Winston's front lawn, and the sight of it just makes me terribly depressed, especially since I no longer have to think about selling ours. None of us have seen Peter Winston over the last few days, but Lauren says that she's seen Keith at school and playing basketball in the driveway, so I'm hopeful that the family will find their way. My own kids are happy right where they are; home in the air-conditioning, cuddled up with blankets on the couch watching *Adventures in Babysitting* for the hundredth time. Even Casey feels the heat. Normally, he'd be following me around on the off chance I might drop some food or throw him a toy, but my retriever is sprawled out on the marble floor, where it's coolest. Then I have a sort of idea. I know where Ken lives, just over the border in Mahwah, so maybe I will just drive by his house and see if he is outside. Besides, the car will keep me in motion and also cool.

I make my way over to his street and go past his house. It is dead quiet there, too, and so I drive by about a million times, even though I feel like I'm sixteen when I'm doing it. I think maybe he will come out to get the mail or something, which is a big stretch since it's Sunday. I have to go so far as to imagine that he *forgot* to get the mail yesterday. What reason I will give for being there, if he does come out, I have no idea. I don't think that far, I just hope that somehow I can put things in motion. When there is no sight of him, I tell myself to stop being such an infant and I get up the courage to park, walk up to his door, and ring the bell. I still have no idea what I will say, so I'm relieved when there is no answer. Good. This is a sign. I start to walk away when I hear something at the back of the house. Very gingerly, I walk along the side of the house and peek into the backyard and there he is, swimming laps in a simple, rectangular pool. Jesus. There is no way I will be leaving now. I am suddenly filled with purpose. I know this man. He's a good guy. He's probably just putting up a few walls to protect himself from getting hurt. With everything I've been through these past few months, what's the big deal about a few walls? Now all I have to do is convince my feet to follow suit.

I am still working on this when suddenly, out of nowhere, there is a ferocious barking and a huge black blob comes bounding toward me. It is so massive and furry that my thoughts turn to magical beasts, à la Harry Potter and Hogwarts. All I can do is freeze. My arms and elbows contract into my chest, my whole body stiffens, and my head turns away as I brace for the assault. At the last minute, the dog lifts its two front feet and pushes them into my chest and knocks me down right on top of what looks like an azalea bush but feels more like a porcupine. Before I even have the time to fear for my life, the largest tongue I've ever seen proceeds to lick the length of my face over and over again.

Maybe because it tickles or because I realize I'm not going to die today, I start to giggle. Ken hops out of the pool and shouts at the dog. "Baxter. Stop!" The dog ignores him. "Baxter. Bad boy! Enough!" By the time Ken comes over and yanks the dog off me by his collar, Baxter has ruined any chance I might have had at looking decent, let alone gorgeous—and as for sophisticated, well, I seem to have done a fairly good job of sabotaging that all by myself. Through the laughter and dog saliva and with Ken's help, I manage to extricate myself from the bush, which will clearly be going to the little landscape cemetery in the sky, and stand up. I am covered with mud and leaves and mulch. There are scratches, tinted green, all over my arms, possibly one on my face. Quite a sight. Ken, on the other hand, is like a big wet Greek God. Except for a bit of gray hair on his chest and the outlines of two adorable love handles, the rest of him is sculpted and fit. He is wearing board shorts, the kind the Abercrombie & Fitch models wear, with blue and white leaves. And he is dripping. I force myself to look elsewhere.

"Are you okay? Sorry about Baxter. As you can see, he listens really well."

"Oh, no problem. Is he always so protective?"

"He's just excited. He's not used to company. It's pretty much just the two of us." I continue to wipe myself off, shaking little azalea leaves to the ground.

"So what exactly is he? Polar bear? Grizzly?"

"He's a newfie. Newfoundland. Really big, I know. He looks kind of scary, but he's a big mush." Just like you, I want to say, as I look into Ken's eyes. But the moment passes, or he turns away, I'm not sure. Ken takes a few steps, acts interested in the shrubbery, and says, "So, this is quite a surprise." His tone is funny—not hostile, but formal. I try to break the ice.

"Good surprise or bad surprise?" He looks back at me.

"A nice surprise. " Still formal, noncommittal.

"I hope so. I wanted to talk."

"Hey, you know you don't owe me more of an explanation. I get it. I always got it. I got carried away, and that's certainly not your fault. We're good." Now he walks over to the chair and retrieves a towel. Too bad.

"I know. It's not that. I wanted to tell you . . . I want to say . . ." I am at a loss. There is so much I want to say, but I don't know where to start. What if I tell him that Alan and I are finished and he doesn't care? What if he doesn't like being pulled in ten different directions? I walk over to a lounge chair and sit down, trying to figure out exactly what to say.

"Look, Barb, I know you're trying to be nice, but I'm a big boy. I'm fine. Let's just move on, okay?"

I take a deep breath.

"Well, what if I say no?"

"No?"

"Yes."

"Yes?"

"No, yes to no."

"What? What are you talking about?"

"I don't know. You're confusing me!"

Ken says nothing, just stares back at me. Then he walks over to the lounge chair next to me and sits down, grabs a T-shirt, and pulls it over his head and looks out into space. He is waiting for me to speak, so we sit there in silence. Baxter has decided to put his big furry head in my lap, which is wonderful, since scratching his ears gives me something to do while I stall for time. I have to get this right. I thought it would be easy to just tell him how I feel, but suddenly I'm afraid. First I tell him that my marriage sucks, then I tell him I have to stay married, now I'm going to say it's over and I just expect him to run into my arms and say yippee? I must be out of my mind. Suddenly, he stands up.

"Barbara, I don't—"

I stand up, too.

"My marriage is over." I blurt this out. "It's . . . over. Alan was cheating on me." I look at him, but his expression doesn't change. "It's crazy, right? I felt compelled to stay with him, and all along he was the one who was cheating. I just sort of walked in on them at the hospital and it was horrible, you know, the surprise and then the knowledge and all that . . ." I turn away now because I'm babbling. Ken doesn't move, but I hear him sigh.

"Barb, I'm sorry. That must have been awful."

"It was, you know? Really awful. But then the funniest thing happened. I stood there looking at Alan and this woman and his *mother,* for God's sake, and instead of feeling worse and worse I suddenly realized that I was"—I look directly at Ken—"starting to feel better and better. In fact I was starting to feel happy."

"Really? And why was that?"

"I was happy because I realized I didn't have to be with Alan anymore. Because I finally admitted to myself that whether he cheated or not, my marriage was a mistake and Alan was the wrong man for me."

"I see."

"Do you?" I walk toward him.

"You have clarity. That's always helpful."

"Except I'm not really clear about everything."

"No?"

"No." I walk right up to him. Really close. I look into his eyes.

"There was another reason I was so happy. It's because there's someone else. Someone I know I want to be with."

Ken looks down. He doesn't say a word. We are almost touching.

"But this has been rough on him, too, and now I don't know how he feels. If he still wants to be with me." There's dead silence. Standing face-to-face, I come up to Ken's chest. I'm breathing right on his shirt, looking into his eyes. I can't tell what he's thinking, but his breaths have gotten shorter, I can feel it. I go on.

"But more than anything I want to be with him." He closes his eyes and takes a deep sigh. I'm thinking, Please don't pull away. Please don't tell me you need some time. Just say what I want to hear. And then he opens his eyes, looks down at me, and smiles. Oh my God. I am almost afraid to believe that it might be true. And then I know it is because Ken wraps his arms around me and lifts me in the air and then we are kissing and hugging and laughing and crying, and before we know it Baxter wants to get in on the act and he is jumping on us and trying to lick any available uncovered skin. I look at Ken and he looks at me, covered in mud and leaves and dog saliva, and suddenly he gets a sneaky look in his eye. Before I can defend myself, he scoops me up and carries me toward the pool.

"Oh no! Don't you dare! Ken! I will kill y—" No luck. I am thrown into the pool and it feels wonderful, even more so when Ken dives in beside me and starts kissing me and pulling me along onto his lap. Baxter, who apparently doesn't like to swim, gives a little reproachful sigh and lies down on the cool deck and I go from splashing Ken to just kissing him and Baxter is whining at us and Ken laughs, looks over at the dog, and says, "Sorry Bax, she's spoken for," and through Ken's kisses I think, "Don't worry Baxter, I know a couple of kids and a golden retriever who I bet will be keeping you company very soon."

EPILOGUE

When the night of my very first pottery show finally arrives in early fall, we are all running late. I have been trying to give the kids dinner, but they've been absorbed in some video game, and they just laugh at me when I threaten to leave them home. The boys, Evan and Bebe's son, Raj, come racing down the stairs first. Since Bebe's children have come to live with us, Evan and Raj have been inseparable, not just because they are the same age, but also because they have the same sensibility. Now, playfully horsing around, they try to elbow each other out of the way to get to the table first. I run through the kitchen, trying to put on my earring and my shoe at the same time and managing to accomplish neither.

"Girls," I yell, still trying to do three things at once, "let's go!" In a minute, I hear footsteps and Jenny Jaikaran dances in, light on her toes, looking like a seven-year-old Indian princess. With her light skin and round eyes, she takes after her mother. Lauren is fast behind, and I notice that Jenny waits to see where Lauren sits and then sits beside her: pure worship. For her part, Lauren softens at the naked admiration, and though she sometimes rolls her eyes, I know she is secretly pleased.

"Is my mom coming home for dinner?" Raj looks to me.

"No, honey, she's going to meet us at the gallery. Tonight is her late class."

"She is smart enough already," says Jenny.

"I agree," I say, stopping to pat the little girl on the head, "but she wants to be a nurse and that takes time."

"How long before she is nurse?" Raj asks, his mouth full of macaroni and cheese. I have to laugh, remembering that when Raj first came to us last month he would eat only rice and beans.

"Oh boy," I say. "You will have to be patient. Maybe one more year after this."

"This, I think, is too long," he says.

"It's less than going to college. That takes four years. I can't wait," Lauren offers.

Jenny looks pained.

"You must not go away, not ever."

"Oh, Jen," Lauren teases, "it's a *long* time from now. Besides, how can you come and stay with me if I don't go away?" Jen beams.

Then Evan says, "Famous saying, 'Whatever you do will be insignificant, but it is very important that you do it.'"

And we all start guessing. "Chickie Soup for Kid's Soul? Camper Soul? Vacation Soul?"

"Actually," says my little scholar, "it's Gandhi. I read it in my social studies textbook."

"I don't want anyone to go anywhere. I don't care if even Gandhi says so." This from Jenny.

Then Evan says, "But you will get your own apartment soon, when your mom starts to work as a nurse."

Raj pipes in.

"Jen is right, this is best house ever, but if we get our own house, then please, Mrs. Barb, teach my mom to make the flat eggs."

"The what?" I ask, half listening.

Evan laughs.

"He means matzo brei."

"Okay, Raj, I tell you what. I will teach your mom how to make matzo brei if she shares the secret of her roti. I can never get that right. Now, will everyone please hurry up and finish and go get dressed?" And to Lauren I add, "And something conservative, please. No hot-body stuff."

My daughter rolls her eyes, but just then another voice pops in.

"Did someone mention me?"

"Hi, Mr. Ken!" Raj stands up, jumps up really, and runs to Ken, then promptly straightens himself and offers Ken his outstretched hand. He is thrilled to know his new principal personally and wants to impress him. Ken bends down.

"And hello to you, Mr. Jaikaran." Ken shakes his hand with genuine formality. "Always a pleasure." Raj beams. Then Evan saunters over, he of the newfound confidence, and high-fives Ken. Lauren stands up, too.

"Ken, will you please tell my mother to join the twenty-first century and tell her that the art world is especially open to alternative fashion?" Ken looks at Lauren, who is smiling, and back to me, who is frazzled, and winks at Lauren.

"Not a chance. I don't mess with a woman who has a run in her stocking."

"What?" I scream, looking down. "Now we're definitely going to be late." Just then, before I can completely go to pieces, there is a crackling and a snapping sound and we all turn to the sliding glass doors and outside there is an amazing sight. Like a stream of smoke, wide bands of glittering diamonds, in a rainbow of colors, are snaking past.

"She's done it! She's reached her goal! I knew she would," Evan yells, and we all rush to the window and watch, amazed.

"What?" asks Raj. "Who's done what?"

"Is it an explosion?" asks Jenny.

But nobody speaks. It is just too beautiful. We all stare at the glittery stream and then, truly awed, I say, "No, honey, it's no explosion," and I look at my family, thinking we are a bit like the stream of color outside, a lovely, beautiful, mixed-up kaleidoscope of a group: a little bit of everything, but a hundred percent committed to one another. I slip my hand into Ken's, and, in unison, Lauren, Evan, and I announce with some respect and not a little delight:

"It's Sparkleworks!"

DEBRA FELDMAN BORDEN grew up in Great Neck, New York. After attending American University, she went to the University of Michigan, where she earned a B.A. in English. Later, she received an M.S.W. from Fordham University. Though she now writes full time, she is a licensed clinical social worker in New Jersey, where she lives with her family. *A Little Bit Married* is her second novel. To learn more about Debra, visit her website at www.debraborden.com.

ABOUT THE TYPE

This book was set in Adobe Garamond, a typeface designed by Robert Slimbach in 1989. It is based on Claude Garamond's sixteenth-century type samples found at the Plantin-Moretus Museum in Antwerp, Belgium.

A Little Bit Married

DEBRA BORDEN

About This Guide

A Little Bit Married's main character, Bitsy Beberman Lerner, could be considered a study in contradiction by some readers, and a throwback or a pioneer by others, but she's anything but uninteresting! An unapologetic full-time wife and mother, Bitsy finds that the choices she's made haven't entirely been the ones to make her happy, and in the book we follow Bitsy's hilarious and poignant journey to self-discovery. The questions below are intended to assist your reading group's discussion of Debra Borden's funny and thought-provoking novel.

Questions for Discussion

1. What did you think of Bitsy at the beginning of the book? How did your opinion of her change as the novel progressed?

2. What do you think of Bitsy's long-held desire to forego a career and be a full-time wife and mother?

3. "Life in the suburbs is not all flower beds and carpools; there are rules." (page 33) What are some of the rules Bitsy is

referring to? Do you agree there is an unspoken code in society, whether in the city, suburbs, or elsewhere?

4. What is your opinion of Alan? How do you think the story would have been different if Bitsy decided to stay with him when he regained his memory?

5. Discuss the various parent/child relationships in the book: the Winstons, Bitsy and her parents, Alan and his mother, Bebe and her children, the Rabinowitzes. What aspects of each make it a good or bad relationship? Why?

6. "But this was not the first time I'd subconsciously adopted Alan's view as my own. After so many years of marriage, it was impossible to experience anything solely with my own antennae, and I often found myself registering Alan's opinion, even when he wasn't there." (page 11) Is this a common occurrence in marriage or long-term relationships? Why do you think this happens?

7. "There was an unspoken agreement in our home: The boys were smart and the girls were pleasant, and throughout my childhood we maintained that myth no matter how many As I racked up or how many courses Eddie had to repeat over the summer or how many math tutors Mitch had to endure." (page 23) How do you think Bitsy's family's prevailing attitude affected her desire to be a full-time mom?

8. Bitsy resumes pottery as a way to gain control over her life, and at the beginning of chapter 25, she says of the hobby,

"As the pottery begins to take shape, so do I." (page 209) What do you think she means by this line? How is pottery a metaphor for her life thus far, and in the future?

9. "Finally, my mother-in-law speaks. 'We've been discussing Alan's release,' she says, straightening herself, 'and he prefers to come home with me.'" (page 210) Did this turn of events surprise you, as well as Bitsy's reaction to the news?

10. How are Bebe and Bitsy's stories similar? What do they ultimately learn from each other?

11. Upon discovering that Alan has a mistress, Bitsy thinks to herself, "And, suddenly, I know. It just all falls apart, like a series of dominoes, one toppling over onto the other, all the pieces coming to rest on a most unbelievable truth. In that moment, I am many things: wife, daughter-in-law, and also 'the last to know.'" (page 266) Was this really an "unbelievable truth" for Bitsy? Do you think she might have figured this out earlier? If so, how?

12. What do you think of Alan's mother? Why do you think she helped Alan hide his affair? What is the reason for her dislike of Bitsy?

13. In describing her sublimated artistic talents, Bitsy says, "I knew that my love for paint, clay, and charcoal could only confuse me, divert me from the road to happiness. Certainly my mother had told me enough times 'to concentrate on finding the right man first. Get your life set—husband, kids. Then

you can worry about what you like to do.'" (page 29) Do you agree with Bitsy's mother's advice?

14. Do you have a talent or skill that you've left unused? What is it? Why don't you exercise it?

15. What does the book's title mean?